LOST
BOY

LOST
BOY

Christina Henry

TITAN BOOKS

Lost Boy
Print edition ISBN: 9781785655685
E-book edition ISBN: 9781785655692

Published by Titan Books
A division of Titan Publishing Group Ltd
144 Southwark Street, London SE1 0UP

First Titan edition: July 2017
10 9 8 7 6 5 4 3 2 1

This edition published by arrangement with Berkley, an imprint of Penguin, a division of Penguin Random House LLC, in 2017.

A CIP catalogue record for this title is available from the British Library.

Printed and bound in Great Britain by CPI Group Ltd.

Did you enjoy this book?
We love to hear from our readers. Please email us at readerfeedback@titanemail. com or write to us at Reader Feedback at the above address.

To receive advance information, news, competitions, and exclusive offers online, please sign up for the Titan newsletter on our website:
www.titanbooks.com

For Henry and Jared and Dylan
For Xander and Sam and Jake and Logan
For all the boys I've known
May you never be lost
May you always find your way home

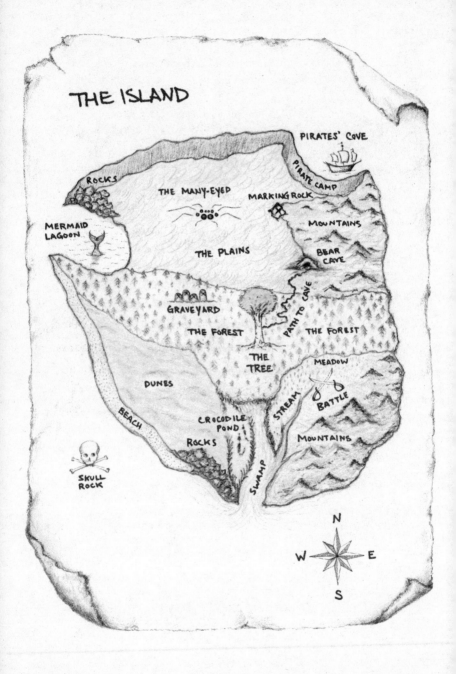

THE ISLAND

PIRATES' COVE

ROCKS

THE MANY-EYED

MARKING ROCK

PIRATE CAMP

MERMAID LAGOON

MOUNTAINS

THE PLAINS

BEAR CAVE

GRAVEYARD

PATH TO CAVE

THE FOREST

THE FOREST

THE TREE

MEADOW

DUNES

BATTLE

STREAM

BEACH

CROCODILE POND

MOUNTAINS

ROCKS

SWAMP

SKULL ROCK

N

W   E

S

PROLOGUE

Once I was young, and young forever and always, until I wasn't. Once I loved a boy called Peter Pan.

Peter will tell you that this story isn't the truth, but Peter lies. I loved him, we all loved him, but he lies, for Peter wants always to be that shining sun that we all revolve around. He'll do anything to be that sun.

Peter will say I'm a villain, that I wronged him, that I never was his friend.

But I told you already. Peter lies.

This is what really happened.

PART I

CHARLIE

CHAPTER 1

Sometimes I dreamed of blood. The blood on my hands and the empty eyes in a white-and-grey face. It wasn't my blood, or blood I'd spilled—though there was plenty of that to go around. It was her blood, and I didn't know who she was.

Her eyes were dead and blue and her hands were thrown out, like she was reaching for someone, like she was reaching for me before that great slash was put in her throat. I didn't know why. I didn't even rightly know whether it was a dream, or something that happened in the Other Place, before I went away with Peter.

If that girl was real it must have happened there, because there were no girls on the island except the mermaids, and they didn't really count, being half fish.

Still, every night I dreamed of flashing silver and flowing red, and sometimes it startled me out of sleep and sometimes it didn't. That night I had the dream same as usual, but something else woke me.

I'd heard a sound, a sound that was maybe a cry or moan or a bird squawking out in the night of the forest. It was hard to tell when you heard something while you were sleeping. It was like the noise came from a far-off mountain.

I wasn't sorry to leave the dream. No matter how many times Peter told me to forget it, my mind returned over and over again to the same place: to the place where she was dead and her eyes asked something of me, though I didn't know what that something might be.

I came awake all at once the way I usually did, for if you don't sleep light in the forest you might open your eyes to find something sharp-jawed biting your legs off. Our tree was hidden and protected, but that didn't mean there wasn't danger. There was always danger on the island.

The piles of sleeping boys huddled under their animal skins on the dirt floor. Light filtered in from the moon through the holes we'd cut like windows in the tree hollow—me and Peter had done it, long ago. Outside there was a steady buzz, the hum of the Many-Eyed in the plains carrying across the forest.

"It's just Charlie," Peter said dismissively from above.

He was curved into one of the holes, his body loose-limbed and careless, looking out over the forest. In his hands he held a small knife and a piece of wood that he was whittling. The blade flashed in the moonlight, dancing over the surface of the wood. His skin was all silver in that light and his eyes deep pools of shadow, and he seemed to be part of the tree and the moon and the wind that whispered through the tall grass outside.

Peter didn't sleep much, and when he did it was just a quick nap. He would not waste a bit of his life in slumber, even though his life was already longer than most, and he hated the way the rest of us succumbed, dropping like biting flies in the summer heat while he pestered us for one more game.

I rose and tiptoed carefully over the other boys until I found Charlie. He was balled up in a knotted tree root like a baby in a cradle, and he was barely older than a baby at that. His face was covered in sweat that glittered like jewels, like a pirate's treasure in the moonlight. He moaned, shifting restlessly in his sleep.

Young ones sometimes had a hard time adjusting when they first came over. Charlie was five, much younger than I had been when Peter had taken me, much younger than any boy he'd ever brought to the island before.

I bent and scooped the smaller boy from the tree root, holding him to my heart. Charlie kicked out once, then settled.

"You're no help to him, you know," Peter warned, watching me shuffle to and fro with Charlie in my arms. "Stop babying."

"He's too little," I hissed. "I told you he was."

I don't know why I bothered, because there isn't a point in saying things Peter won't listen to anyhow.

Peter usually chose boys who were about the same age I was when he picked me—around eight or nine. Peter liked that age, for boys were old enough to have the spirit of rebellion and the will to follow it. By then a boy would have gotten a good taste of adulthood—through work or schooling, depending on his class—enough to know that he didn't want to spend his days toiling at figures or in the fields or fetching water for some rich man.

The last time we went looking for new boys, Peter had spied this tiny one wandering through the piles of filth in the alleys. He declared that the child would be a splendid little playmate, and I argued that he would have been much better off in a home for orphans. Naturally, Peter won. He wanted the boy and Peter got what he wanted—always.

And now that he'd got him, Peter had no use for him. It wasn't any fun to play with someone too small to fight and roughhouse with the bigger boys. Charlie couldn't keep up when Peter trekked us through the forest on an adventure, either. More than once I'd suspected Peter of trying to leave Charlie somewhere so the little boy might get eaten, and then Peter would be free of the trouble of him. But I kept one eye on Charlie (though Peter didn't like it), and as long as I watched out for him and carried him home there wasn't much Peter could do about it but complain. Which he did.

"You should have left him by the crocodile pool," Peter said. "Then his crying wouldn't wake you up."

I said nothing, because it wasn't worth my breath. Peter never lost an argument—and not because he wasn't wrong; he was, and pretty often too—but because he never got tired.

He'd keep coming back at you no matter how right you were until you threw up your hands and let him win just so you'd have some peace.

Peter didn't say anything else and I went on walking Charlie until his breathing told me he was properly asleep again. I tried to replace the boy in the pile of skins he'd been sleeping in, but he whimpered as soon as I tried to put him down. Peter sniggered.

"You'll be up all night with him, walking him like a mama with her babe," Peter said.

"What would you know about it?" I said, as I rubbed Charlie's back again to get him to settle. "There's never been a mama here, and you don't remember yours."

"I've seen them at it," Peter said. "In the Other Place. The little babies wail and the mamas walk to and fro and shush and jiggle them just like you're doing now. And sometimes the babies quiet and sometimes they don't and when they don't the mamas will cry and cry themselves because those little wailing things won't shut it. I don't know why they don't just put those babies under a blanket until they stop. It's not as though they can't make more."

He didn't mean it, not really. At least, I didn't think he meant it. To Peter all children were replaceable (except himself). When he lost one here on the island he would go to the Other Place and get a new one, preferably an unwanted one, because then the boy didn't miss the Other Place so much and he was happy to be here and to do what Peter wanted.

Those who didn't listen so well or weren't happy as the singing birds in the trees found themselves in the fields of the Many-Eyed without a bow or left near the pirate camp or otherwise forgotten, for Peter had no time for boys who didn't want his adventures.

After a while I sat and leaned against the bark of the tree, humming a quiet tune that I learned once, long ago, before Peter, before this island. I didn't know who had taught me that song, but it had stayed in my head all these long years. The song irritated Peter, and he told me to shut it, but I sang until Charlie's breath grew soft and quiet and even, his chest rising and falling in time with mine.

I stared out the window, past Peter, to the untouchable moon. The moon was always full here, always looming like a watchful eye.

Two staring eyes. Small hands covered in blood.

I pushed the dream away. It did me no good to remember it. That was what Peter always said.

I had been with Peter longer than I'd been in the Other Place, longer than I could count, anyway. The seasons did not pass here and the days had no meaning. I would be here forever. I would never grow up.

Peter's whittling knife danced in that white light until the moon disappeared behind my closed eyes.

* * *

was smaller then, and Peter was big and brave and wonderful. He said, "Come away and we'll have adventures and be friends always," and I put my hand in his and he smiled and that smile went into my heart and stayed there.

We ran through the streets of the city where I lived, and Peter was so swift and silent I could hardly believe it. He ran like the wind was part of him and his feet barely touched the ground and I thought, watching him run in the dark, that he might take off and fly and take me with him. It would be lovely to fly away from the city and into the stars, for the city was dark and dirty and full of big people who would grab at you if you were small and say, "Here, now, what's all this?" and cuff you around the head just because they could and they would take your bread and your apples and leave you with your insides all twisted up and then throw you back in the mud and laugh and laugh.

But Peter said he would take me away from all that; he was taking me to a place where there was all the food you could eat and no one would hit you and there was no one to tell you what to do and when to do it and to get out of the way and go sleep in the trash where you belong. He said that on his island you could sleep in the trees and taste the salt from the sea on the air and there was treasure and fun all day long.

I wanted to go there. I couldn't wait to go there. But I was scared about getting on a ship to go to the island. I'd never been on a ship before, but I'd seen them in the port. Peter might not like me if I told him I was scared so I didn't say anything, but I *was certain that once we got out to sea a monster would come and break the ship into a thousand pieces and we would fall, fall, fall to the far bottom of the water and never be seen again.*

Peter tugged me along and I was getting tired and he said, "Come on, Jamie, just a little more and we'll be there," and I wanted to make him happy so he would smile at me again, so I ran and tried to be as fast and quiet as he.

I thought we would go to the docks, but Peter was taking us away from there and I tugged on his hand and said, "Aren't we going to a ship?"

And Peter laughed and said, "Why would we go to a ship, silly?" But he said it in a way that didn't hurt and didn't make me feel stupid—more like he had a secret and was laughing because he was going to share it with me soon.

We went away from the city, far away from the place where I slept, and I didn't know where we were or if I would ever find my way home again, and then I remembered I didn't want to go home anymore because home is where they hit you and you sleep in the dirty straw and she screams and screams and screams . . .

The scream was still in my ears when I was roused by Peter's cock-crow just as the sun emerged over the mountains. His cry and her scream twisted together into one sound and then the scream faded away as my eyes opened and I saw him perched in the window.

He had ginger hair that was always dirty, for he hated to bathe, and was dressed in a shirt and leggings made from deerskin, the hide grown soft and white with age.

His feet were bare and filthy, the toenails broken and torn from scampering over rocks and through trees. Peter was silhouetted in the window, legs wide apart, hands on hips, crowing with great vigor.

"Cock-a-doodle-do! Cock-a-doodle-do!"

My eyes had opened immediately, accustomed to Peter's morning antics. Several of the newer boys groaned and covered their heads with their arms.

Charlie blinked sleepy blue eyes at me. "Get up now, Jamie?"

"Aye," I said gently. I placed the younger boy on his feet and rose, stretching. I felt somehow taller today than yesterday—not a lot, just a smidge. It seemed my hands were closer to the roof of the hollow than before. I didn't have much time to trouble about it, though, for Peter's next words shook it from my mind.

Peter clapped his hands together. "We've a raid today!"

"What for?" I asked, not troubling to keep my annoyance hidden.

I didn't think this was the time for a raid. We'd only brought the last six boys over a few days before. Most of them were not even close to ready.

"The pirates need raiding, of course!" Peter said, like he

was giving the boys a huge pile of sweets.

Nod and Fog, the twins, cried, "Hurrah!"

They were both whippet-lean and strong with it, little ropey muscles on their arms and legs, matching shocks of blond hair darkened by their mutual dislike of washing. I'd never been able to tell if they hated to wash because Peter did or because they liked feeling the bugs in their hair.

Nod and Fog had been on the island longest except me, and raiding the pirates was their second-favorite game after Battle. There was nothing the twins liked better than an excuse to shed blood.

A long time ago Fog had taken down a wolf with only a sharpened rock, a feat that Peter so heartily approved of that he made Fog King of the Tree for a week. Fog made a kind of band for his head out of the tail and attached the wolf's ears to it, and turned the rest of the skin into fur leggings. He'd briefly contemplated a cape, but dismissed it as too awkward for fighting.

Not to be outdone by his brother, Nod had promptly gone out and slaughtered one of the big cats that prowled in the mountains on the east side of the island. Now he wore the cat's yellow ears and yellow furred leggings, and was still inclined to complain that Peter hadn't made *him* the King of the Tree.

Some of the other boys tried to copy Nod and Fog, and got eaten by a cat for their trouble. And when we lost a boy we would go collect a new one from the Other Place, for Peter had particular ideas about how many boys should be about him at all times.

There were fifteen of us in all, including Peter and me. We lost a few every year to Battle, and to the raids, and some to illness or animals. Ambro had died coughing up blood, and now Del was looking thin and white. Soon he would start coughing too, and then Peter would send him outside to sleep.

Peter had complained incessantly about the noise when Ambro was dying, as if the boy could have prevented it. And if he could have stopped it, he would have, for we all loved Peter, even when he was cruel. His approval was hungrily sought, and his derision cut sharper than the blade of a pirate's sword.

Peter hopped down from the window, landing lightly on his feet despite the height. Sometimes I thought that Peter couldn't be hurt, and that was why he didn't bother so much when others were, for he couldn't understand their pain. And Peter was bound to the island in some way that the others weren't. He understood the land, and it understood him. That was why I had grown a bit and Peter hadn't.

It was the island that kept us all young, though some of us wouldn't stay that way. Some of the boys, for reasons none of us could comprehend, grew up like normal. It didn't happen too often, for Peter was pretty good at choosing the right sort of character for the island, and I think that had something to do with it, the desire to stay a boy and do boy things for always.

But when Peter noticed the boy turning into a man, that

boy was cast out, no looking back, no second chances. Those boys ended up in the pirate camp if they made it across the island alive, and became unrecognizable bearded faces, no longer our little friends.

I reckoned I'd been about eight, same as Nod and Fog, when Peter found me. I'd be long dead if I'd stayed in the Other Place, for one or two hundred seasons had passed. I wasn't sure exactly how many because it's easy to lose track if you don't pay attention. I looked about twelve, a few years older than I was when I arrived.

Nod and Fog, too, had grown a bit. Peter had started out eleven, and had stayed eleven. There wasn't a part of him not exactly the same as it had been when he took me from the Other Place so long ago, his first friend and companion.

Sometimes I worried, just a little, that I would grow up and be sent to the pirate camp. Peter always cuffed my ear when I said things like this.

"You'll never grow up, you fool. I brought you here so you wouldn't."

But I was getting a little older just the same, and Nod and Fog too. We lost too many of the other boys to tell if only the three of us felt the minute creep of age. Sometimes at night, when the nightmare clung to me, I wondered if Peter's assurances that I would never grow up were only assurances that I would die before such a thing happened. I wondered if that were better, to die before I became something withered and grey and not wanted.

Our leader crouched on the ground with a stick and drew a quick map of the island, and then a detail of the pirate camp. Our tree was in the very center of the forest and in the very center of the island. The forest cut through the middle of a mountain range on the east side. It crossed the whole middle of the island and emptied out to the ocean on the east side, and a sheltered lagoon on the west.

In the northwest part were the plains in which the Many-Eyed lived. We didn't go there if we could help it.

If you went straight south from our tree, you would run into the crocodile pond and then the swamp. The swamp became a green marshy place that met the ocean.

The southwest corner of the island was mostly big sand dunes, giant things that took a long time to climb up and then down again. Past the dunes was a sandy beach, the only one where we could safely play and collect coconuts. On the northern side of this beach, hidden by the forest that wrapped around it, was the mermaid lagoon.

The pirates had staked out the beach on the north end of the island, near the cove just where the border of the plains and the mountains met. There was no beach on the east side at all, only sheer rock face from the mountains and a towering cliff where the forest ran up to the sea.

The boys crowded around Peter. I had no need to. I knew the island by heart, better than anyone except Peter. I'd been over every root and rock and plant, crept around every wild thing, seen all the mermaids a hundred times over and pulled away from the snap of a crocodile's jaws more than once. I didn't like having a raid so soon, but I knew my part if one was to happen.

Charlie stayed with me, one of his little hands safely buried inside mine. He stuck his other thumb in his mouth, not interested in the map or what might happen next.

I sighed softly. What would I do with Charlie in a raid? It was a certainty that he wouldn't be able to defend himself, and I half suspected Peter of devising this trip just to get rid of the smaller boy.

Most of the new boys seemed unsure as they collected around Peter, except for a big one called Nip. He was almost as tall as me, and I was easily the tallest boy there. Nip had the look of a boy who liked to be the strongest and the fastest, and he'd been eyeing me since he'd arrived. I knew Nip would pick a fight soon. I just hoped I wouldn't have to do Nip serious harm when it happened.

There wasn't any malice about this; I didn't wish the boy any more harm than he wished me. But I was the best fighter. Peter knew it. All the boys who'd been around longer knew it. Even the pirates knew it, and that's why they tried their damnedest to kill me every time there was a raid. I'd learned not to take it to heart.

The pirate camp was about a two-day walk from the tree,

depending on how fast you could hurry along a pack of boys, and though Peter made it sound like an adventure to the new boys, I knew well enough that there was as much work as play. There would be supplies to gather and carry. The Many-Eyed patrolled through the plains we had to cross. To top it off, the pirates might not even be in port. This time of year they were often away raiding themselves, stealing gold from galleons at sea and crying girls from cities they burned.

To my way of thinking this was not a smart idea. Not only did I have Charlie to worry over, but the new boys were untried. We didn't even know whether half of them could fight at all, much less against grown men who made their living by the blade.

And Del might not make it. I could already imagine the boy sicking out puddles of blood on the way, blood that would attract the Many-Eyed to us when we took the path that bordered their lands. It was a risky plan, probably wasteful. Even saying that all the boys made it to the pirate camp, it was unlikely all would make it back. We never did come back with the same numbers that we left with.

I let Charlie go with a reassuring grin. The little one gave me a half smile in return when I told him to stay where he was put. I sidled around to Peter, who energetically slashed at the ground, making marks to indicate who would go where in the pirate camp. I had to try, though nothing was likely to come of it.

"I don't think—" I began under my breath.

"Don't think," Peter said sharply.

Some of the boys snickered, and I narrowed my eyes at each face in the circle. One by one their gazes fell away, except Nip, who stared insolently at me until I growled. Nip dropped his eyes to the ground, a red flush climbing his cheeks. I answered to no one but Peter, and the sooner the new ones learned that, the better.

"I know what you want," Peter said, his green eyes bright and intent on his drawing. "Stop babying."

"It's not babying to wait till they're ready," I said.

"Stop babying," Peter repeated.

And that was that. Peter had spoken, and we would all do as he wished. It was his island. He had invited us there, had promised us we would be young and happy forever.

So we were. Unless we got sick, or died, or were taken by the pirates. And it was of no nevermind to Peter if we did. The boys were just playmates to help him pass the time, though none of them knew this. They all thought they were special in his eyes, while the only one who was special was me. Peter had picked me first, had kept me at his right hand for so many years. But even I had no power to make Peter do what he did not want.

Peter wanted a raid. We would have a raid.

I stuffed my hands under the waist of my deerskin pants and hooked my thumbs over the edge. I listened to Peter's plans with half an ear. I had heard it all before, and I knew what I would have to do anyway. I always fought the first mate.

I'd killed most of them, and the ones who lived carried my mark. I cut off the right hand of all my victims, living and dead, so they would know who I was, and remember. I always used their own swords to do this, for I carried only a dagger, and I thought it hurt them more if I used their weapon.

Peter always fought the Captain. There had been a few Captains over the years, although this new one had been about for quite a while. I didn't think Peter tried very hard in a fight sometimes. He seemed to like taunting the Captain better than killing him.

After a bit Peter stood up and dusted his hands. "Go and get something to eat, boys. Then, after, we'll get on to our mission."

Most of the boys filed out of the small notch that served as both entrance to and exit from the tree. The tree was enormous and completely hollow inside, large enough to fit thirty boys lying side by side on the ground. The roots twisted up along the floor, making chairs and beds for those who wanted them, though most nested in piles of skins.

The new boys still wore the clothes that they had when they came from the Other Place, and the rest of us wore a mishmash of animal skins and clothes we'd stolen from the pirate camp. I had a red coat buttoned over my chest, taken from one of the Captains a long, long time ago, when he'd foolishly left it hanging on a washing line. It was too big in the body and I'd had to cut the sleeves and the tails a bit, but it was mine.

For a while Peter was inclined to be jealous of this, for it was a good prize, and to wheedle and imply that I ought to give it to him, but I wouldn't. I'd seen it before he had and snatched it off the line while he was looking for something shiny to take, as always. He just couldn't bear to think I'd beaten him at anything. Then he decided the coat was a stupid thing and that it looked foolish on me because it was so big, but I knew he wanted it.

Charlie waited where I had left him, until I went to him and gave him a nudge with my knee to follow the others outside.

The little boy looked up at me with grave eyes and spoke around the thumb in his mouth. "Are you coming?"

"In a minute," I said, and patted Charlie's shoulder. "Go on, now."

I wanted a word with Peter away from the others. When I turned back Peter had his arms crossed and watched the twins with mild interest.

"What's this about?" I asked.

Peter shrugged. "What is it ever about? They like to hit one another."

Nod and Fog rolled on the ground, each punching the other in the face as hard as possible. One of the twins—it was hard to tell who was who when they were tangled up and rolling in the dirt—was bleeding, and the blood dribbled and splashed away from their flying bodies.

We watched the twins for a few moments longer. Peter

would have let them bash about until they were both dead, but I didn't want them breaking limbs just before a raid. Peter didn't think about these things. He said that was why he had me, so I would think about them for him and save him the trouble.

Fog had snapped Nod's wrist once, and though I had tried to set it with a piece of bark and some rope made from a twining plant, it hadn't healed quite right. The wrist was just slightly off straight, and if you touched it where the break was, there was a knot of gnarled bone underneath.

Nod wasn't bothered in the least by the break or the less-than-perfect healing, but he'd had a fever for several days after, and things had been touch-and-go. I watched over him during that time, made sure Nod got through. But if one of the twins broke another bone right before a raid, Peter wouldn't let me stay behind to watch over him. I had my job to do, and nobody else would look after Charlie. We'd return to a corpse that used to be a twin, and I'd bury it with the others in the clearing in the woods.

I thought all of these things while the twins spun and pummeled. After a moment I stepped forward to break them up.

I heard Peter mutter, "Spoilsport," but the other boy didn't stop me. Maybe he, too, was thinking about the harm they might do each other. Or maybe he'd lost interest in watching them fight.

One of the twins had pinned the other's arms with his knees and was pounding ferociously on his brother's face.

The latter had a broken nose, the source of the blood spattered about on the roots and dirt.

I hooked the attacking twin—I could see now it was Nod, by the yellow cat's ears—under the neck of his leather vest and hauled him off Fog. Fog immediately jumped to his feet, tucked his head under like a goat and ran for his brother, head-butting him in the stomach.

Nod dangled from my hand with his toes just brushing the floor, and he let out a great whoosh of air as Fog's head caught him just under the ribs.

"None of that now," I said, tossing Nod to one side so I could catch Fog by the shoulders as he made another run at his twin.

"He took my best knife!" Fog shouted, his arms spinning like a windmill.

One of his hands caught me in the chin, just clipped me a bit. It wasn't enough to hurt, not even close, but it set me off when I was already in a foul mood about Peter and the blasted raid.

"That's *enough*," I said, and hauled off a good one right in Fog's mouth.

The smaller boy fell to his bottom on the ground, wiping blood from his lip.

Nod cackled at the sight of his brother chastised in the dust. I turned on the second boy, lifted him from where I had tossed him in the tangle of roots, and gave Nod the same treatment I'd given his twin.

The two of them sat side by side in the dirt, identical pairs of pale blue eyes staring up at me from blood- and muck-encrusted faces.

I heaved a deep breath, my hands clenched at my sides.

"Sorry, Jamie," the twins chorused.

I pointed at Nod. "Give him his knife. He worked on that blade for days."

"But . . ." Nod began, but stopped at the look on my face. Nod and Fog both knew better than to get on my wrong side.

Nod pulled the stone knife from under his vest and handed it to Fog, who tucked it lovingly into a leather sheath at his waist.

I jerked my head toward the notch. "Go eat something."

They scampered to their feet, seemingly none the worse for wear. By the time they reached the notch, the argument had been forgotten, and Nod playfully punched Fog in the shoulder.

Peter chuckled softly. "That's why neither of them play against you in Battle."

I took another deep breath, waiting for the red to recede, so that I wouldn't turn on Peter.

For a moment I'd thought about pulling my own knife, the metal one I'd stolen from the pirates. Then I'd knock Peter to the ground, grab his jaw and squeeze it together until Peter's tongue lolled out, and slice it off as neat as the edge of a pirate's sail.

Then the mist drew back a bit, the crazed burning in my

blood cooled, and Peter stood there, grinning, unharmed, unaware of what had passed in my mind.

It startled me, it surely did, for I loved Peter—at least most of the time—and spent the better portion of my life trying to make him smile at me the way he did when we first met.

"They try me sometimes," I said, after a bit. I was returning to myself again, the Jamie I knew.

Peter slung his arm around my shoulder. "You'll whip the new boys into shape. And we'll have an excellent raid."

"There should not be a raid at all," I said, trying once more, though I knew it was in vain.

"It'll be a lark," Peter said, and he nudged me toward the notch in the tree.

Outside a few boys scampered in the clearing around our tree, chasing and tagging one another. Some of them had plucked the fruit from the trees and stacked it in a pile. Del showed the new boys how to peel the skin from the orange-yellow fruit before eating it.

"The outside bit, that'll make you sick if you eat it. But the inside is nice and sweet," Del said, holding the fruit up to his lips and biting into it. Juice spilled over his chin. The sticky yellow stuff stood out against his white skin, like a warning.

I paused, my hand on the trunk of the tree. Peter emerged beside me and followed my gaze.

"Del won't last much longer," I said. "He won't last a raid—that's for certain."

Peter shrugged. "If he's sick he can stay behind. Better he coughs out that muck when I'm not here. I don't want to listen to it."

This was more or less what I expected, but I felt a surge of that same strange anger I'd felt a few moments before. It made me speak when I would have held my tongue.

"What if I was the one sicking out my lungs?" I said. I felt the temper perilously close to the surface, lurking just underneath my skin, hot and wild. "Would you leave me behind?"

Peter looked at me, just the faintest of questions in his eyes. "You never get sick, Jamie. All the time you've been here you've never had so much as a sniffle."

"But what if I was?" I persisted.

I wasn't sure whether I should be angry with Peter or not. There was no harm in his feelings. Peter would like it if Del was alive, but it wouldn't bother him if Del wasn't. He didn't wish the other boy harm.

"You won't be," Peter said, and he ran off to join the running boys. They were practicing swordplay with sticks now, jabbing and slashing at one another with the long branches that fell from the fruit trees.

I stared after him, felt that familiar mix of love and worship and frustration that I often felt with Peter. You couldn't change him. He didn't want to be changed. That was why Peter lived on the island in the first place.

I crossed to the circle of boys gathered around the pile of

fruit. Most of the lads were fine, but Charlie struggled with the small stone knife that one of the older boys had lent him.

I knelt beside him on one knee, took the unpeeled fruit from Charlie's little hand.

"Like this, see?" I said, making quick work of it and handing it back to Charlie.

The smaller boy looked up at me with shining eyes as he bit into the fruit. "'S good," he said.

I ruffled Charlie's hair, yellow-white in the sunlight. He was like a little duckling with his head all covered in fuzz, a little duckling who'd follow behind me and expect me to keep him safe. There was nothing to be done about it now. I would just have to make sure to keep him with me until the smaller boy got bigger, or smarter.

I stood and called Nod and Fog to me. The twins were busy beating at each other with sticks, but they quit as soon as they heard my voice, coming to attention before me like soldiers.

"Take Kit and Harry and check the traps," I said.

We'd need the meat while crossing the island. Some to eat, and some for the things we might meet on the way. I didn't like the way the Many-Eyed had been acting lately. They were bolder than they'd ever been before.

"'Kay," the twins said.

"And take the new boy, Nip, with you," I said.

Nip looked like he might be working up the gumption to come at me, and I was not in the mood for fighting just then. Best if the other lad were busy.

Nod and Fog collected the others, including an obviously reluctant Nip, and disappeared into the trees. I looked up at the sky, calculated they would be back by midday.

I rounded up the other boys and set them to tasks— cleaning and collecting the knives and bows, rigging up carrying pouches for food, laying out strips of fruit to dry in the sun. Peter frowned when he realized all his playmates had been taken from him for chores.

"What's the idea?" he said.

"You want a raid, don't you?" I said, turning away so he wouldn't see the gleam of satisfaction in my eye. If he wanted his raid he could have all that came with it, including the work.

"Aye," Peter said.

"Then there's work to be done."

"Not for me," Peter said. He planted himself defiantly in the shade of a fruit tree and took out the piece of wood he'd whittled at the night before, one he'd turned into a little flute. He whistled, watching me from the corner of his green eyes.

I gave Peter my back, and went about my business. Peter watched me closely, though I pretended not to notice, watched me as a mother might watch over her child, or a wolf might watch something that was between it and its prey.

CHAPTER 2

The trap-checking party was back just before the sun was highest, as I had expected. All the traps were full, which was an excellent surprise. It meant we could do less hunting on the way to the pirate camp. There was always plenty of food in the forest, but much less once we reached the border of the mountains and the plains.

Peter, of course, wanted a bit of rabbit for lunch as long as there was so much to go around. And I, though my inclination was to save for the upcoming journey, didn't argue.

I was pleased to see Nip looking so bedraggled after trekking around the forest with the twins, who'd doubtless kept up an unaccustomed pace for the tall boy. If Nip were tired out from exercise, he would, I hoped, be too tired to cause trouble.

Soon we had a fire crackling in the clearing and a couple of the fattest rabbits on spits, watched over carefully by Del, who was the best thing we had for a cook. Del sprinkled a bit of sweet-smelling leaf he'd collected over the rabbits, and my mouth watered.

The best of the meat was given to Peter first, and then me, followed in order by the size of the boy, the length of time he'd been on the island, and his current position of favoritism in Peter's mind. Thus Nip and Charlie were the last two to get fed, and they had the smallest portions.

Charlie bit into the rabbit with relish. The tiny piece of meat was more than enough for a boy his size, especially as he'd been eating as much yellow fruit as he could get his hands on all morning.

Nip narrowed his eyes at the scrap Del held out to him. "What's all this, then? Where's the rest of it?"

Del looked uncertainly from Nip to me to Peter. Peter was not inclined to do anything about Nip at the moment. His face was buried in the best piece of meat and he smacked his lips with every bite.

I didn't like to step into every confrontation between the boys. First, it would mean I'd spend my whole bloody day solving problems and I had better things to do. Second, the other ones would never learn how to get along if someone always fixed it between them. So I waited. I didn't care for Nip, but Peter had picked him and the boy needed to find his place in the group just as Del needed to defend his.

And Del is going to die soon anyway. It was a heartless thought, and it made me feel a little sick to think it, but it was true.

It wouldn't matter what happened now, not really, because Del would be dead before we came back from the pirate raid. He would cough out all the blood in his lungs or he would be too weak to defend himself from the pirates or maybe, if he was lucky, one of the Many-Eyed would take him and kill him fast and use what was left of Del to feed its children.

So when Del looked at me I just looked back, and waited to see what happened. I liked Del better than Nip, but I didn't think Del would get away from this one. Del was a good fighter—leastways, he had been before he was sick—but I didn't like his chances against the bigger boy.

Del swallowed, like he knew what was coming, and said with only a little stutter, "It's your share of the meat."

Nip knocked it away with a hand that seemed twice the size of Del's, Del being so thin and pale that he was half ghost already, and Nip hearty and strong from knocking boys down and taking their food in the Other Place.

"That's no share," Nip said, leaning over the fire to push his face in Del's. "I want yours."

Del had fairly allotted his own pile when his turn came up—it was larger than Nip's, though not as much as Peter's. He'd been on the island for some time, and he'd cooked it all besides. He looked at his food, then at Nip, and his chin came up.

"You're new. You get your share last. That's how it is here. If you don't like it, you can get your own food."

"Or," Nip growled, "I can take it from a skinny little rat like you."

Nip's big hand was already reaching for Del's share, but he was looking at Peter to see if our leader approved. That was stupid, because he was so busy looking at Peter instead of Del that the big lug didn't see Del shift, shift so his foot was closer to the hot coals of the fire.

Good for you, Del, I thought.

Del kicked the red coals into Nip's face with a sideswipe of his foot. Some of the boys near Nip got some ash on their food and shouted at Del about it, but their complaints were drowned in Nip's scream.

The flaming coals touched his eyeballs and he made a noise like something dying. Nip immediately showed his brains were made of pudding by doing the one thing guaranteed to make it worse—he clapped his hands over his eyes and rubbed at them, shouting all the while and stumbling away from the fire like a blind bear.

Most of the boys had stopped eating to stare while Nip threatened Del. Now that there was no fight in the offing they went back to their rabbit, ignoring Nip.

Del calmly picked up his own meat and tore into it with his teeth. When he glanced at me I winked at him to show he'd done fine. Del gave me a half smile in return. I thought again how pale he looked and how powerless I was, even with the power to live forever, to stop what was to come.

Charlie paused in his eating and with big eyes watched Nip bellowing and blundering about. "Should we help him, Jamie? He's hurt."

"He got what he deserved for trying to take Del's share," I said, and patted his head to take some of the sting out of it. Too little, and too softhearted on top of it. Charlie would never make it unless he toughened up, unless he lost something of what made him Charlie.

Just for a moment I felt the weight of that bear down on me, and I could feel the deadweight of his small body in my arms as I carried him to a grave I spent all morning digging.

The vision was so real, so painful to my heart, that I lost where I was until Peter said, "Someone ought to make that noise stop. It's hurting my ears," and the spell was broken.

I sighed, knowing an order when I heard one, shoved the rest of the rabbit in my mouth and stood up. Nip shouted and flailed and staggered closer to the forest's edge.

Really, I wondered what Peter saw in him. If I had been with him the last time he went to the Other Place (and I wasn't because Ambro had just died and I'd taken his body out to the border where the Many-Eyed lived, in hopes that it would keep them satisfied. We did this now and again, when it seemed they were tempted to go into the forest), I would have advised against Nip. Peter had gone for just one boy, one especially to replace Ambro, and come back with this. He wasn't half the boy Ambro had been, to my way of thinking, and because Peter took a trip just for Nip, he had a false sense of his own specialness.

But I was the only one who was special, truly special, for I was the first, and would be the last if it came to that. It would always be Peter and me, like we were in the beginning.

I watched Nip for a few moments. He made such a fuss I was embarrassed for him. My own inclination was to spin him around and point him to the path through the forest and come what may. If he got eaten by a bear or stumbled over a cliff, that was all right with me. But Peter hadn't said to get rid of Nip, only to shut him up.

The other boy blinked as I approached. I could tell he was trying to get his eyes to focus on me, that I was nothing but a blurry shadow moving toward him.

"Here, now," Nip said, his fists up. He sensed, I think, the dark thoughts in my mind. "Don't you come near me. I didn't do nothing wrong. That pasty little runt threw fire in my eyes and he's the one who ought to . . ."

Nip didn't finish, because my fist connected with his temple, hard enough that his ears would ring the next morning. That might not have been enough on a regular day, but Nip was already tired from checking the traps, sore from the coals in his eyes and hungry because he'd been too busy trying to take Del's food to eat his own.

One punch was all that was needed for now, though I didn't fool myself that it would be enough when Nip came looking for turnabout, as I knew he would. He was that kind.

Nip went down hard, face-first in the dirt, like a toy soldier kicked over by a careless boy. I went back to the fire.

"Quieter now," Peter remarked.

You could still hear the buzzing of the small flies, and the soft sigh of the wind through the branches of the trees, and the crackle of wood burning in the fire. The sun was past its high midday point and the shadows were lengthening, though it was still a long time until night fell. The boys were eating and laughing and pushing and shoving one another, the way they did, and I was happy to be there, to see them all that way.

Then Peter got that look in his eye, the one that said he wanted to stir the pot. I don't know why it was so but Peter just didn't feel right when everyone was content. Maybe it was because he wanted all eyes on him or maybe it was because he wanted everyone to feel the way he did all the time. He told me once that when he sat still he felt like there were ants crawling under his skin, that if he wasn't moving, running, planning, doing, it was just as though those ants would crawl right up inside his head and make him mad.

He leapt to his feet, and they all turned to look at him. I saw the satisfaction on his face and thought of a group of mummers I'd seen once in the Other Place, long ago, when I was very small. The leader of the troupe had the same look when he jumped on the box in the center of the stage, a feeling that must be like all the stars circling around the earth only for you.

"Who wants to hear a story?" Peter said.

All the boys chorused yes, because they were feeling fed and warm and because Peter wanted to tell a tale, and if Peter wanted it, then they did too.

"What kind of story? A pirate story? A ghost story? A treasure story?" Peter hopped around the circle, scooping up a handful of dirt as he did.

"Something with lots of blood and adventure," Fog said.

"Something with a mermaid in it," Nod said. He was partial to the mermaids, and went often on his own to the lagoon where they liked to splash and show their tail fins above the breaking waves.

"Something with a haunt walking and scaring folk to death," Jonathan said. "I saw a story like that once. This fellow killed a king so he could be king and then the old king's ghost stayed about and sat in the new king's chair."

"What would a ghost want to sit in a chair for? Ghosts don't need chairs. They fall right through them," Harry said. He'd been around the island for a while, and I'm sorry to say that being bashed around in Battle and at raids had done nothing very good for his brains.

"So he could scare the new king for killing him in the first place," Jonathan said, punching Harry in the shoulder.

"Killing who in the first place?" Harry asked.

"A ghost story," Peter said, effectively squashing the argument before it got properly started. He smeared the dirt he'd scooped up across his face. It made him a wild demon in the shadows left behind by the lowering sun.

Charlie's cold hand grasped for mine. He stood up so my ear was close to his mouth. "I don't like ghosts," he whispered. "There was one in the house where we lived before. It was in the wardrobe and my brother said if I opened that door the ghost would take me away to where the dead people live."

I squeezed his fingers, partly to comfort him and partly to cover my surprise at his words. A brother? Charlie had a brother? And an older one, by the sound of it. Where was he that day we found Charlie wandering lost and alone? Why hadn't Charlie told us about him?

Charlie crowded closer as Peter spoke.

"Once there was a boy," Peter began, and his eyes glinted when he looked at Charlie and me. "A very little boy with yellow hair like baby duck feathers."

I brushed my hand over Charlie's downy blond head and gave Peter a look that said I knew what he was about.

"This little duckling was very foolish. He was always wandering away from his mama, and his mama would squawk and find him again. And she would scold him and say that he had to mind her and stay close, but whenever they went walking in the woods he never did."

"I thought this was a ghost story," Harry said. "What's all this about a duck?"

"Shush," Jonathan said.

"One day the duckling and his brothers and sisters and mama were walking in the woods, and the foolish little duckling saw a jumping grasshopper. He laughed and followed the hopper, trying to catch it with his fat little hands, but he never could.

"He kept on chasing and laughing until he noticed, all sudden-like, that there was no quacking of mama and brothers and sisters all around him and it was silent as his grave. It was then the foolish duckling saw how he'd lost the path and there was nothing but the great big wood closing in."

I felt that this duckling boy was shortly to be eaten by one of the Many-Eyed. I frowned at Peter, but he didn't much care about the message I was trying to send.

"The silly little duckling quacked then, quacked loud and long, and waited for his mama to quack back, but she never did. Then the little duckling started to cry, walk and quack and cry all at the same time the way a baby will. The other creatures of the forest watched the duckling pass by and shook their heads, for the boy had been so foolish and hadn't listened to his mama when she told him to stay close and mind her.

"It started to get dark, and the duckling was scared, but he kept walking and crying, thinking that around every corner there might be his mama, ready to scold and hug him all at the same time."

"My mama was never like that," Harry said to Jonathan in a low voice. "She only did the yelling and the hitting, none of the hugging."

Peter gave no sign that he noticed this remark. "After a long time the boy came to a clear pond in a little valley. The water was so fresh and still that all the world reflected in it, like the shiniest looking glass you ever did see."

Ah, I thought, *it's to be a gobbling by a crocodile, then.* I pulled Charlie a little closer to me and put him in my lap, like I could protect him from Peter's story with my arms.

"The little duckling went to the water and peered in, and inside the water was the valley and the trees all around and the white face of the moon and the white face of another little duckling, fuzzy yellow hair and all. The duckling quacked 'hello,' for he was very pleased to see a friendly face after walking and crying so long in the woods on his own. The other duckling in the pond said 'hello' at the same time, which made them both laugh and laugh. The duckling reached through the water, toward his new friend, and their fingertips touched.

"At that very moment the smooth surface of the pond rippled and the sneaking, peeking eyes of a crocodile broke through. The croc wasn't far from where the little duckling and his friend were laughing together. The duckling started up and shouted to his friend, 'Oh, get away, get away or you'll be eaten.'

"He ran a little way and looked over his shoulder to see if his friend followed him like he hoped, but the other duckling wasn't there. Then the little duckling's heart was in his

LOST BOY47
mouth, because he was so scared but he didn't want to leave
his friend to be gobbled up by the crocodile. Those sneaking,
peeking eyes still lurked in the same place, so the duckling
thought he had time to get his friend from the water."

"How come the bird was so stupid?" Harry asked. He
seemed to have forgotten that the duckling was actually a
boy in Peter's story. "Don't he know the pond only shows
what's put in it?"

This didn't really make sense but we all knew what Harry
meant. A few of the others nodded.

Charlie hadn't forgotten the duckling was actually a boy.
He pressed his face against my chest, like he was trying to
climb inside my skin, trying to find a place where he could
be safe from the story. Only Charlie and I seemed to know it
wasn't to end well, and only I knew the story was meant for
me. Charlie was dead scared of the crocodile pond, and he
was right to be. Those beasts could gobble a little one like
him in one bite.

"Haven't I said he was a foolish little duckling?" Peter
said, responding to Harry's question. "Everyone knows we
stick together in the forest."

"If you go out alone you won't come back," a few of the
boys said together.

"'Cept Jamie," Fog said.

"Yeah, 'cept Jamie," Nod said.

"Nothing in the forest would be dumb enough to try and

hurt Jamie," Peter said, with a fierce kind of pride.

That pride would have made me swell a little were it not for Charlie's small voice. "But what about the duckling?"

"Right you are, Charlie," Peter said. "That little duckling crept back to the so-still pond, where Mr. Crocodile waited. He gathered all his courage and looked into the water and saw his friend there, so very close to those watching eyes."

"I thought this was a ghost story," Billy said. He didn't seem much impressed by the tale of the little duckling. "Where's the ghost?"

"Aye," said Jonathan. "I thought a proper ghost story would have bloody white creepers covered in chains and all."

"If you don't shut it we'll never get to the ghost bit," Peter said, temper snapping in his eyes.

That's all right, I thought. *Charlie and me, we don't need to hear the end of this story. We don't need to know how the crocodile chomped the little duckling into its jaws while the boy cried for his mama, because Charlie and me, we already see it.*

Peter cleared his throat so all the boys would pay attention again. There was no thought of leaving, of doing something else, of taking Charlie somewhere he wouldn't hear. And the boys who were bored wouldn't leave either. It was Peter's island, Peter who'd brought us here, and in the back of every boy's mind was some form of the same thought—*He could send me back, if he wanted.*

They didn't know that Peter wouldn't ever let anyone

leave. Once you came to the island, you stayed on the island. That was the rule. You stayed there forever.

And none of them wanted to go back, for they'd all been alone or as good as, running from the smell of ale and dirty straw and the fist that made your teeth fall out. Anything Peter had on offer was better than that, even if there were monsters here.

Except, I thought, *maybe for Charlie. Charlie didn't belong. Charlie might have a brother, a brother who teased about the ghost in the wardrobe but who might look out for him too, and maybe Charlie had been that little duckling following a grasshopper the day we found him. Maybe we should have just turned him around so he could find his way back to the path, instead of taking him away with us.*

"The duckling reached for his friend in the water, and his friend reached back. Just as the duckling was about to grasp hands with the other boy his fingers somehow slipped past and into the water."

"How can a bird have fingers?" Harry asked Billy, and Billy shushed him at the look in Peter's eye.

"The sneaking, peeking crocodile eyes hadn't moved, so the little duckling thought there must still be time to save his friend. He reached in the water and the other boy reached back and his face was scared but their hands did not touch. The little duckling knew then his friend was trapped beneath the surface and that meant he would be eaten for certain.

"No wonder the crocodile hadn't lumbered from the pond to chase the duckling, for his meal was only a snap and a clap away, no need to run after little boys on land."

"Here, now, where'd the boy come from?" Harry asked.

"The little duckling thought and thought, and then he dragged a large branch to the pond and pushed it in for his friend to grab. It splashed and crashed and the old fat croc blinked his eyes, but he did not move, and the duckling's friend was still stuck beneath the water, his face as pale as the white moon.

"The duckling saw a vine on a tree and he ran to the tree and tugged with all his might, always checking over his shoulder to make sure the croc wasn't about, but the croc just stayed where he was put, like he was sleeping with his eyes open.

"The vine came loose with a ripping noise and the duckling tumbled back, rolling so far so fast that he almost went right into the pond with the friend he was trying to save, and what would happen then? Who would save them if they both were trapped under the surface?

"He threw the vine in the water and told his friend to grab hold of it and he ran away from the pond as fast as he could, holding his end of the vine and hoping, hoping, hoping he was pulling his friend from the reach of the crocodile's teeth. After a while he looked back and saw he had gone far from the water and the sneaking, peeking eyes but he was all alone. The end of the vine trailed along behind him, wet and dirty and friendless.

"The little duckling cried then, for he was scared of the croc and the water and of being by himself in the woods and he just wanted his mama, just wanted her to come and put him under her wing and take him home."

Peter looked at me, and I knew this last part was for me—a warning, maybe, or a foretelling of the future? Charlie started to shake then—he couldn't bear it another second—and I turned him around so his head was on my shoulder, just like he was my little duckling and I was his mama, putting him under my wing. I gave Peter a look that said, *Do your worst.*

"But though he was a foolish duckling he was still, deep down, a brave one too. He wouldn't leave his friend behind. The little duckling decided finally he must dive into the water and push his friend out, and the thought of this made him tremble all over and made the downy yellow fuzz on his head stand up. He stood on the shore of the pond, watching that sneaking, creeping crocodile, who was so still the duckling almost thought he wasn't even alive.

"Just as the duckling had worked up enough courage to leap into the water, he heard something, something so far away but so longed for that he was sure he imagined it. It sounded like Mama, quacking and quacking his name.

"The little duckling forgot about his friend in the water and turned and called for her, and she called back and now his heart was full and happy and he started away from the pond, running across the clearing and shouting and shouting for her. Everything would be all right now that his mama was here.

"But, oh, that peeking, sneaking crocodile, he knew his time had come. The little duckling's back was turned but if he had looked over his shoulder he would have seen that old crocodile moving fast now, faster than anyone would have thought possible. His tail whipped that giant monster's body through the water in a trice, and though he splashed as he clambered onshore, the little duckling did not hear. He could only hear one thing—the voice of his mama."

Charlie trembled all over, his body vibrating against my chest, and he covered his ears with his little hands. He didn't want to hear because he already knew, and so did I. The other boys leaned forward, their eyes shining in the afternoon light, for Peter had them well and truly caught now.

"And what do you think happened then?" Peter asked, for he never lost a chance to perform for the audience.

"He got eaten!" Harry said. "And he turned into a ghost!"

I sniggered a little at the look on Peter's face, for although it was obvious where the story was heading, he clearly felt that Harry's delivery left something to be desired.

"The little duckling's mama broke through the trees and saw him running to her, and she saw, too, the crocodile behind, his eyes so hungry and red. She shrieked and reached for her duckling but it was too late, far too late. That sneaking, creeping crocodile had hold of the duckling's leg and the little duckling was too surprised to cry out, too surprised to do anything at all.

"His mother, she was quacking and squawking as the little duckling was dragged away, but she should have kept a better eye, shouldn't she? Isn't that what mamas are supposed to do?"

"Don't remember our mama," said Nod, and Fog nodded his head up and down in agreement.

"I do," Billy said, and it didn't seem the memory brought him any particular joy.

"I do," said Charlie, but it was a tiny whisper, just for me. "She used to rock me and sing to me and hold me so tight."

"That mother duck, she ran after the crocodile, but he disappeared under the water of the pond, taking the little duckling with him.

"Now, you might think that the little duckling turned into a ghost that haunts that old crocodile pond," Peter said, his eyes hard and bright as he glanced at the shivering Charlie in my arms.

"Didn't he?" Harry asked.

Peter shook his head side to side, a long, slow "no" that had all the boys peering at him in confusion.

"What's all this duck business about, then, if he didn't turn into a ghost? Where's the bloody ghost in the ghost story?" Harry asked, but there was no rancor in his voice, just confusion.

"The mother duckling stood at the shore of the pond, weeping and weeping for her little lost one. Her tears were so great and so many that the waters of the pond rose and flooded around her feet and ankles, and she sank deep into the mud there until the water covered her to her knees. On and on she wept, for she knew it was all her fault for letting her little boy get lost in the first place. After a very long time her tears ran dry, but by then her legs had turned into stems and her yellow hair into the petals of a flower, and so she stands there until this day, crouched over the crocodile pond, hoping forever to see the face of her little duckling again. And sometimes, if you go to the crocodile pond late at night, you can hear her voice on the wind, crying his name."

Peter said this last bit very quietly and dramatically. I didn't know what the rest of the boys would make of this tale—they mostly looked confused and slightly disappointed—but I knew that Peter meant it for me. But was I the little duckling's mama in the story, or was I supposed to return him to her before something happened to Charlie? I wasn't sure.

Peter's eyes were dark and full of blood, but the wet on my shoulder was from Charlie's quiet tears.

CHAPTER 3

After that strange little interlude, the boys were full of energy and ready to run, so Peter decided we ought to set off for the pirate camp though the sun was lowering. As usual, my objections were overruled.

"The sun will be up for a while longer," Peter said. "Anyhow, the boys are already gone."

It was true. As soon as Peter had given them leave to go, all the boys had collected their supplies and weapons (following the lead of Nod and Fog, who were always happy to order the new boys about). Then the twins whooped and hollered and ran into the woods, and most of the others had followed them with varying degrees of enthusiasm. Del's face was less pale than usual, and I could tell he still felt some lingering pride at having fought Nip off at lunch.

Maybe he would make it. Maybe he wouldn't die slowly coughing out blood. Maybe.

Everyone left except Nip, who was still passed out where

I'd left him, and Peter and Charlie and me. Charlie had one hand attached to the tail of my coat and the thumb of his other hand was stuffed in his mouth.

Peter eyed the little boy with distaste, though after the story he'd told, Peter could hardly expect Charlie to scamper happily after the others.

"Go and kick Nip," Peter told Charlie. "If he doesn't get up he'll have to stay here on his own while we raid the pirates."

Charlie looked up at me, which I could tell bothered Peter no end. He was used to having his wishes granted without question.

"I'll do it," I said. I didn't want Nip to wake up swinging and punch Charlie in the face, although I was pretty certain that was precisely the goal Peter had in mind.

"I'm not minding him while you're about it," Peter said, just as if Charlie weren't there at all.

"It's fine," I said. "Come with me, Charlie."

Peter frowned, this outcome apparently not at all what he'd wanted.

"Go on after the others," I said to Peter, and his frown became fierce. Not only was I taking the risk of harm away from Charlie but I'd just dismissed Peter like one of the other boys. Like he was ordinary.

And Peter never wanted to be ordinary.

"I don't want to go yet," Peter said.

"As you please," I said, and hid my smile as I turned away.

Charlie kept his hand on my clothes, but as we approached Nip he tugged at the hem. I glanced down at him and he shook his head at me.

"You don't want to get closer to Nip?"

Charlie's thumb popped out of his mouth. "He scares me."

"Do you want to go back to Peter?"

Charlie shook his head no again, but didn't offer any explanation this time. I had a fair idea that Peter's "ghost" story had taken some of the shine off the other boy for Charlie.

"Just stay here, all right? I'll just go give Nip a kick and come right back for you."

Charlie shook his head, his eyes big and blue and full of feelings he couldn't put into words, but I could see the story of the lost duckling swimming around in them.

"I promise I'll be back," I said. "I don't want you to get hurt if Nip wakes up like an angry bear, right? And you can see me all the time I'm gone."

Charlie turned this over in his mind, and finally nodded and let go of my clothes. He snagged one hand firmly in his own shirt hem and put his other thumb back in his mouth.

Peter stood near the fire where we'd left him, his brow creased as he watched us.

Whatever trouble Peter seemed to think Charlie might cause, it was nothing, in my mind, to the trouble Nip *would* cause. He was that kind of boy, the kind who'd always be slugging the others and taking their food and generally disturbing the peace. Not that there was so much peace, really, with more than a dozen boys about, but the roughhousing was usually in a friendly spirit.

I'd seen Nip's eyes when he went for Del at lunch. There was a piggy kind of meanness in them, a cruelty that didn't have a place in our little band of lost boys—at least I thought so, though clearly Peter didn't, else he wouldn't have chosen him.

That made two mistakes Peter had made in the last collection—Charlie and Nip. I knew what he thought he'd get in Charlie—a sweet little toy to play with. I wondered what he thought he'd get out of Nip.

All this was drifting around in my brain as I stood over the prone boy, and so I didn't do any of the things I might have done with one of the others—shake him awake, or roll him over so that the sun on his face made him open his eyes. No, I did exactly as Peter had told Charlie to do—I kicked him.

I kicked him good and hard in the ribs and if I didn't crack any bones it wasn't for lack of trying.

Nip rolled over with a cry and came to his knees. His face was smudged with dirt and ash from the fire and his eyes were reddened from the coals. It took him a moment to realize where he was, what had happened and what I was doing there. When he did he stood up—staggered up, really, and his hand went to his head like my last blow was still ringing there.

None of this stopped him from putting up his fists in clear invitation.

I hadn't wanted to fight him earlier, so I'd sent Nip off with Nod and Fog. Now I wanted to fight. It'd been boiling in me all day.

First the dream, and Peter's insistence on a raid that would probably kill half the boys, then Nip's bullying of Del and that thrice-bedamned story about the duckling that Peter told to terrify Charlie half to death. I'd been holding back so as not to scare the little boy who trailed behind me, but now Nip offered a chance to beat him good and bloody and I was going to take it.

It wasn't fair of me, not really. Nip was about the same height as me, and he had more weight on him, but he was still staggering-stupid from before. It wasn't an even fight.

I didn't care if it was even or not. I just wanted to beat the piss out of somebody.

So Nip put his fists up and I smiled at him. And when I smiled he dropped his fists a little and asked, "What are you smiling about?"

His nose was broken before he realized why I was smiling.

Then his cheekbone—I heard it crack—then I kicked in his stomach and he staggered back, puking his guts up.

I would have done more. I could have done more. The red haze was riding hard in my blood and I wanted to peel his eyelids back and pop his eyeballs out. I wanted to put Nip down for good.

But then I heard Charlie's tiny gasp as the bigger boy

retched out what little he'd eaten that day. When I looked back I saw his eyes as giant pools of blue in a face as white as a seabird's wing feather.

There was blood on my knuckles from where I'd busted Nip's nose open, but I knelt and opened my arms to Charlie and he ran into them. I felt that hard anger receding—not disappearing, for it never disappeared entirely but waited for the right feeding to bring it back to life.

Nip retched again, his breath harsh and shallow. He started to speak but I stopped him.

"You leave off the other boys, you hear?" I said. "Else there'll be more of the same for you."

Nip's eyes narrowed at me, full of resentment. "What's it to you? Who do you think you are, anyway? Peter picked me himself."

"Don't go thinking that makes you special," I said. They were all the same. They all thought they were special, but only I was. I was first and none of them could take that from me. I was first and best and last and always. Peter could do without them but not without me. Never without me. "You're here to be part of our band, and we all work together here."

"I'm not taking orders from you," Nip said.

"Then you can leave," I said. "Go live with the pirates and see how you like that."

"Try and make me," Nip said, and sneered. His face was spattered with blood from his nose, and his left cheekbone moved in a very wrong way when he talked. He must have been full of vinegar to keep gabbing at me through that. "Don't see how you can when you're playing nanny."

Charlie was nothing to do with this, and I wasn't going to let this new boy bring him in.

"I can kill you with one hand," I said, and let Nip see it in my eyes.

"Can you really?" Charlie whispered in my ear.

I nodded once, and wondered if Charlie would be scared of me now. But instead he gripped my neck tighter, like he knew for certain I was strong enough to look after him, to keep him safe. And I was.

Nip watched me, his mean little eyes going from my face to the back of Charlie's head resting on my shoulder. I saw him working something out that I didn't care for.

All this happened while Peter watched and waited by the dying embers of the fire. The sun's slanting rays were longer and longer by the minute. I wasn't keen on starting off after the others in the dark.

"Leave off the other boys, and do as you're told," I said to Nip. "Or else you'll pay for it."

I turned away then, for he was the sort of boy who would learn his lesson only after hard knocks, so there wasn't any point in standing there bandying words with him all day.

"Now can we go a-raiding?" Peter asked in a singsong voice, skipping around me like a child asking his father for a sweet. "If we don't catch up to the rest soon they'll get eaten by the Many-Eyed without you there."

"Nod and Fog can look out for them," I said mildly, though I privately agreed. Nod and Fog could take orders, but too often they got caught up in their own concerns to take proper care of the other boys. "Besides, they'll stop at the cave for the night before they get to the fields."

"Then let's go!" Peter cried, and ran into the woods after the others.

Nip had pushed up to his feet. He looked a right mess and none too steady. I hoped he fell off a cliff or wandered into the mouth of a bear on the way and saved me some future trouble, for he was staring at me with that trouble in his eyes.

"Are you coming or not?" I shouted to him.

He didn't say a word to me, only went after Peter.

Charlie had picked up his head to watch the bigger boy. "Maybe he'll get lost," he whispered hopefully.

"Maybe he will," I said, and rumpled his hair. "You don't like Nip, do you?"

"He tried to take Del's food," Charlie said as I placed him on the ground. He immediately grabbed the hem of my coat as we went toward the path after the others. "He would have eaten mine if you weren't there."

He understood this instinctively, understood that because he was small there would always be those who tried to use their size against him.

Nip and Peter weren't far ahead of us on the trail and I

didn't fancy the four of us walking together like a happy family. "Do you want me to show you something, Charlie?"

"What?" he asked.

"A shortcut," I said.

"A shortcut to what?"

"I know where they'll stop for the night," I said. "And anyway, all those boys don't know how to be quiet when they're together. We'll hear them before we see them."

"And we won't have to walk with Nip," Charlie said, his eyes lit up at the thought of a shortcut, a secret for only him and me.

That was the magic the island had—rocks to scramble over and trees to climb and mermaid lagoons to swim in and, yes, pirates to fight. I didn't want to take the boys there today, but fighting pirates was some of the best fun you could have. The whole island was a great wide playground for boys like us to run in, to make secret places, to go where we wished and when we wanted with no adults to stop us or make us mind.

And Charlie, he needed that magic. I was pretty certain that we'd taken this little duckling from a mama who loved him.

Peter didn't think very much of mothers—it had been far too long since he'd had one to remember, and most of the boys had the kind of mothers you wanted to forget.

Peter said mine was like that too, that she'd harangued and beaten me, but I didn't remember her. I didn't remember too much from before, only flashes, and sometimes the songs that made my heart ache and Peter frown.

I knew the boys would stop at Bear Cave for the night, so named because the first time Peter and I went there we found the bones of a huge bear. Peter had loved that snarling skull so much that he mounted it on the wall and we dug a fire pit beneath it like some altar to an ancient god. When the fire was lit the flames played strangely on the skull, making it seem that at any moment it would live again, devouring us all.

I spared a thought for how those dancing shadows would frighten Charlie, then let it pass. I couldn't keep things from scaring him, only from harming him.

The boys would stop at the Bear Cave, because there was good cover there and it was well before the fields of the Many-Eyed.

Nod and Fog, for all that they both seemed fearless, were both terrified of the Many-Eyed. I'd never shame them for this; nor would anyone on the island with sense. Even Peter, who liked to tease and play on the others' fears, wouldn't mock this.

The boys wouldn't try to cross the fields without Peter or me, and it was pure foolishness to try at night in any case. That was asking to get eaten.

Charlie followed me off the path and into the dark thicket of trees. It was cooler away from the main walk where the sun beat down on the exposed trail. Here under the canopy of leaves the small flies didn't buzz and bite, and the shifting shadows welcomed those with a heart to explore.

Little soft things scurried in the undergrowth, rabbits and field mice and miniature foxes with overlarge ears and watchful eyes. I liked the soft loam of the earth here, the wet green smell of the ferns mixed with the pungent sweetness of fallen fruit.

The trees arced over our heads far above, the long broad leaves tangling there like they stood arm in arm, protecting us.

"I like it here," Charlie said, kneeling to push his fingers into the dirt. He laughed when several fat pink earthworms poked their heads blindly through the surface, waving about like they were sniffing for an intruder.

All we needed to do was cut through the forest and we would come out alongside the rocky cliff that led up to Bear Cave. The footing was narrow there, but Charlie was small and I'd climbed it so many times I could do it in my sleep.

We'd easily beat Peter and Nip there if they stayed to the path, for the path they followed twisted and rambled all through the forest and countryside before stopping at the point of Bear Cave, where the mountains met the plains.

And Nip wasn't all together in his mind and body either. The memory of his broken cheekbone moving out of time with the rest of his jaw made me smile to myself.

Charlie ran ahead of me, giggling and flushing birds out of their nests in the ferns so that they chirped angrily at him.

It was the first time I'd seen him free and happy since he'd arrived on the island.

When night fell and the woods grew dark, he came back to me. It didn't feel that this was because he was scared, just a little unsure where to walk.

Bigger animals moved in the dark around us. We heard the soft pad of hooves and spotted the gleam of white antlers.

Later, we heard a bear snuffling toward us, big and broad and smelling of the last thing he killed. Bears mostly left us boys alone, but the reek of this one warned me of its approach and I decided not to risk it, pushing Charlie onto a tree branch and following after him.

We waited until the bear's shadow passed underneath the branches we perched on and its grunting bulk gradually moved away.

"Would it eat us?" Charlie asked. I was glad to hear that he didn't sound frightened, only curious.

"Probably not," I said. "Bears have much better things to eat on this island than skinny boys, and that one has already had a feast."

"I smelled the blood," Charlie said. "It probably had some rabbits, like us."

"A rabbit's nothing but a mouthful to a big old grunter like that." I laughed. "He's been at deer or elk or maybe some of the fat silverfish that live in the ponds and streams. All those kind are much better food for a bear than us, but a bear is something that kills, and being something that kills, the best wisdom is to avoid its teeth and claws."

"Are you something that kills?" Charlie asked. "Nod and Fog say that you are. They say no one's killed more pirates than you."

"I've lived here a long time," I said. "Peter's lived here even longer."

I shifted uneasily as his bright little eyes studied me in the moonlight. Both of us knew quite well that I hadn't answered the question.

I'd killed more pirates than I could remember, and for longer than I could remember. The pirates hated Peter but they hated me more, for I was a plague to them, a plague that cut away their best and youngest mates. No older pirate was quick enough to face me, so they sent their bright things to try to take me. But no bright young man, for all that he has the strength of a man, was as fast as a twelve-year-old boy. And I had experience on my side, though I did not look it.

You'd think that after all these years of losses to us, the pirates would choose another island when they wanted to stay in port, but they returned to ours season after season. One time, long ago, I asked Peter why they kept coming back.

"Because they want to know why we never grow up, silly," Peter said, and cuffed the back of my head. "They think we have some special treasure that keeps us young, and they want it."

I frowned at him. "If they want it, then why don't they ever go past the beach near their ship?"

"They think they'll catch one of us when we come a-raiding," Peter said.

I snorted a laugh, and Peter smiled at me, and when he smiled like that it was just the two of us together, brothers forever.

Charlie's voice brought me back to the woods and the dark, his voice and the fear in it. "Will I have to kill a pirate?"

"Not if you don't want to," I said. *Not if I have anything to say about it, you won't.*

"I don't know how to fight," Charlie said.

"You're not the only one," I said, thinking of the other new boys, the ones who'd never handled a sword or a knife. "Just stay with me and you'll be fine."

I hopped off the branch and reached up for him, and as I set him on the ground I decided. Peter wouldn't like it, but I wasn't going to let Charlie anywhere near the pirate camp. I was going to tuck him up in a tree or a cave like a baby in a cradle and keep him well away from any fighting. If I was lucky, Peter wouldn't notice.

Except Peter notices everything.

There was always a first time, I reasoned. He might be so busy with the raid that he wouldn't trouble to keep track of Charlie, though since the little boy was almost always attached to my sleeve that was unlikely.

Charlie's silence told me he was worried about the pirates,

and the joy had gone out of the adventure in the woods.

Too damned little, I thought for the dozenth time that day. *Too little for all of this.*

We emerged from the forest right at the bottom of the cliff path. The boys up in the cave had a fire lit and the smell of burning wood and meat had led us to them for a good mile before we reached the cliff. They were having a raucous time of it, too—screeching and laughing and jumping about.

"They're having a jolly time," I said, smiling down at Charlie.

He stared up the path at the leaping shadows and beyond, into the cold white eye of the moon. He didn't seem to think it was very jolly up there, and his fist wound into my coat again.

I detached him gently. "You have to go ahead of me. There's not room for us side by side."

He stubbornly rewound his fist and shook his head. "I don't want to."

I felt the first stirrings of impatience. "You have to."

"I don't want to," Charlie repeated.

I deliberately peeled his hand out of my coat and pushed him toward the path. "You have to. We can't stand here playing about all night."

He wriggled away from my hands, shaking his head, his mouth set in an obstinate line. "No."

I didn't know whether this was about Peter or Nip or that he was afraid of the dark or the cliff path or what. I just knew that I wasn't of a mind to deal with his nonsense. I didn't care about Charlie's reasons at that moment; I just wanted him to *mind* me.

I was angry and let him see it. "You have to go up there. If you don't, I'll leave you here."

His face went shocked and white. I could have smacked him and hurt him less, I reckon. "The duckling," he whispered. "What about the duckling?"

"The bloody duckling didn't *listen*, didn't *mind*," I said, starting up the cliff path and leaving Charlie there, staring after me.

Peter was right. I didn't do them any good when I tried to take care of them. I wasn't Charlie's mama and it wasn't down to me to be one. If that stupid little boy fell in the crocodile pond or got eaten by a bear or wandered into the fields of the Many-Eyed, it was no nevermind to me because he wasn't my problem, not my responsibility.

Peter was the one who'd wanted the little brat. Let him look after Charlie, let him . . .

My steps slowed, then stopped. I was about halfway up the path, the raucous shouts of the boys in the cave practically inside my ear, they were so loud. I looked back.

Charlie stood at the base of the path, his face upturned in the moonlight, tears streaming from his eyes.

He appeared frozen, his muscles locked, unable to follow, unable to do anything but wait. Wait for me to return for him.

I sighed, and my anger went out with that sigh. Peter chose the boys, yes, he did. But he didn't care for them. He didn't look after them. He didn't teach them how to find the best mushrooms or how to string a line to catch a fish. He took them to fight the pirates but didn't teach them how to do it properly so they wouldn't get killed. He didn't show them how to skin a deer for clothes or comfort them when they cried in the night or bury them when they died. I did that.

Peter was good for showing you the quickest path to the mermaid lagoon and for picking teams in Battle and for sneaking through the pirate camp at night, stealing shiny things that he stored in a hollow in our tree like he was an overgrown magpie. Peter was for fun, for play, for adventures. Me, I kept his playmates alive—even when he didn't want them anymore. Like Charlie.

I went back down the path, sure-footed despite the narrow track and the crumbling edge that promised a hard bruising fall, if not a broken bone.

I wasn't sure Charlie would forgive me, but as I approached he broke into a run and leapt at me. I stumbled a little until I had his weight, saying, "Hey, now, you'll make us both fall," but not in a gruff way.

Charlie's wet face pressed against my neck and he said over and over, "I'm sorry, Jamie, I'm sorry. I'll listen. I'll be good. I'm sorry, only don't leave me."

I patted his back and told him I wouldn't. And I wouldn't.

I was better now. I would look after him.

I wished I could promise him he wouldn't be hurt. But you can't make promises like that—not on the island, not in the Other Place. Boys got hurt. They fell. They bloodied one another's noses. They called one another cruel names. Sometimes they got eaten by crocodiles. Sometimes they got stabbed by pirates.

I wouldn't lie to Charlie. But I could promise not to leave him.

CHAPTER 4

Just before we crested the top of the cliff I set Charlie on his feet and wiped his face. My hands were dirty and left streaks on his cheeks.

"Can't let the others see you like this," I said.

"Boys aren't supposed to cry," Charlie said. "My brother Colin said so. He said only babies and girls cry and I'd better quit it. That's why he sent me outside."

"Outside?" I asked.

I was only half listening until then, my head cocked to one side to see whether I could hear Peter's voice amid the chorus of noise coming from the cave. I wanted desperately to beat Nip and Peter, to prove somehow that Charlie was worth more than Peter thought he was, to show that Charlie wouldn't drag him down. I didn't hear our fearless leader, who usually liked to be the loudest.

Charlie spoke again. "Yes, he put me outside because he scared me and I was crying. Mama told him to watch me, only he didn't. He hid in the cupboard and knocked on the inside of the door and pretended he was a ghost and then he jumped out and scared me. He scared me and I cried and he said, 'Shut it, I don't want to hear your noise; only babies cry like that,' and when I didn't stop he sent me outside and shut the door. I hit the door and I cried and told him to let me in but he only made a face at me from the window and went away. Then I stopped crying and he still wouldn't let me in and I was thirsty. I was going to get a drink from the pump—it's in the square—only I got lost and couldn't find it and I was crying and so thirsty. Then I got tired and stopped crying but I couldn't find home again. Then you and Peter found me and said we could have an adventure and I couldn't find my way home so I came with you."

I stared at him. This was the most words Charlie had ever said in one go, and they confirmed the great wrong I'd suspected. We hadn't saved Charlie from an unhappy home or a life in an orphanage. We'd stolen him from a mama who'd probably cried every day he was gone, just like the mother duck in Peter's story.

I don't know what I would have said or done then, though my first inclination was to scoop him up and take him home straightaway, damn Peter and his pirate raid.

But just then a sound reached me, a chittering, clackety sound, a sound that should not be so close to the Bear Cave, should not be so close to this part of the island at all.

"What's that?" Charlie asked.

"Sh," I said. "Stay close and do as I say."

He didn't ask any more questions. Maybe it was my manner or maybe the memory of me leaving him at the bottom of the path, but he listened. Charlie huddled close to my legs as I strained, trying to figure where the noise was coming from.

It wasn't from the forest or the path we'd just climbed; I was certain of that. It hadn't somehow gotten around behind us.

Anyway, that didn't make any sense. They wouldn't come from that side, the forest side. They'd come from the other side of the cave. There was a downhill track there that went along through the foothills that bordered the plains. The Many-Eyed lived in the plains, and usually stayed in the plains.

Lately we'd been finding one or two on their own, probing into the forest like scouts. We would chase them off when we found them there, using our slings to throw rocks and scare them away. It was easy to scare them when we were in the forest, for we could climb trees and stay safely out of reach.

I'd proposed more than once that we should just kill them if they came in our territory, that it would send a message to them to stop sniffing about that part of the island. But Peter thought they would see a killing as an act of war, and that it would invite an angry invasion of Many-Eyed upon us. Peter knew the island best of us all, so we listened, and didn't kill them.

But now one was nearby, far from its home in the plains. The Many-Eyed nested in the very center part of those plains, and that made it easy to avoid most of them. One had never come as far as Bear Cave, mostly because they didn't seem to like climbing—or so we thought. The mountains were the one part of the island where there had never been any sign of them.

The clicking and chittering drew closer, and I was certain now that it was coming up the track—the track we would take the next morning to go down to the pirate camp. I hoped there was only one—maybe a young one that had gotten lost and just needed to be encouraged to go back to its proper home, far from us.

The boys in the cave shouted and screeched and seemed entirely unaware of what was happening. I tugged Charlie toward the cave. I had to get him inside and hidden, for he would be nothing but a little sweetmeat to a Many-Eyed.

We moved quickly and quietly across the flat rock outcropping that led to the cave. My heart pounded in my chest. I wasn't scared for myself; I was scared for Charlie and the other boys. The new boys, especially. They'd never seen a Many-Eyed, and might panic, and that would make things harder when I wanted them to be safe.

If Peter were there, he might say they needed to learn on the run. I said that left a lot of dead boys and that was wasteful even if he didn't care about any of them. But Peter wasn't there. I was.

Charlie and I rounded the lip of the cave and at once I saw why they hadn't noticed the noise or anything else.

Somebody had killed a deer—Nod, by the look of it, for he wore the deer's head and part of its skin over his shoulders. They'd made quick work of the dressing and were roasting the deer's haunches over the fire.

Somewhere along the way they'd all stripped down to their bare skin and painted themselves with blood. They were dancing and jumping and whooping around the fire.

I thought, *Peter will be sorry to have missed this*, for Peter loved it when the boys were wild things. It tied them to him better, made them forget the Other Place, made them belong to Peter and the island.

Then I thought, *All the blood will bring the Many-Eyed right up to our door. It might have already.*

I put my fingers between my teeth and whistled, a sound that echoed into the depths of the cave and made Charlie clap his hands over his ears.

All the boys stopped, staring at Charlie and me in the entry.

"There's a Many-Eyed coming," I said.

For a moment they paused, and I thought how vulnerable they looked, without their clothes and their weapons, and how the fresh blood looked like paint, like a dress-up game, not like they were the mighty warriors they thought they were.

Then Nod pushed off the deerskin and ran for his breeches

and his sling and his knife, and Fog did too. The other boys who'd been on the island for a time followed, their eyes reflecting various degrees of fear, grim determination or panic. The new boys—Billy and Terry and Sam and Jack—milled together, mostly confused.

"What's a Many-Eyed?" Terry asked.

"A monster," I said, pulling Charlie into the cave.

I brought him over to Del, who could be trusted to be sensible. Besides, I wanted Del to avoid making himself any sicker. If he coughed out blood it would attract the Many-Eyed right to him.

"You stay here with the new boys," I said to Del.

I put Charlie's hand in Del's free one, for he had just straightened up holding a small metal sword. He was proud as the devil of that sword, and well he should be, for he'd taken it out of a pirate's scabbard while the fool slept on the watch.

Del's brow wrinkled, and I could see in his face the question he wanted to ask—*Why do I have to stay here and nanny?*

"I need you to look after them," I said. "In case the Many-Eyed gets past me."

Del gave me a look that said he thought that was unlikely and he knew what I was about, but he rounded up the new boys anyway and pushed them to the back of the cave. Charlie looked slightly panicked at being separated from me but he went without protest.

"You too," I said, pointing to Kit, Jonathan and Ed.

"Help Del look after the others."

The other three looked relieved. That left Nod, Fog, Harry and me.

I wished Peter were there. Me and Peter, we could take one Many-Eyed by ourselves, and then I wouldn't have to worry about the others.

Harry wasn't any too bright but he was strong and followed directions without question, which was why I'd kept him with me. Nod and Fog were terrified of the Many-Eyed but they were also brave as anything. They wouldn't run from the fight.

I indicated they should follow me out of the cave. We crept to the mouth, listening, me in front, then Harry, Nod and Fog. I had my dagger in my left hand, though I didn't remember taking it off my belt.

Now that the boys were quiet the clicking of the Many-Eyed's fangs seemed incredibly loud, filling up all the empty space, crawling inside our ears and down our throats and into our hearts. It was the sound of something hunting, something hungry.

The echoing quality of the sound made it impossible to tell whether the creature was still on the foothill track or just on the other side of the cave wall, ready to turn in on us at any moment. I stepped forward and my foot slid in something slick.

Unlike Peter, who preferred to go barefoot, I wore ankle-high moccasins made from elk hide. The bottom of the right one was now coated in deer offal I'd trod in without noticing. That gave me an idea.

"Fog," I whispered, as he was now standing in it himself. "Pass me some of that."

Fog obligingly scooped up two handfuls of guts and carried them to me. I took the unidentifiable mess from him and peered around the cave wall.

The Many-Eyed was just clambering on the rock shelf. Its full body hadn't cleared the edge yet. One of its hairy legs was testing the space, ensuring there was room for the rest of it.

For a brief moment I contemplated rushing the beast with the other boys, grabbing hold of that leg and pushing it from the side of the cliff. Its bloated body would burst on a protruding rock, and the Many-Eyed wouldn't be any the wiser about why one of its own had died.

But Peter would know. Just because he wasn't there wouldn't mean not finding out, and he didn't want to be at war with the Many-Eyed. He'd made that very clear. He would happily be at war with the pirates, and he didn't mind—no, he even encouraged in the form of Battle— fighting among ourselves.

But we were not to start trouble with the Many-Eyed, no matter that they were a monstrous and unnatural scourge that was clearly (to my mind) creeping farther into the forest every day. Soon enough, I thought, we'd have a war with them whether we wanted it or not.

There was something about the Many-Eyed that stirred a primal sense of wrongness in me, though they were nothing more than part of the island to Peter. Their fat round bodies, covered in shaggy hair and swollen with the blood of their meals; their legs—eight of them, far too many, and the strange bent way they moved, gliding and awkward at the same time. They were alien, everything a boy was not.

"Harry, get a torch from the fire," I said.

I squeezed the deer organs in my hand. The wet flesh slid between my fingers.

Harry darted back in place behind me, holding a long, thick piece of wood blazing at one end.

"Right," I said. "I'm going to toss this mess to it and see if it will take it. Harry, you use the fire if it seems like it's getting too close. Nod, Fog, you spread out behind me with your slings. If it gets going past me or Harry, then you take out its eyes with rocks."

Even Peter couldn't object, I reasoned, if a Many-Eyed fell over a cliff and died because it was blind. At least, he could object (and usually did, loudly, when not getting his way), but we wouldn't have actively killed the thing and therefore would have followed the strict letter of Peter's law.

My own inclination to wipe the Many-Eyed off the island would, too, be at least partially satisfied.

With my knife in my left hand and the deer guts dripping through my right, I jerked my chin toward the opening of the cave. The others followed me. I heard Harry's breath coming in short, sharp pants. The torch he held dripped sparks on my neck, but I couldn't cry out.

The Many-Eyed had cleared the cliff face and was fully on the rock shelf. There wasn't very much space between it and us, and it seemed bigger to me than any Many-Eyed out in the plains with the wide blue sky above.

Here the darkness pressed down, and the rocks and cave made it feel like we were trapped in a closed room with the thing. The deer guts in my hand reeked, making my eyes water.

The Many-Eyed gave a long hiss when it saw us and pounded each one of its eight legs on the ground in a kind of ripple, starting with the back leg on each side and circling up to the front leg. I'd seen Many-Eyed do this before, when they were scared or uncertain.

I didn't flatter myself that it saw four boys as a threat, but all Many-Eyed fear fire, and Harry's torch was a good size for threatening. Harry moved to my right side while Nod and Fog stayed behind.

If it seemed like the creature would get around Harry and me, I wasn't going to wait until Nod and Fog took out its eyes with slingshots. I was going to grab that torch and chase it off the cliff, Peter's rules be damned. A giant monster wasn't going to eat all the boys even if Peter did think one was as good as another.

The Many-Eyed took some tentative steps toward us, hissing through its long fangs all the while. I judged that it was a juvenile, not fully grown for all that it seemed so big on the rock shelf. The moonlight showed clearly that it didn't have the silvery-grey fur that developed in adulthood; nor did it have the extensive scarring that resulted from the merciless fighting for food. There were always more Many-Eyed than could possibly be fed, given the astounding number of babies that spilled out of their egg sacs.

Only a young one, I reasoned, would have strayed so far from the rest of the pack, or been so foolish as to climb a cliff. Really, it could have fallen off a precipice and died before it ever reached us. I wondered what had pushed it on to even try.

And a juvenile would be distracted by the deer meat, and frightened by the fire. Or so I told myself.

I tossed the offal at the Many-Eyed, as far as I could throw, and as I'd hoped the deer guts skidded past its legs, close to the edge of the cliff.

It clicked its fangs together, and a little venom dripped off the edge of one, sizzling on the ground. You didn't want to get that poison on you. It burned right through to your bone. I knew—I had several small round scars on my left arm where a Many-Eyed had splattered me years before.

The Many-Eyed looked toward the pile of blood and guts. I waited, hoping it would accept the offal as an offering and leave. That's what an adult would do.

Its dozens of pupilless eyes rolled back and forth above its fangs, almost like it was considering. Harry raised the torch threateningly and the beast took two or three steps backward, resuming its hissing.

The creatures didn't have any kind of noses that we could see, but they seemed to smell things all the same. It turned its bloated body toward the offal. I blew out my breath, only half aware that I'd been holding it.

When I was on my own there was no fear, only the sure sense of what needed to be done. But when the other boys were around—especially new ones

(*especially Charlie*)

I found myself worried on their behalf, and part of my brain always taken up in their safety. Which, I suppose, was one of the reasons why Peter told me to stop babying them. He never worried about them, not for a minute. Nor about me, come to think of it.

Suddenly the Many-Eyed turned back toward us, having ignored our offering, and made a high-pitched sound like a scream.

Fog gasped behind me and swallowed it just as fast, and I knew he wanted to scream too.

I stepped forward with my left foot and jabbed the knife in my left hand toward the Many-Eyed. I wasn't trying to hurt it yet, only to make my intentions clear. It reared back, front legs in the air, and screamed again.

Far away, far, far across the plains, came an answering cry, so faint I almost thought I imagined it.

It's calling for help, I thought.

And then I imagined dozens of Many-Eyed crossing the

plains, climbing the cliff, surrounding the boys and wrapping them in silk and dragging them back to their colony to feed their babies.

"No," I said, and charged it.

I hadn't given any indication to the others what I would do, and Nod or Fog (sometimes it's hard to tell who is who) shouted after me to stop.

His voice barely penetrated the tidal roar of blood in my ears. I knew the belly was the most vulnerable part, and I didn't want to be within biting distance of those fangs.

The Many-Eyed's shape made them seem awkward—that fat body balanced on all those legs—but they were quick as hell and could turn faster than you could blink. They couldn't twist, though, so if I got behind it I might be able to slide under it before it realized what was happening. At least, that was what I intended.

"Harry, get that fire as close to it as you can!" I shouted.

And as I said that the Many-Eyed charged at Harry, right *at* the fire, screeching all the way.

For a moment we all froze, for none of us had ever seen a Many-Eyed run toward fire before.

I thought, *This one is broken. It goes to fire instead of away from it. It climbs mountains.*

I needed it to be broken, to be different from all the others, because if it wasn't, then the Many-Eyed were developing new and frightening behaviors—and those behaviors didn't bode well for us boys.

Then it knocked the torch aside with its leg and bit down on Harry's shoulder, sinking its fangs into his chest. Harry screamed, screamed and screamed, and his scream unfroze my brain.

Blood spurted and venom poured, burning his skin wherever it splashed and spilling into his muscles and bones.

The belly, the belly, I thought, and knew I wouldn't have another chance. It was distracted by Harry but it wouldn't be for long. Maybe, maybe, I could still save him despite all the blood and the poison and the way his scream was fading away like he was waving good-bye.

I ran behind it, skidded to a stop near its stinger and leapt forward with my arms in front of me, belly down, sliding underneath its body.

It smelled of foul death there, so rank I nearly choked on it. I flipped to my back so I could see the bloated mass shaking above me as it killed Harry.

I slid the blade into the Many-Eyed's belly, jerking the blade parallel to its legs to make a long slice in the thick hairy skin just like I did when I slid down a pirate ship's sail holding on to the handle of my knife.

The Many-Eyed reared back on its legs and there was a terrible rending noise as its fangs tore free from Harry's body. I rolled free just as hot liquid poured out of the slash I'd made. It stung where it touched my hand and arm and shoulder—I wasn't quite quick enough to escape without getting burned.

The thing screamed again, that terrible high-pitched, inhuman sound. I thought I'd finished it, but it wasn't quite done yet.

I rolled up to my feet, my knife in front of me, dimly aware that one of the twins had run to Harry and was dragging him toward the cave.

The Many-Eyed turned to me now—all of those red eyes mad and rolling, Harry's blood coating its venom-spitting fangs, and its own blood running in angry rivers all over the rock shelf.

If I lunged for it, my moccasins would slide in the mess. They might even slide me straight under those sharp, sharp teeth.

The creature pounded all its legs on the ground again and I knew it was going to charge me. I'd gotten turned about while underneath it and now I was essentially in a corner with the cave wall on one side and the cliff face on the other.

There was a little jutting bit of rock shelf about waist high in front of me that made a kind of momentary shield, but it wasn't enough to stop the Many-Eyed; nor was there enough of it for me to crawl into and hide.

Besides, I'd never hide while it went for the rest of the boys.

The Many-Eyed ran at me, though I don't know how with its guts spilling everywhere like that. I didn't have much space, but I got a running start and leapt onto the rock shelf. I lost the temporary protection of the shelf and was completely exposed atop it, but I was only there for a moment before leaping again.

It was going too fast to stop, and I don't think it quite realized what had happened in any case. I jumped on its back before it realized I was above it and not in front.

I mirrored the slashing action I'd used on its belly, this time stabbing hard in the center of its body and sliding over it and down, just like I really was on a pirate's sail this time.

More of the creature's blood and venom spurted out, shooting upward in fountains. I crashed to the ground behind it, narrowly avoiding the stinger, and scrambled out of the way before it decided to sit on me.

The Many-Eyed thrashed its legs in all directions as it screeched, all of its insides erupting out. I flattened against the cave wall, covering my ears as it shrieked out its final death throes.

That noise will bring every Many-Eyed on the island, I thought in despair.

I had to get the boys away from there, back to the tree. And maybe I could lay a false trail with the dead Many-Eyed's blood back to the pirate camp, so if any of its fellows came looking for it they would go after the pirates, not us.

I felt a little sick at the thought of the pirates paying for my deed, turning into meat for the Many-Eyed's children.

But truly—it would be better that it was the pirates, who just stayed on the island to torment us or to try to nab one of us to discover the secret of our youth. Better the pirates than one of my boys.

I thought all this as the Many-Eyed shook out its last drops of blood and then stilled. I could send Nod and Fog back to the tree with the others while I laid the trail to the pirate camp. I could burn the body first, too, and stink up the area, make the Many-Eyed confused about just who and how many had been here.

And then a voice rang across the rock shelf, sharp and clear and angry.

"What have you *done*?"

CHAPTER 5

It was Peter, his words like frost on the air. I'd half forgotten he was on his way, likely delayed on the path by Nip and his injuries. Peter's green, green eyes burned in the moonlight.

Most of the other boys stood silently behind him, their faces unsure. Everyone's expressions said they were glad the Many-Eyed was dead, but Peter quite obviously was not glad and so they didn't know how to feel about this.

"It attacked Harry," I said, feeling angry and slightly ashamed, and then angrier because I thought I shouldn't have to feel sorry about the Many-Eyed. "I thought it was going to kill him."

"It did kill him," Peter said.

His tone said this was of no consequence to him whatsoever. I closed my eyes for a moment so I wouldn't scream at him in front of all the other boys.

"You should have left and taken the rest of the boys with you while it ate him," Peter continued.

"Why? So it could follow us and eat the rest when it realized just how delicious we are? Peter, it was calling the rest of them. They would have swarmed all over this place."

"Now they *are* going to swarm all over," Peter said. "Because of what you did they will follow us into the forest and hunt us until we are all dead, and that will be the end of Peter and his boys."

He was making me feel more foolish and embarrassed with every word. This was the first time any of us had killed a Many-Eyed, though we had fought them before and the monsters had eaten their fair share of boys over the years. I'd never understood why Peter only let us wound them, or why he would never explain.

"Why?" I shouted, unable to restrain my temper before the boys. I kept hearing Harry's scream fading away, the last breath leaving his body. "Why are they allowed to take as many of us as they like but we're not permitted to do the same for them? They should have been burned out years ago. We should have scorched the plains and chased the rest of them to the sea. We should never have let monsters stay on this island."

"They've been here as long as I have," Peter hissed. "We had a treaty! And you, you fool, you broke it and now they'll come for all of us."

I went very still. "What treaty, Peter?"

Peter's eyes shifted away.

"How can we have a treaty with monsters, Peter? How can you have a bloody damned treaty that none of us have heard about before when we don't even know *how to talk to them*?"

I saw it in his face—he'd said something he hadn't meant to, and it was bad enough that I knew but worse that it was revealed in front of the others.

How had I not known this? How could I have lived on this island for scores of years and not known that Peter could actually speak to the Many-Eyed?

Worse, how could he treat with them like they were our equals? They *ate* us. They didn't fight us fair and face-to-face like the pirates. They treated us like dumb animals, nothing but blood bags for their survival. They'd eaten more of the boys than I could remember all down the years.

And yet, and yet . . . Peter never let me kill one of them. Not one, no matter how many of my boys they took screaming to the plains.

The others were murmuring now, as some of the brighter ones fitted the jigsaw together.

"I never said I could talk to them," Peter said in that careless way of his. Sometimes I could ignore it, but just then it made me see red.

I stalked toward him, splattered in the Many-Eyed's burning blood, still gripping the knife that had saved the others and me from being eaten alive. I wondered, for the first time, why I'd ever followed him through the door in the Other Place, all those years ago.

When he'd smiled at me and told me we would have adventures, I thought we would be friends always, that it would just be Peter and me, like brothers. But now I saw— and it was so strange that after all this time I finally did see—that I wasn't enough for him, had never been enough.

I didn't mean anything to him, and not even I was special if he could keep a secret like this. And it made me love him a little less, and the memory of that smile hurt deep down in the place where I kept all my secrets and my sorrows.

Peter must have seen some of this on my face, or guessed it by my silence. I saw a little flare of panic in his cool eyes, where he thought no one could see. If he wasn't careful, he would lose the boys. The others would follow me and he knew it, for I was the one who looked after them, looked out for them—not Peter.

His adventures wouldn't matter when it came down to it. The boys wouldn't enjoy starving to death just because Peter didn't want to be troubled about gathering food.

"Well," he said, as if I were not standing less than an eyelash's length from him, covered in blood and fury. "It's all done now and I suppose I will have to forgive you. After all, you didn't know about the treaty and I really think I could make an argument to their chief that you were provoked. I must speak with him about his soldiers coming into the forest anyway."

"I thought you said you couldn't talk to them," I said

through gritted teeth, and I was certain I'd never sounded quite like that before.

The boys knew it too, for they went completely still and silent, as if abruptly aware of the presence of a bear, or something else large and sharp-toothed and hungry.

I felt something coming off Peter—not anger, exactly, but something strong and powerful, something I'd never felt him direct at me before. That power rolled off him, pushed against the haze of red all around me, sparked against it.

A few of the boys gasped and backed away. There was a rising scent in the air, that almost-burning smell that came before a lightning storm.

A little drop of blood rolled from the corner of Peter's mouth, but whether it was wrought by my will or his effort against me, I never knew. All I knew was that something deep and savage inside me howled, howled for more blood, said there could never be enough.

"You're allowed this one time," Peter said, and I had a sense that only I could hear him now. "Just this once, because you're Jamie and I can see you're upset. But never again. If you try to take them from me, I'll cut off your hand."

"Don't ever lie to me," I said. "Don't."

I didn't threaten him, for even as that submerged piece of me raged for more of his blood, there was still a part of me that hurt when I remembered just the two of us, and how we were happy.

Peter sensed the shift, the throttling of my anger, and gave me a crooked smile as he turned away, not worried in the least that I might plunge my knife into his neck.

"I'm going to burn the Many-Eyed," I told his back. "And leave a blood trail to the pirate's camp, away from the forest. At least it might confuse the Many-Eyed for a time, especially since they think we *have a treaty*."

Peter turned back to me, ignoring my dig, his face transformed. The light of adventure glinted in his eyes. "That sounds marvelous fun! So much better than a silly old raid. I'll laugh myself to death if a big old Many-Eyed lumbers into the pirate camp and eats that fat pirate Captain. He's gotten so fat he's hardly sport at all. What do you think, boys? Shall we lay a trail for the Many-Eyed to follow?"

There followed a series of reluctant murmurs instead of the cheers of delight Peter clearly expected. Most of the new boys (and a fair number of the old) darted their eyes between the corpse of the Many-Eyed and me. It was obvious they didn't wish a repeat of this encounter, particularly if it meant they would end up like Harry—burning from the inside with venom and bleeding out white.

"It won't work if we all troop through the plains and the beach leaving a trail behind us," I said. "It's really a job for one or two."

"Then we can be the two," Peter said, slinging his arm over my shoulder like nothing had happened between us.

I shrugged out of his embrace, nodding my assent because I still didn't trust my voice, not entirely. He wasn't acting any way that he didn't normally act, but it bothered me more than usual.

Peter pretended he didn't notice my cut, but I knew he did. "Nod, Fog, you take the others back to the tree."

He waved his hand, dismissing them. They all looked relieved to be going home instead of with us. The fun had gone out of the adventure for most of them when the Many-Eyed appeared.

It made me worry, again, about taking the new ones to the pirate camp. Just because we didn't go today didn't mean we wouldn't go another day, when Peter got it into his head again that it would be fun to have a fight. The pirates, like the Many-Eyed, weren't interested in mercy for small boys.

The only one who looked disappointed was Nip, whose bruises appeared worse than they had the afternoon before. The broken cheekbone had swelled and was pushing up to his eye, making it look even smaller and meaner. *Someone ought to fix that,* I thought, *push the bones back together so they'll heal properly.* But the only person who knew how was me, and I didn't much care to.

Nip's good eye watched me, and I saw the waiting in it. He would wait for his chance to hurt me and then take it.

I didn't care about that as long as he stayed away from Charlie and the others. What Nip might do to me—or, rather, try to do—was no worry to me.

I went into the cave to see if I could salvage some of the burning wood from the bonfire. The boys followed me to collect the sacks of supplies and the weapons they'd left there.

Nod jerked his head at the deer carcass they'd spitted. It was scorched on one side and dried out on the other, entirely uneatable.

"Waste of good meat," he said sadly. "And I took it down with one shot, too."

"Aye," I agreed, though I wasn't really listening.

Harry's body had been dragged off against the wall of the cave. He looked like some rubbish that had been shifted aside so people wouldn't have to look at it.

And that was how Peter thought of him, really, now that Harry was gone, and his big stupid face was stupid and empty now, and I wanted to weep but knew I couldn't as long as the other boys were there. So I put that weeping feeling inside, next to the place where Peter's lie about the Many-Eyed had burrowed into my heart and curled up there, waiting.

I carried an armful of dry wood out to where the Many-Eyed's corpse lay, seeping fluids that steamed in the night air. It was almost impossible that it was still night, that the sun had not yet risen to end that seemingly endless darkness. It was a very long time ago that I'd woken in the night to the sound of Charlie's cry, though a full day had not passed.

I returned back to collect some of the burning wood to

use as torches. Charlie stood in the mouth of the cave, his gaze half on me and half on the other boys, shuffling his feet.

Before I could ask what was wrong, he burst out, "Can't I go with you?"

I could just imagine what Peter might do to Charlie if we brought him along—tie him up and leave him in front of the pirate Captain's tent when I wasn't looking, or "accidentally" push him over a cliff, or some other horror I couldn't imagine. No, it didn't bear thinking about.

Besides, it would do Charlie some good to be away from me, with the other boys. It would help him find his place, and he needed to find it if he were to stay on the island.

"I won't be gone long," I said. "You just stay close to Del. You like Del, don't you?"

"Not as much as I like you," Charlie said, and then he beckoned me closer.

I put one knee down so our eyes were level, and he covered the side of his mouth with his hand as he whispered, "And I'm afraid of *him*."

He cut his eyes toward Nip, who leaned against the cave wall with his arms crossed, watching us. There were burn marks around his eyes and that swelled cheek and I didn't like the way he looked at Charlie, not at all. We'd crossed him, to his way of thinking, and he wanted his own back. He would take it out on Charlie when I wasn't there.

Del had crossed him too, I realized, and rethought the

idea of having only Del watch out for Charlie while I was gone. I couldn't trust Charlie entirely to the twins, though, for the twins liked to run and fight and play too much—they didn't have it in them to look after a little one.

"I can't take you with me, Charlie," I said. "We'll have to move very fast, and there might be more Many-Eyed."

"I . . . I can fight and run fast," he said.

He could do neither, which we both knew very well, but he was trying so hard to be brave I didn't have the heart to crush him. "There's no shame in going back with the others," I said. "They can run and fight too, but this is a job for just two."

One, really, for there was no reason for Peter to come along except to pretend he knew what to do when he didn't.

"I have to get back to it," I said, so that he would know there would be no more discussion.

Nagging in the back of my mind was the worry that the Many-Eyed would track the smell of the dead one before I had a chance to lay the false trail. I hoped, too, that burning the corpse would keep the rest away entirely.

They all feared fire, and the scent of smoke should drive them away instead of arousing their curiosity. Though that juvenile had run right at the fire . . . but that one was stupid or sick. It had to be.

"Okay, Jamie," Charlie said, his voice very small. "I'll mind you. I'll be good."

I smiled at him, and rumpled his duckling-fuzz hair, and he smiled at me in return.

"Stay with Del," I said. "Don't wander off on your own."

"I won't," he said, and there was the shadow of a sneaking, peeking crocodile on his face.

I went to have a word with Del. "Keep Charlie close to you."

He was the only one of the boys who were left that I could trust completely to follow his task and not get distracted like a magpie.

Del coughed, a cough that started off low and ended with him spitting out a great gob of blood on the cave floor. His cheekbones were sharp enough to slice you open but his eyes were steady as he said, "I will."

"Nip's got it in for Charlie and for you," I said. "I'll be back as quick as I can, but watch yourself until I am."

"I'm not afraid of Nip," Del said, his fingers wrapped tight around the pirate's sword. "But come back soon, anyway, Jamie."

Del went to Charlie, who stood exactly where I'd left him, watching me. Del took Charlie's hand and then called to the other boys to follow as he led them back down the path.

Nod and Fog, who were supposed to be leading the group at Peter's decree, were squabbling over something in the back of the cave.

Charlie glanced back at me as Del led him away, and I felt a stab of fear. He was so little, so vulnerable, and so much could happen while I was gone. I was the only one who could really look after him properly.

And we never should have taken him in the first place. That was what ate at me, really. Charlie wasn't one of our boys. He wasn't lost, not in the way that Peter preferred. He had a family.

That, I couldn't solve. Once you came to the island you could not leave—that was one of Peter's most fixed rules. If you weren't happy, then you could go to the pirates or feed yourself to the Many-Eyed or toss yourself into the mermaid lagoon and drown, but you could never go back to the Other Place.

So I went to Nod and Fog, because I would need them to keep Del and Charlie and the others safe from that look in Nip's eye, the one that said he was only waiting for his chance.

The twins hadn't noticed the others departing. They were arguing (I really did not care to know about what), and while they hadn't gotten to the point of rolling on the ground punching each other, experience told me this was in the offing.

Before they could get started I smacked them both in the back of the head. They looked up at me with innocent eyes.

"We weren't doing anything," Nod said.

"Yes, we were. He took . . ." Fog started, but I cut him off.

"Listen to me," I said, and lowered my voice though no one was about. Peter could be outside, lurking, listening. "What do you think of that new boy, Nip?"

"Don't like him," Fog said immediately.

"He's a bully," Nod agreed. "And he wants a fight with you, Jamie. We all can tell. Do you want me to put biting bugs in his clothes? I can do that. He'll go mad from the itching."

"Never mind that," I said. "Don't worry about me. It's Del and Charlie I'm worried about."

"Charlie's never done nothing to him," Nod said. "But Del got that Nip good."

"He was roaring around just like a big old bear when Del threw the fire in his eyes," Fog said.

He jumped to his feet and started on a credible imitation of Nip staggering around with coals in his eyes.

This was precisely why I couldn't leave Charlie alone with these two. They went off on their own adventures and forgot everything around them.

"Stop," I said.

Fog quit his antics and Nod stopped laughing and sat up straight.

"I want you to keep an eye on Nip," I said.

This was better than asking them to watch Charlie, which they were unlikely to do well. They'd forget about him in an instant. But if they thought there was a chance they might get to tease Nip or harry him or fight him, they wouldn't forget.

"If he tries for Del or Charlie, you stop him."

"*How* do you want us to stop him, Jamie?" Nod asked.

I knew what he was asking. Did I want them to hurt Nip or kill him? If they killed Nip outside of Battle, then Peter would come down on them—might even try to exile them, despite all the time they'd been on the island. I'd never let it come to that, of course. I'd never let them take a punishment meant for me.

Besides, if someone was going to kill Nip, then I wanted to do the deed myself. Nip, I felt, had brought something rotten to the island. He was a worm inside the sweet fruit, and when you found a worm you tossed it to the ground and stomped on it.

"Don't make it forever," I said. "But I don't mind if you bloody him while you're at it."

They grinned at each other, already planning their sport.

"Now get *on*," I said. "The rest of the boys are already gone."

"We'll catch up to them faster than a mermaid can flip her tail," Fog said.

"Don't let Nip do anything to Charlie," I warned. "Or there's always Battle."

The twins never fought me at Battle. Never. It had likely contributed to their long life on the island.

The same fear blazed up in two identical sets of eyes. I knew they would mind me, and keep a sharp watch on Nip. They collected their things and chased out after the others.

The bonfire had burned down to nothing but glowing coals, but a few pieces along the edge of the pit were unburned at one end and burning on the other. They'd serve my purpose.

The first seeking fingers of dawn were stretching over the plains when I rounded the cave wall. Peter was perched on the little rock shelf, whittling at a piece of wood.

The shape of his creation was just forming—a round ball at the top that spread down into a kind of bell shape. It looked like a child's toy—a doll, perhaps.

We didn't have any toys on the island, for all that we were a band of boys. Despite his fear of growing up, Peter likewise disdained child's toys, which were from the country of babies. Our toys were knife and sword and stick and rock, the kind of playthings that bit.

I stopped and narrowed my eyes in suspicion. Was he planning some trick on Charlie?

"What's that?" I asked.

Peter tucked it away and resheathed the knife before I could get a good look at it.

"Nothing really," he said easily, and his too-unconcerned manner set the hair on the back of my neck rising. Before I could say anything he spoke again. "Didn't you want to burn that mess and lay a false trail? Are you going to wait until the whole tribe of Many-Eyed are climbing the cliff in search of it?"

Of course he was right, and I did want to return to the others. But he was hiding something. He had that look.

The sun was halfway to its zenith before I got the Many-Eyed burning well. It's not as easy as you'd think, burning a dead creature. Flesh and skin want to cook and crisp and char rather than ignite. If you want to get a body burning, you've got to build up the fire around it good and hot and then keep watching it to make sure it stays aflame. Once that fire is hot enough, though, the body will burn right down to the bones.

Peter, naturally, watched me running to and fro while he continued to whittle at his piece of wood. Each time I passed him I tried to get a good look at it, but he would cover it with his hand or tuck it away so I couldn't.

As soon as I realized this game was amusing him, I stopped trying to sneak a peek. Thereafter both he and I would feign indifference when I passed, though Peter looked sulky when I stopped playing.

An enormous column of black smoke rose in the sky. I wondered if the pirates would see it and come investigate.

They never strayed too far from the camp, at least as much as we could tell—and certainly never as far as the mountains. But perhaps the smoke would draw them. If it did, all the better. They would lie in their own scent trail and do half my work for me.

"Peter," I said, wiping my forehead with my arm. I'd taken off my red coat and laid it to one side, for the work was hot and we were exposed on the rock shelf.

He didn't respond, seemingly absorbed in the whittling, but I knew Peter. His hands might be busy but he watched me intently from under his eyelashes.

"Peter," I said again, sharply so he would know I was on to him.

"Mmm?" His knife flashed in the sunlight, winking silver.

"What if you went ahead of me to the pirate camp, and drew some of them out along the trail?"

Peter looked up then and frowned. "They never leave their camp, because that Captain is a cowardly codfish. Anyway, even if I could get them out, I wouldn't want them so close to the forest. They might get ideas about where our tree is."

"Not likely," I said. "You've said yourself that this is the dumbest lot that's been at the camp in many a year. Besides, we don't want them to come all the way to the cave. I just want them to follow you partway, to make a scent trail for the Many-Eyed."

Peter's eyes gleamed as he understood. "And then their scent trail will meet your blood trail, and when they go back to camp they'll take some of the blood with them."

I nodded.

"What fun!" he said, tucking his knife and his whittling project in the pouch he wore at his belt. Then he scowled at me. "But you might have thought of this before, so I wouldn't be so bored watching you burn this thing."

Sometimes I thought I would bite my tongue bloody not saying the things that Peter needed to hear. Needed to hear, but wouldn't hear, so I saved my breath and didn't point out that he might have helped.

"I'll bring them out to the marking rock," Peter said. He was already off the rock shelf and bounding toward the path that led down the other side of the cliffs, the side the Many-Eyed had climbed up in the first place.

The marking rock was a boulder that was taller than me and Peter stacked on top of each other. It was on the path that ran alongside the plains of the Many-Eyed, and it was close enough to the pirate camp that Peter might be able to lure them there.

"How will you get them out of the camp?" I shouted after him.

His voice floated up from the path, echoing off the rock, full of mischief. "Oh, I'll find a way!"

And then I was alone, and glad that he was gone. I'd never been glad at Peter's absence before, and something inside me seemed to shift. My legs hurt like fire for a minute, and then it was over, and I distinctly felt that I was taller than I'd been a moment before.

CHAPTER 6

I wondered whether Peter would notice. I wondered whether I should worry about growing up. I hadn't grown for such a long time, and never in such a dramatic way. It was more a creeping sort of growing, usually, the kind you didn't realize had happened until one day you noticed Peter's eyes were below yours and they didn't use to be.

Then I realized I hadn't time to worry about getting taller, for Peter could run fast and light when he was on his own and if I didn't hurry, the trail wouldn't be laid in when he got to the marking rock.

I didn't want to leave Harry in the cave, nor the remains of the deer, both of which would attract bears or big cats. Though I was loath to put Harry in the fire with the thing that had killed him, I knew I must. There wasn't time for burying, and burning was better than being picked over by whatever creature sniffed out the rotting meat that used to be a boy.

I dragged Harry over to the bonfire of the Many-Eyed

and heaved him atop the monster's corpse, getting a mouthful of smoke for my trouble. Coughing and pounding my chest, I backed away from the fire and went back for the charred remains of the deer.

Harry and the deer and the Many-Eyed burned. I collected blood in a coconut half shell that I carried in my coat pocket for cupping water from streams, so I wouldn't have to touch the blood and possibly be burned. There were pools of it that had splashed around the Many-Eyed in its death throes. Then I left Bear Cave and the rock shelf behind, following the path Peter had taken.

The mark of his foot was barely visible in the dirt track and sometimes not present at all for several steps, as if he'd taken a huge leap and landed soft as down floating on the wind. I ran quickly, and though I was not as light as Peter, I could travel nearly as fast.

With a troop of boys crossing to the pirate camp, this path would take hours to traverse, but the sun was just past overhead by the time I reached the path that bordered the foothills on one side and the plains of the Many-Eyed on the other. Several times I marveled that the juvenile Many-Eyed had made it to Bear Cave in the first place. The trail was narrow in several spots, occasionally bordered on both sides by sheer faces of rock. How the creature had managed to make it through and sniff us out at the cave was a wonder.

I balanced the coconut shell in my hand and dropped no

blood until I reached the plains. It was important that the other Many-Eyed not consider the hill path at all, but think that the pirates had killed their young here on the border and dragged it back to the camp.

This part of the trail was the most dangerous, for while almost all Many-Eyed stayed in the central plains, there was always a chance of coming upon a soldier walking near the edge of their territory. They might even be looking for the one that was now dead and burning in the distance.

The smoke was barely visible above the foothills from here, but it would be clearer from other parts of the island. It might make the pirates curious, and help Peter in his task.

I listened, hearing nothing but the sounds of the wind, the cries of the birds, and the buzzing of the Many-Eyed ever present but distant, as it should be. When they gathered together in any group larger than two, they would naturally make this noise—a steady kind of buzz that seemed incongruous with their fangs. Still, it was useful as it kept us from being overwhelmed by their numbers. The buzzing that preceded them made it easy to avoid a large pack.

The distance of the noise forced me to wonder if I'd been overcautious about the juvenile in the first place. Perhaps with so many babies (and they did have so many—I'd snuck close to their camp once to get an idea of their numbers and later wished I hadn't) one missing young was no nevermind to them.

Still, it didn't pay to take risks with the boys' lives,

especially if this business of a treaty was true. I would follow
through with the original plan.

I splashed some blood along the trail, then deliberately ran to
and fro, dragging my heels in the dirt and making a lot of
footmarks. I pulled out handfuls of tall yellow plains grass so it
would appear to the pirates or the Many-Eyed that there was some
kind of struggle. It wasn't certain how much the Many-Eyed
would understand of my charade, but they were smarter than they
appeared; that, I knew. They weren't just dumb animals.

Proceeding with caution, I followed the path and kept my
ears open for sounds of the Many-Eyed or the pirates that
Peter was to entice out of camp. I splashed more blood here
and there and scratched up the ground in different places.

The blood was not as skin-burningly potent as it had been
coursing fresh from the Many-Eyed, but it hissed a little
when it touched a rock or leaves or dirt, and sometimes a
small curl of steam emitted from a tiny droplet.

Even though I was listening close, I didn't hear Peter's
approach. I crouched just inside the long grass across from
the marking rock, waiting for him. The last of the Many-
Eyed's blood was splashed at the foot of it.

One moment I was alone and the next Peter appeared,
seemingly out of nothing. He saw the blood around the rock
and turned on the spot, looking for me.

"Here, Peter," I whispered, parting the grass so he could
see my eyes.

He dashed in beside me, his face wilder and fiercer and happier than I'd seen it in a long while.

"Are they coming?" I asked.

"Yes," Peter said, and it seemed he was resisting the urge to clap and scream with joy.

"What did you do?"

"Set the camp on fire!" And then he did chortle, delighted with himself and unable to hide it.

"Set the . . ." I started; then my voice trailed away.

I hadn't noticed the smell of smoke on him at first for my nose was full of the reek of burning bodies, but I caught it now.

"You burned their camp down."

Peter caught the disapproving tone. "What's the matter? You don't think it was a wonderful notion? It got that fat old Captain good and riled, all right. He's waddling after me now, waving his sword and cursing about what he's going to do when he catches me. Which he never will, of course. He looks just like a plump never-bird egg, rolling along."

He laughed again, and my frown deepened, which made Peter's laugh fade away.

"Come, now, Jamie, how is burning their camp any worse than stealing from them or killing them?"

"Well . . . it's not fair play, is it?" I said slowly.

I wasn't sure if I could explain my feelings, even to myself. Yes, we and the pirates fought and killed each other. But that was man-to-man, as it were. We faced one another and we all had a fair shot.

Burning the camp—it was sneaky, somehow sneakier than a little theft. And it was cruel. Peter hadn't just taken their jewels or their swords—he'd taken their home.

The pirates would have a much greater motivation to leave the seaside and hunt us across the island if their camp was gone.

Peter's actions put us all in danger—much more so, I thought, than anything I might have done to anger the Many-Eyed.

I was about to tell him all this when he clamped his hand over my mouth. "They're coming," he whispered.

His hand was dirty and his body vibrated with excitement. I didn't hear so well as Peter—a few moments passed before the shouting and cursing of the pirates reached me.

The marking rock (so called because Peter or I scraped a mark on it every time we went on a pirate raid) was at a place where the trail to the beach rounded the foot of the mountains, turning east; we heard them long before we saw them.

The Captain's voice was loudest, booming, "Get on, you dogs, and FIND THAT BLASTED BOY! I'll string him from the yardarm and keep him there until his face turns blue! Catch him! Catch him!"

From the ruckus they made it seemed like the whole camp was turned out to find Peter, but as they passed our hiding place I saw there were only five, plus the Captain. The first mate was not among them.

I hadn't cut off the new mate's hand yet, but the previous first mate (a man they called Red Tom because he had red hair—pirates are very unimaginative) was with them. I'd taken his hand some months before. The stump was wrapped in a striped bandanna, though, like it was still fresh—or like he was ashamed of it. Perhaps he was just ashamed that a boy had done it.

The group of pirates continued on, cutlasses drawn, and I felt sure that if they found Peter, there would be no dragging him back to the camp. They'd surround him and cut him to pieces and carry his head back as a trophy. Peter had gone too far this time.

The Captain panted along behind the others. He wasn't truly as fat as Peter made him out to be, though his belly did seem to get in his way when he fought and he wasn't very fast.

Given this, it was a certainty that Peter could have killed the Captain several times over, but he hadn't. Peter could be a cat sometimes, letting a mouse think it was all right to crawl out of the mouse hole until one day it suddenly was not and the mouse found itself pinned by sharp claws.

"How far do you think they'll go?" I whispered once all the pirates had missed our hiding place.

They had never come so far before, all the way out here to the plains, and they appeared very determined. What if they went through the foothills and tracked our steps back to the Bear Cave? From there it wouldn't take much to find the trail that went back to our tree. Dozens of boys had walked that trail for dozens of years. It was a clue that even a foolish pirate Captain couldn't miss.

"They won't cross the mountains," Peter said. "Can you imagine that Captain even climbing up to Bear Cave? His face will turn red and his heart will blow up before he gets halfway there."

"He might send the others on," I said, trying to make him feel the urgency of the situation. The boys would be in danger. But Peter didn't care about the boys. He only cared about his fun.

So I would make it fun—at least, Peter's idea of fun.

"What if they went into the plains instead?" I said.

Peter's eyes glowed. "Now, that would be an adventure. They'd stumble right into the Many-Eyed's nest."

"And then the Many-Eyed would never think it was us that killed their child," I said.

"It *wasn't* us. It was you," Peter said.

Peter enjoyed laying blame, particularly if he hadn't earned any in the process.

"But you're right—the pirates would distract them," he continued. "I'd better be the one to go into the fields, though, since the Many-Eyed don't know you."

It wasn't like Peter to express interest in the well-being of others. I stared at him.

"I wouldn't want anything to happen to you, Jamie. You

were the first, and you're still my favorite."

Then he smiled, and oh, that smile. It was that smile that had stolen me away from the Other Place, the smile that made me want to do anything for him.

I was suddenly sorry I'd grown, even if it was only a little, and wished I could be smaller again and that it was just Peter and me, running and climbing and laughing, back when the island was ours.

He clapped me on the back. "You can help me, though. I'll go ahead here in the grass until I'm in front of them. You creep up behind and kill any that try to go back to the camp for help. The best thing will be if the other pirates don't even know what happened. They'll think the island ate up their crewmates."

Peter's grin grew wider and fiercer. "How I'll love to feed that Captain to the Many-Eyed. He's grown so *boring*."

I could have pointed out that he could slay the Captain anytime he wanted a new one (that was how we always got new ones) but I didn't. I didn't care how Peter did it so long as he kept the threat of the pirates away from the boys.

He stood, and he was small enough that his head didn't clear the tall yellow grass, though his ginger hair was just visible.

"You go on back to the cave after I lead them into the plains," he said. "I'll meet you there."

I didn't want to wait at the cave for Peter. I wanted to go on, to get back to the tree, to assure myself Charlie and Del hadn't been caught out by Nip. But Peter wanted me to wait, and I would wait because he'd smiled and made me remember.

He was gone the instant after I nodded, so light and free and unbound to earth that the grass barely rustled as he passed.

I waited a few moments, then followed. I could be quiet, but not as silent as Peter. A rabbit was startled by my appearance and darted out of the grass toward the path. I was certain Peter had walked by it a moment before and the little creature had not even noticed.

After a while I stopped and listened. The sun was hot and making me drowsy, for I hadn't slept in more than a day now.

I think I did drift off for a bit, crouched there in the grass with my eyes closed and the sun beating down and the lovely earthy, grassy smell all around me.

There was a voice then, an accusing voice that sounded like Peter's—"What have you done?" I thought he was angry about the Many-Eyed again, but that wasn't it.

She was there again, whoever *she* was, the she who was in my dreams every night. Her eyes were blank and blue, and dark hair curled around her head. Her mouth was open but there was a smile too, a smile in the wrong place, a smile that ran under her chin from ear to ear. There was a wink of silver in the dark, like a darting fish in a stream, and then I was awake, eyes wide.

The pirates were shouting curses, and I heard Peter's laughter on the wind. After a moment I was able to trace the sound. They were headed west, into the fields, and from the ruckus they made it seemed certain they would find the Many-Eyed.

The noise also told me all the pirates were after Peter. That meant I could relax and walk along the path instead of crabbing along in the grass. I stood, brushing the sticky bits of grass seed from my coat—I was inclined to be a little vain about that coat, though it was covered in blood and dirt and who knows what else. I was vain about it because Peter wanted it, and because it still bothered him that I'd thought of getting it first.

I drifted along the trail back to the cave, thinking of nothing in particular except perhaps a nap. The thrumming urgency that plagued me earlier was gone. The sun had beaten me into a sense of dreamy lassitude. My only thought was to reach the cave before Peter returned so that I could sleep for a time.

Because I was walking slowly and not listening properly, the pirate was practically upon me before I noticed him.

The trail wandered this way and that along the bottom rim of the foothills, and there were many blind turns and curves. I should have heard him—he pounded down the dirt in those heavy boots all the pirates wore—and his breath came in sharp puffs as he ran. But I didn't hear him. I was thinking of my dream, and the voice, and the silver knife.

I rounded a corner and he was there—only a few strides away from me—and my sudden appearance made him draw up and jump away with a frightened yell.

"You," he said, for of course it was Red Tom.

Red Tom who hated me. Red Tom who'd lost his hand to me. Red Tom who was no longer first mate because of me.

That hazy, drifting feeling shook off in an instant. I had my orders from Peter. No one was to go back to the pirate camp.

When he'd passed by earlier, Red Tom had his sword out, ready to slice Peter apart. Now it was gone. He must have dropped it in the fields. Red Tom *had* entered the fields; I knew that much. I saw the clinging strands of long grass on his clothes.

His face was white as the cold moon though he'd been running hard. He made as if to charge me, but my words stopped him dead.

"You saw one, didn't you?"

He gulped air, his skin more bloodless than before. "It were horrible . . . The Captain . . . It bit the Captain in two and his blood were everywhere. Everywhere."

Red Tom closed his eyes, and I was sure he could see that vision of his Captain eaten alive on the insides of his eyelids. That was just enough time for me to pull my dagger out and lodge it in his throat.

His eyes flew open, and he gurgled, and blood pooled in his mouth and spilled over his lips. His hands scrabbled uselessly in the air as he fell to his knees, and then Red Tom was no more.

His body slumped to the ground. I pulled the knife out,

wiping the blood on my deerskin pants.

The sun was heading down in the west. I shielded my eyes with my hand as I gazed over the long fields of yellow grass. There was no sign of Peter, the pirates, or the Many-Eyed. I thought they must have been quite near for Red Tom to be returning so soon to the camp.

Then again, I reflected, I had dozed in the grass. Though it had seemed like only a moment, it may have been longer. The noise that woke me could have been from farther away than I thought. Sounds traveled strangely on the island.

Red Tom's corpse attracted flies almost immediately. I grabbed his arm and dragged him into the grass, leaving a trail of sticky blood behind. Sweat poured down my neck and back. It always amazed me how *heavy* grown-up corpses were compared to boys', even if the grown-up in question was as skinny as Red Tom.

I left him just inside the edge of the fields, so that any passing Many-Eyed would find him and eat him. If any of the other pirates came looking this way for their lost companions, the only evidence they would find would be that trail of blood. With luck even that would be washed away in the next rain before anyone went searching.

Then I started on the trek back to Bear Cave. I entered the path through a narrow cut in two rock faces. The trail wound steeply upward before settling into an ebb and flow across the foothills and linking up with the cliff path to Bear Cave.

Once you were partway up the trail you could look out pretty far over the fields, and I did just that, turning back to see if I could catch a glimpse of Peter before the sun went all the way down.

I can't run as fast as Peter; nor can I hear as well. But I can see clear and far, and the only limit to the accuracy of my shooting was how far arrows could fly.

To my surprise, Peter wasn't terribly far away at all—perhaps a quarter of an hour's walking. I saw him very clearly, not far inside the borders of the plains. Several blue and pink flowers sprouted nearby, bobbing around his head. He stood there, clearly unconcerned that he might be seen or caught by anyone.

His face was in profile, and he was—talking to his hand? At least, that was what it seemed like he was doing. I squinted my eyes and thought I saw a little golden light bobbing in his cupped palm.

A firefly? Why would Peter be talking to a firefly? That was strange, even for Peter. He turned away, toward the center of the plains and the Many-Eyed's nest. I watched him, wondering what he was doing and why he wasn't turning back toward the cave, toward me.

That was the first time I saw him fly.

He rose out of the grass gently, so gently, his bare feet wriggling in excitement. Soon enough he was almost level with my height on the trail. If he turned around, he would see me. But he didn't turn around. He soared away, over the golden fields and toward the sea.

I felt the burn of envy deep in my chest, scorching hard enough to bring tears to my eyes. When had he learned such a thing? Why hadn't he shared it with us?

Why hadn't he shared it with *me*?

The warmth I'd felt when he smiled at me was gone. I didn't know Peter anymore, not the way I used to. We used to share everything. Peter would never leave me out of an adventure.

But now he had treaties with the Many-Eyed and he knew how to fly. He kept secrets. I didn't need to wait at Bear Cave for a boy like that, someone who said I was special but only said it so I wouldn't look too closely at what he was doing.

I ran, all fatigue forgotten then, and when I ran I tried to forget all the times we'd teased the crocodile and splashed with the mermaids and made a fool of the pirate Captain.

All I could think of—all I could see—was the sight of Peter flying, flying, flying away.

Flying away without me.

CHAPTER 7

He didn't catch up with me until well past the Bear Cave. The sun was gone, the moon was up again, and the urgency I'd lost earlier while sleeping in the heat of the day had returned in force. I'd been away too long. Anything might have happened to Charlie by now.

I'd chosen the less direct trail the boys took earlier because I didn't want Peter tracking me down on my shortcut. That was my special way, mine and Charlie's now, and I didn't want Peter knowing too much about it.

I heard Peter approaching, but only because he whistled the tune of a pirate sea shanty. The night was cloudless and the moon so bright, as always, that it was like daylight on the path once you were away from the shadows of the trees.

"Jamie!" he called to me, once I came into his view. "Jamie, you should have seen it!"

He didn't seem to notice that I'd ignored his dictate to wait at Bear Cave, and that burned inside me too, all mixed up with my jealousy over his flight.

"Jamie!" Peter said, as he caught up to me and matched his strides to mine easily.

This irritated me also, as I was half a head taller than Peter and my legs much longer. Only a short while before I'd lamented growing. Now I was bothered that my height gave me no advantage over the boy who always loved to win.

"Did you feed the pirates to the Many-Eyed?" I asked, my voice cool.

Peter didn't notice at all. "Did I!" he said, so full of glee his body hummed with it.

He then described what was no doubt a thrilling adventure that involved Peter being daring and brilliant to rid himself of his enemies. I listened with only half an ear, for if you've heard one Peter's-daring-and-brilliant story, you've heard them all.

I picked up a smooth rock from the path and tossed it from one hand to the other, then tossed it in the air with my knife hand and caught it in the same one several times. I found another rock that was about the same size and juggled the two for a while, until I felt I'd gotten the hang of it, then added a third rock in.

Peter stopped talking about how wonderful Peter was and laughed at my trick.

"You could be in a traveling fair, Jamie, flipping torches lit on fire," he said, clapping me on the shoulder.

"When have you ever seen a traveling fair? It's not as if we have them on the island," I asked, curious. I remembered seeing one myself, long and long and long ago, just a washed-out memory of men in brightly colored silks capering across the square.

"We should," Peter said. "We should have mummers and dancers and magicians to come and entertain us in the evenings. The boys would love that. And we can clap and throw flowers at the performers while they bow."

He was already off in his own mind, imagining how wonderful it would be, but it did not escape me that he hadn't answered my question. Peter did that when he didn't want you to know something. He'd just pretend he never heard you in the first place, and shouting in his ear wouldn't make him budge.

"We should have taken a magician from the Other Place instead of Charlie," Peter said. "A magician would have been useful. At least for a while. When he wasn't useful anymore, we could feed him to the crocodiles."

"Why do you hate Charlie so?" I asked, ignoring these musings about a magician. Peter would never bring an adult to the island. "You picked him. I told you to leave him behind."

Peter stared into the sky, giving the impression he was not listening at all, but I knew that he was. We had been together long and long, Peter and me, and I knew his ways as well as he knew mine.

I waited, knowing he would say something sooner or

later, for Peter loved to fill in empty space.

"He takes up all your time," Peter finally said, and I saw an uncharacteristic frustration wrinkle his brow. "It's always 'Charlie this, Charlie that, Charlie's too little, he can't fight, he can't keep up.' Where's the fun in that? I brought him here to play and he's useless."

"I have to look out for him *because* he's small," I said slowly. "Because he shouldn't be here. We shouldn't have taken him, Peter. He still has a mother."

Peter flipped his hand at me. Mothers were of no concern to him.

"If he takes up so much of my time, if he annoys you so much, then you should let me bring him home, back to the Other Place. He doesn't belong here," I said.

"No," Peter said, and his voice was sharp as the blade he carried. "You know the rules. Once you come here you can never leave. Nobody leaves. Nobody goes home. This is his home now."

"But if he—" I began.

"No," Peter said. "Anyway, it doesn't matter, as Nip will have . . ."

He trailed off, suddenly realizing what he said.

"As Nip will have what?" I asked.

Peter said nothing, only turned away and feigned interest in a black-and-emerald butterfly that landed on one of the fat white night-blooming flowers that bordered the path.

Anger snapped inside me, mixed with dread. I dropped the stones I'd been playing with and jerked him roughly around to face me.

"What have you done, Peter?"

"Oww, Jamie, that hurt," Peter said, rubbing his shoulder.

"WHAT HAVE YOU DONE?" I roared.

"Only what I had to," he said, and he was serious in a way that I rarely witnessed. "Nobody will take you from me, Jamie."

I could have killed him then. The rage surged up, pulsed in my blood like fire. I *should* have killed him then. It would have prevented everything that came after.

Peter took a half step back, just a little shuffle, but he'd never retreated from me before. Never.

He realized this immediately and stepped back toward me, but I was already turning, already running. Charlie was more important than dealing with Peter.

"I don't know why you're bothering to run!" Peter shouted after me. "It will be already done by now!"

I didn't care what he said. Until I saw Charlie, I wouldn't believe Nip had succeeded in whatever task Peter set him. I believed—I had to believe—that Del and Nod and Fog would look after him as I asked.

I ran, and the terror swamped my anger, and the fear that I would be too late drove me on, faster and faster. I cut into the forest, never wishing so much that I could fly as Peter did at that moment.

My legs burned and my chest heaved and my hair was soaked in sweat and I ran. The forest held no joy for me now. It was only an obstacle in the way, a thing that kept me from Charlie. I'd promised him he'd be safe. He had to be all right. He had to be.

I ran, and Charlie's tiny face turned back to look at me as Del led him away, and his face said he was trying so hard to be brave. I didn't think about his blue eyes empty or his yellow duck-feathered hair matted with blood. I didn't think of those things, and I ran faster.

I burst into the clearing before the tree, gasping for air, and I was so wild with anxiety that it took me a moment to realize what I was seeing. All the boys were gathered in a still, silent circle—all but two of them.

One of them was tied to a stake that was driven into the ground. His face and chest were a mass of purpling bruises, but he was still alive. The other one lay on the ground.

He was white and still and he would never get up again. The pool of blood underneath him told me that.

"Oh, Del," I said, and knuckled away the tears, because I didn't cry in front of the others. "Oh, Del."

His sword was in his hand, lying limp in his open palm. He'd fought, or tried to. I was proud of him for that.

"Jamie!" Charlie ran to me and I picked him up without even thinking about it. He trembled all over and his eyes were red and swollen because he was too small to stop himself from crying in front of the boys.

"He saved me," Charlie said, weeping into my neck. "He protected me."

I let Charlie cry because I couldn't, not just then, not while the boys were watching, not while Nip was watching me with a sneer in his eyes even though he was tied to that pole.

Nod and Fog separated themselves from the others and came to me. They seemed unsure whether to be ashamed about Del or proud that they'd caught and tied up Nip.

"He went for Charlie so fast," Nod said.

"Didn't even think he could move that fast," Fog said.

"Del was right next to Charlie and he was taking out his sword as he got in Nip's way," Nod said.

"Nip never got a finger on Charlie," Fog said. "Not one. Del got off one slash"—here he pointed at an ugly wound in Nip's thigh—"but Nip got Del's throat before Del could do anything else."

"Then we caught on to what was happening and jumped on Nip, and us and the others pounded him good and proper, 'cause we can't have boys just killing other boys. That's not how it works here."

The rest of the boys murmured in agreement.

"We were just having a trial before we hung Nip, because that's what you're supposed to do, Billy says," said Nod.

"You're supposed to tell your story in front of a judge and then the judge says you're guilty and then you're hung in the town square," Billy said proudly. "I saw a hanging once. The fellow's neck didn't break when he fell like it was supposed to, and his legs were kicking around and his face was purple for a long time before he died."

All the boys turned to look at Nip, as if imagining him kicking and turning blue at the end of a rope. None of them seemed particularly troubled by the idea.

"We were just deciding who should be the judge," Nod said.

"I think it should be me," Fog said. "'Cause I noticed him killing Del first."

"No, I did," Nod said, and punched Fog in the shoulder.

"No, I did," Fog said, punching back.

I knew it was a short walk from this to the two of them rolling on the ground bloodying each other's noses. I shifted Charlie to my left arm and moved to break them apart with my right.

Nip's laugh, slow and congested (he was laughing through broken teeth), cut in before I could. We all turned as one to stare at him.

"Ain't none of you going to judge *me*," he said. "Peter told me to do it, and he's not about to let me swing from any rope when I'm just doing what I was told."

Nod broke away first, running at Nip and punching him in the face. Nip's head cracked against the pole from the force of the blow.

"You're a liar!" Nod shouted.

Fog, who hated to miss out on anything his brother did, followed suit, punching Nip's other cheek and shouting, "Liar, liar, liar! Peter would never do that!"

"That's outside of the rules," Nod said.

"It's not fair play," Fog said. "If we have something to settle, we go to Peter or Jamie, and if fighting's needed, real fighting, we save it for Battle."

"Yeah, we don't stab the other boys just 'cause we feel like it," Nod said. "And those are Peter's rules, so we know you're nothing but a dirty liar."

The other boys nodded, and the general feeling was that Nip's lie about Peter was almost worse than his killing Del.

I knew it wasn't a lie. I knew, but I wasn't about to save Nip.

Nip's eyes darted around the closing circle of boys, all of them ready to carve their piece of flesh from the liar in their midst.

"It's true!" Nip shouted, desperate now. The sneer was all gone, and the knowledge that Peter might not be back in time to save him was dawning.

He was a wreck of himself, covered in the evidence of two beatings, but his strength—or fear—was so powerful that he was able to shift the stake a little as he wrenched to and fro, trying to break free from the ropes that bound him.

"I'm not a liar!" he screamed.

Nip looked right at Charlie and me, who'd ceased his

sobbing and stared at the bigger boy with blank eyes. Charlie didn't much care if they hung Nip either.

"Peter told me to take care of that little brat, and if he was here he'd tell you so! If you hurt me you'll be sorry!"

"No, we won't," Nod said, shaking his head. "You broke the rules."

"Jamie knows the rules better than anyone," Fog said, and turned to me for assent.

"Yes, you broke the rules," I said. I didn't say that Peter would never tell Nip to go after Charlie. I couldn't bring myself to speak the lie.

Fog nodded. "Jamie's passed judgment. We'll hang you now."

"I'll get some rope," Billy said happily, and ran off to the tree.

We stole rope from the pirates regularly, as it was handy for things like setting snares and much sturdier than the vine ropes we sometimes wove.

In a trice Billy had fashioned a hangman's noose and thrown it over a branch of the tree. He fixed the rope around the branch in such a way so they could toss it over Nip's neck and then pull the rope (with Nip in it, of course) up from the ground, sort of a pulley with Nip on one end and the boys on the other.

The rest of the boys surrounded Nip. Fog cut him loose from the stake. Nip immediately tried to fight his way out of the crowd, but he was so wild that none of his blows landed.

The boys were able to subdue him easily and dragged him, screaming incoherently, to his noose.

"Stop making so much noise," Fog said, and stuffed a filthy rag from his pocket into Nip's open mouth.

Nip's eyes widened and he tried to shout through the rag, the result being a kind of intense grunting that made the other boys laugh. A couple of them picked up sticks and poked him to see what other noises Nip might make.

"I don't want you to look when they string him up," I told Charlie. I was reluctant to put him down again, sure that if I did, I'd find out that it wasn't Del's body in the middle of the clearing but his.

"Okay, Jamie," Charlie said. "I'll mind you."

I remembered the way I'd lost my temper with him at the bottom of the cliff path. It seemed so long ago, and it was only yesterday.

"I don't want you to have nightmares," I said, by way of explanation.

Charlie nodded and turned his head away when the boys finished poking at Nip and put the rope around his neck.

Nod and Fog and three others grabbed the trailing end of the rope and pulled. Nip let out his longest scream yet, muffled by the rag.

They only managed to pull him far enough so his heels dragged in the dirt, even with five of them putting their backs into it. Nod gave a count to heave again in three, two, one . . .

. . . and Peter bounded across the clearing in two jumps. If any other boy had been looking, they would know his secret in that instant. It was quite obvious he wasn't leaping like an ordinary boy.

He pushed into the fray and cut Nip down before the others realized he was even there.

Nip collapsed in the dirt, clawing the noose off his neck and yanking the rag from his mouth. All the other boys chorused, "Awwwwww," for Peter had spoiled their fun.

"What's all this, then?" Peter said sternly, looking around at all of us.

His eyes rested on Charlie a moment longer than the others. I saw the flicker of disappointment in them, but then, I was looking for it.

Nod and Fog rushed to tell what happened. I'd been standing a little apart from the rest, but now I set Charlie down and joined them. Of course the smaller boy immediately wound his fist into my coat, but I couldn't blame him for that after Del.

Peter avoided my gaze. He also didn't glance at Del once. Now that Del was dead, he was no longer interesting to Peter. If anything, Peter was likely relieved that Del had died before coughing out his lungs and annoying him with the noise.

Nip smirked up at the others. He obviously thought that Peter's last-minute rescue confirmed his specialness. I had a feeling he was in for a big surprise on that front.

Nod and Fog finished telling the story, tumbling over each other in the rush to be first, but Peter got the sense of it. When the twins finished, Nip broke in before Peter could speak.

"I told them," Nip said, "that I was only doing what you told me to do."

I think he would have liked to drawl this out in a self-satisfied way, but the effect was ruined by his swollen face, missing front teeth and the need to spit out blood every third word or so.

Peter's eyes went wide when Nip finished speaking. He appeared astonished at this news. "I?" he said, pointing his thumb to his chest. "I told you to kill Del? I never did!"

His outrage was almost believable, if you didn't know what I knew. The other boys were nodding and muttering that they knew Nip had lied about that.

"No," Nip said, his face twisted in frustration.

He still believed Peter would support him, that Peter would tell the truth when it came down to it. He didn't know Peter the way I did.

"You told me to take care of that little yellow-haired brat. And I was trying to except that skinny one got in my way." Nip jerked his chin in the direction of Del's corpse.

"I told you to *take care* of Charlie," Peter said with exaggerated care. "Look after him! He's very small and you're very big. I never told you to *lunge* at him with a *knife*."

I saw then how Peter had done it, that he'd likely said

those precise words—"take care of Charlie." This was how he'd set Nip to the task instead of doing it himself—so he could deny it all if Nip failed.

Nip scowled at Peter like he couldn't believe what Peter was saying. "You never did! You told me to take care of the brat and you knew just what you were telling me to do, and it wasn't anything to do with 'looking after'!"

"Don't call Peter a liar!" Nod said, and ran at Nip.

He landed on the bigger boy's stomach with his bony knees. Nip *oof*ed out all his air and had no chance to get it back as Nod pounded his face.

"Peter's no liar! You are!"

Peter pointed to Jonathan and Ed. "You two, get Nod off him."

He put out a restraining arm to stop Fog from joining in the scrum. Jonathan and Ed dragged Nod off Nip, though it seemed to me they did so very slowly. Nobody was much interested in Nip's well-being.

"Get up," Peter told Nip.

Peter wasn't concerned for Nip's well-being either. I knew how Peter thought. Nip had failed, and now he was no longer valuable to Peter. The other boy would have to prove his worth again, or else spend all the rest of his days on the island on the wrong side of Peter's attention.

Nip struggled to his feet, his nose freshly bloodied, his mean little eyes in their swollen sockets darting around for an ally and finding none.

"Now," Peter said, his hands on his hips, and gave us his best angry glare. "Rules have been broken. First rule is that we don't kill each other outside of Battle. That's not our way."

Nip opened his mouth to speak, to defend himself, to say again that he was only doing as he'd been told. Peter waved a dismissive hand at him and talked louder.

"Nip killed Del, but the rest of you were going to hang Nip for it, which means you broke the rules too."

All the boys seemed slightly ashamed now—not for hurting Nip, necessarily, but for getting carried away.

"Nip's done wrong, and so have you. That means there must be a Battle."

A murmur started up immediately. The new boys weren't sure what Battle was, and the older boys speculated that Battle wasn't quite fair with Nip in the condition he was in.

"You're right," Peter said. "Nip should have a chance to heal, so it will be fair."

He put his hand on his chin and twisted his mouth this way and that as he took in Nip's injuries. "What do you think, Jamie? Thirty sleeps?"

That was overly generous, to my way of thinking, though there was always the hope that Nip would catch a fever and die before Battle day.

"Twenty," I said, just to show Peter he couldn't lead me by the nose.

He shook his head. "Thirty. We'll mark the days off on a

board. One of you find a good piece of wood for marking."

This was exactly the sort of task I'd like to set Charlie on, but his hand clung to my coat in a way that said he would never let go. Anyway, I didn't want him out of my sight until after Battle was over. I wasn't so sure Peter wouldn't plan something else now that his first idea had failed.

One of the new boys—Sam, I think—scampered off to find a board. I realized with a pang that there were now as many new boys as old—we'd lost both Harry and Del in the last day. It was down to me, Nod, Fog, Jonathan, Kit and Ed. The rest had been there less than a week.

And knowing that, knowing they didn't know a damned thing about Battle, I knew what would happen when next Peter spoke.

"When Nip's healed up, one of you will fight him to death in Battle. Then this disagreement will be ended forever."

"I will," I said, before Nod or Fog could volunteer.

They both loved Battle, whether it was in play or to the death, and surely both of them had more cause to fight than me. I hadn't even been there when they tied Nip to the stake.

But it was my lot to stand for the boys, to look out for them. Nod and Fog were good fighters, but Nip was much bigger than them. And he'd have more reason to fight and win, for he'd feel his reputation as truth-teller was at stake. There was a slyness about him, too, that told me he'd try for any advantage in a fight.

Nod and Fog weren't sneaky fighters. But I was. I'd do whatever was necessary to survive. We were the same that way, Nip and me.

And it came down to this—I wouldn't lose the twins too, not after what had passed in the last day.

"Jamie, no," Charlie whispered, tugging at my coat.

Peter gave me a curious look, one that I couldn't read. "Why should you be the one, Jamie? You weren't even here for the first part of it."

"Aye," Nod said. "It ought to be me."

"No," Fog said, "it ought to be me."

Of course the expected thing happened. I shouted over the noise of them punching and arguing.

"It will be me, because I'm the one who passed judgment," I said, and they stopped trying to hurt each other to stare at me. "I stand for all the boys."

"But, Jamie—" Fog said.

"No," I said. "It's me."

They both sighed.

"I suppose it's only fair since you were the judge," Nod said.

"But, Jamie, I could take him," Fog said. Fog knew—or thought he knew—why I was putting myself in front of him.

"I know you could," I said. "But it will be me all the same."

Nip squinted at me, and I could tell he was already working out the best way to kill me. His thoughts were so plain anyone could read them without trying.

I showed him nothing. I knew better. Anyway, he'd have a hard go of it, trying to kill me. I'd been on the island much, much longer than he knew.

Peter looked from me to Nod to Fog to Nip and then heaved a great sigh, as though he hadn't intended for it to end that way all along. Me against Nip, his right hand against the boy who wanted to take my place.

"Very well," he said, in that pretend grown-up voice he used when he wanted to be serious. "Nip against Jamie, thirty sleeps from now. Sam, you're in charge of marking off the days. When you wake up in the morning put a line on that board with a rock."

Sam nodded. He looked eager to be a part of this, but glad that he had a meaningful part to play that wouldn't involve blood or death.

The circle of boys broke up, and nobody seemed to know quite what to do with himself. The game was supposed to end with Nip kicking from the end of a rope until he was still.

Since it hadn't ended that way, none of the boys wanted to look Nip in the eye. I wondered what would become of Nip until Battle day. He hadn't made a place for himself among the boys before this, and he seemed unlikely to now. It's hard to make friends with someone who tried to hang you.

Del's body lay in the center of the clearing and Peter pretended it wasn't there as he walked by.

"Who wants to swim with the mermaids?" he shouted, just as if nothing of import had happened.

There was a loud "hurrah" from Billy, and the others joined in the chorus. They appeared relieved that Peter was giving them something to do besides think about recent events.

I didn't point out that it was nearly sundown, and that sharks sometimes swam into the lagoon after dark, making the mermaids scatter. I didn't say that the boys had just returned from a long, pointless trek to Bear Cave and back and needed to sleep and eat so they wouldn't do foolish things that might get them killed.

I didn't say anything at all, though it was clear Peter expected me to do so. He wanted so badly to tell me off for babying them, for spoiling their fun, but I wouldn't bite his bait.

I watched them go, Peter in the lead, the rest already forgetting Del.

Soon the only boys left in the clearing were Charlie and Nip and me. Nip turned and limped inside the tree to lick his wounds, just like a bear—and just as dangerous.

I picked up Del's body—he was already cold and stiff—and carried him out to the place where I buried the boys we lost.

Charlie trailed behind me, a little yellow-feathered duckling, and he patted my shoulder when I put Del in the ground and wept like I would never stop.

CHAPTER 8

The boys didn't return until almost morning. Charlie and I chose to sleep outside in the clearing by the fire. Nip was likely too damaged to be much of a threat, but I wasn't risking Charlie over that belief. It was only sense to stay away from him when the others were gone.

The night was fine and cool, the never-birds calling to one another in long singsong cries. Charlie tucked himself right up against me like a roly-poly bug and went to sleep. I lay awake for a while, listening to him and the night breathing all around me, and wondered how Peter could fly.

I thought we would take a boat to the island, but Peter took me to a secret place, so-so-so secret that it didn't look like anything at first and I thought he was teasing me. We had to go outside the city, a long way, and I was tired when we got there, so tired, but Peter kept smiling and clapping and telling me it would be wonderful, so I kept going even when I wanted to close my eyes and fall down. When we got to the secret place, there was a big tree, and a hole between two thick roots that jutted out of the ground.

"In there," he said, and pointed.

I thought for sure then that he had tricked me. "That's nothing but a hole in the ground," I said, and could hear the tears in my voice.

"No, no, it's not!" he said, and he was so earnest that I believed him again. "It's magic, and only we know that it's here."

He came next to me and put his arm around my shoulder and pointed up over the top of the tree. The tree was very big, bigger than some of the houses in the city, and right above it were two stars. One of them was very bright and one of them was smaller.

"It's because of that star," he said. "The second star to the right. That star shines over my island, and shines over this tree, and if you go inside you'll come out on the island on the other side."

He must have seen me doubting, because he said, "I'll go first, and you follow."

That seemed a little better to me. If he went first, that meant that he wouldn't stand outside the hole and pour dirt on me and laugh, which had seemed a possibility. He dashed into the hole and slithered inside so fast I hardly saw him. I stood there, unsure if I should follow or not as there still seemed the chance of a trick.

His head popped out of the hole again like a jack-in-the-box,

and his green eyes gleamed in the starlight. "Come on, Jamie,
follow me. Follow me and you'll never grow up!"

I took one step, and then another, and then I was inside and
the earth seemed to close all around me.

The whooping and hollering woke me first, and then the
wind brought the smell of the sea ahead of them. They
tumbled wild-eyed out of the forest, and many of them just
collapsed once they were within sight of the tree.

I sat up and grabbed Fog's ankle as he danced by, full of
mermaid songs. "Where's Peter?"

"Went to the Other Place," Fog said. "Said he had to find
new boys to make up for Harry and Del."

I let Fog go, and he fell to his knees and then flat on his
face, snoring before his nose even touched the dirt.

Peter had gone to the Other Place without me—again.
The last time he'd brought back Nip, a choice he'd known I
would never approve. It was clear now that the reason for that
was to find a boy with just the right qualities, one who
wouldn't be troubled about slashing a five-year-old's throat.

I soothed Charlie down again—the ruckus of the boys'
return had him sitting up and rubbing his eyes—and soon
he was asleep like the others. The air filled with the sleeping
breath of boys, their dreams dusted by the glow of the moon.

I stayed awake the rest of the night, watching that cold

eye, and wondered what sort of boys Peter would return with this time.

There were three of them, not just two to replace Harry and Del. The extra one was, I perceived, to replace whichever of us (Nip or me) was lost in Battle, and Peter was trying to get ahead and save himself a trip later.

The first was called Crow, and he was in the Nod and Fog mold—small and energetic and liked to roughhouse. Soon enough he was always a part of their games and fights, and it was just as if they'd been born three instead of two. We found ourselves saying "the triplets" instead of "the twins" before we knew it.

The second boy was Slightly, and we called him that because he was thin and slow to talk and generally more thoughtful than the other boys Peter picked. We could have used a boy like Slightly in the long run, but it wasn't likely that he would have lasted long with those qualities. At least, that was what I told myself later, when I was burying him.

And the third boy was Sal. Sal wore a brown cap over a head of short black curls and had blue eyes that were always laughing at me. They told me in a thousand ways to stop being so serious and to have more fun; that was what the island was for.

Yet Sal was also kind and good to all the boys, especially

Charlie, and that made me like him, for no one else thought much of Charlie. The others wouldn't hurt him, but he couldn't keep up with them and so they didn't think of him. Sal did think of him, and waited for him, and walked next to him while the little boy shyly showed him the best places to dig for worms.

Soon enough Sal was a favorite of everybody's, for he had a way about him of making everyone feel like they belonged. Sal could make you feel happy just by smiling—those tiny white teeth flashing always made me warm in my belly. Some of the happiest days I had on the island were those days before that awful Battle day, when Sal and Charlie and I would break away from the others and go off roaming on our own.

Peter watched all this and pretended it was fine, that he wasn't bothered in the least that this new boy had taken me away from him even more than Charlie had. He even pretended not to mind about Charlie so much.

He pretended, but I caught him watching.

He watched Sal and Charlie like that sneaking, peeking crocodile in his story, the one who waited for his time to come.

Peter brought Sal to the island, and Sal changed everything for all of us forever, though I couldn't know that would happen.

I was only a boy then.

PART II

BATTLE

CHAPTER 9

I knew that business with the pirate camp burning would cause more trouble than Peter thought it would. He'd burned their camp and fed their Captain to a Many-Eyed and thought that nothing would change between us and them. We'd come a-raiding and they would try to kill us, but it would all be in good fun.

Though none of the group that followed Peter that day had survived to tell the tale, it was a certainty that the remaining pirates knew who was at fault. I thought that meant they'd know who to come looking for when it was time for revenge, and said so.

"No," Peter scoffed. "They'll leave. They'll go off sailing somewhere else. Why would they stay? Their camp and all the supplies in it are gone. I didn't burn their ship, and I could have. I left it there so they could go away and find a new Captain. Then they'll tell him that he can find the secret to staying young forever on this island and he'll sail back here and then we'll all have a grand time fighting each other again."

He laughed, and clapped my shoulder. "Did you know that they think it's some kind of spring? I don't know where they could have gotten such a notion, but I heard some of them talking about it when I was setting the tents on fire. They think they'll dump out their rum bottles and fill them with 'the water of youth.' Pirates are so *stupid*."

I didn't really think the pirates were all that stupid, and anyway, who was to say it wasn't the water that kept us all young? I'd lived there for years and didn't know for certain why I was still a boy. I didn't think Peter knew for sure himself.

That wasn't a secret I was interested in, anyway. I wanted to know how Peter flew. I'd not mentioned it to anyone else, not even mentioned to Peter that I'd seen him. I tried following him a few times, if I saw him sneaking off on his own, but he always disappeared before I caught him. I was reluctant to spend much time chasing him, as I was still nervous about leaving Charlie alone for too long. Nip did his best to glare death at Charlie and me whenever we drifted into his view.

Sal was the best, most reliable boy to leave Charlie with if I was away, but much as I wanted to discover Peter's secret, keeping Charlie safe was more important. And I didn't want Sal to fall under Nip's fury either.

Since the day the boys had tried to hang him, the others mostly avoided Nip. He spent almost all his time in the tree, watching his purple bruises turn yellow. He tried to reset the bone of his cheek himself, pushing the broken pieces more or less in place and tying a long strip of cloth from his sleeve around his jaw.

The necessity of not being able to move his teeth too far to chew meant he couldn't eat much besides soft fruit. That meant he was constantly hungry and roared at any boy who walked too near him.

I knew how to make a broth out of deer bones and some certain green leaves that would keep any boy strong. I'd used it plenty of times when the others had a fever and it saw them through. It would have helped Nip heal faster, but that wasn't any secret I'd be sharing with him. If he got weak, or even if he starved to death before Battle, it would save me the trouble of killing him later.

If I worried about Peter—which I didn't, because Peter could take care of himself—I'd have worried about the way Nip watched him too. The bigger boy resented Peter for denying their plot. More than once I caught him squeezing his fingers together while he stared at Peter, like he was daydreaming a strangling.

It didn't trouble me as much as it ought to, for Nip couldn't catch Peter on his best day, and Nip was far from his best day. But still he watched, and planned, and waited.

On the day we saw the pirates, Peter took us south through the dunes and to the beach near Skull Rock. This beach was a very long stretch of sand—perhaps a mile or two—with jumbled rocks at the east end. On the other side of the rocks was a wet marshy place where the swamp emptied into the sea.

At the west end was a jutting promontory of forest that curled around the mermaid lagoon. The lagoon wasn't visible from the beach—it was on the other side of the trees, which were thick and took the best part of an hour to cross if you went from the beach to the lagoon.

Skull Rock was a flat grey rock that looked like a skull facing up out of the water—the top end of the rock curved just like a human head, and it even had two large round depressions set roughly equidistant from each other that seemed to be blank eyes staring up in the sky above the sea.

The rock wasn't that far from shore, but you had to swim through some very deep water to get there, and the waves could be rough. It was shallow from the beach for about twenty or so steps and then suddenly the bottom dropped away, which took a lot of the boys by surprise the first time. The rock was a good place for catching fish, though, and Peter had declared he was sick of deer and rabbit meat.

Nip didn't come with us, naturally—just stayed in the tree and brooded. It was eleven days since the almost-hanging, and he was probably well enough for the trek through the dunes, but nobody was inclined to persuade him to come along.

He'd taken to going off in the forest for short stretches,

always returning with something to eat that he didn't share with the rest of us—a rabbit or a bird or a squirrel. His jaw had healed enough for him to eat meat again, but eating it hadn't improved his disposition.

Several of the boys were not very good swimmers, which wasn't any trouble when splashing in the shallow mermaid lagoon but quite a bit dangerous in the water near Skull Rock. The mermaids would sometimes help boys who struggled in the lagoon, giving them piggyback rides around. Of course, sometimes they also thought it was fun to watch the boys almost drown. You never could tell with mermaids.

Sal cheerfully rolled up his trousers—he wore baggy brown wool trousers from the Other Place, and couldn't be persuaded to cut them into something shorter and better suited to the climate of the island—and waded in as far as his ankles.

"I can't swim at all," he said, and turned his cap around so the brim was on the back of his head. "How about you, Charlie?"

Charlie shook his head.

"That's all right. The water's nice and cool here, and look, there are crabs," Sal said, beckoning to the smaller boy.

He looked at me, then at Sal, who'd crouched in the water to peer at the crabs hidden in spiky pink shells all along the shore.

"Go on with Sal. I'm going out to the rock," I said, taking off my coat and deerskin trousers. I carefully laid my knife belt on top of these things and dove into the water.

The sea was warm, but the first splash of it was chilly after the heat of the island. I flipped over in the water when I was halfway to the rock and just floated on my back, letting the waves push me this way and that before turning back on my stomach to swim the rest of the way.

Nod and Fog and Crow and Peter had stripped down to their skin and swum out to the rock as soon as they reached the beach, yelling about who could get there fastest.

We stashed a collection of fishing gear in one of the skull's eyes, covered by a tarp weighted down with heavy rocks. There were nets and lines and hooks—all stolen from the pirates, of course, including the tarp. You could take almost anything from them without them noticing, really.

In the early days Peter and I used to steal things from them but not fight them, sneaking about their camp in the dead of night. They'd wake in the morning and wonder if the island was haunted, and we would watch them from the cliffs above their camp and laugh silently into our hands.

This was before they knew that we lived on the island, when the pirates first came there because it was a good place to hide from other pirates, and also from those who would hang them for their crimes.

When I climbed onto the rock, the triplets already had the net out. Peter flopped on his back with the sun on his face and let the others go to the trouble of catching the fish he wanted.

He squinted at me as I shook the water out of my hair.

"Where's your little tail?" he asked. "Did he get eaten by a shark? What a shame that would be."

I pointed toward the shore. "He's on the beach, crab-hunting with Sal."

"Oh, at least that's useful," Peter said. "I like crabs. And perhaps he'll lose a finger if one snaps at him."

Kit and Ed were swimming out our way, and a few other boys had gathered around Sal and Charlie. The rest scampered over the beach, collecting coconuts that had fallen from the long-leafed beach trees. They had a fairly sizable pile, though I knew from experience that they wouldn't last long. There was nothing sweeter on a hot day than the milk out of a coconut.

"Can't he swim?" Peter asked, in a would-be casual voice. "All my boys must be able to swim."

This was patently untrue and he knew that I knew it. Plenty of our boys over the years were unable to swim, and it never bothered him before.

"I won't let you drown him, Peter," I said, my voice mild.

"Who said anything about drowning? I just think it would be safer for him to *know* how to swim, being that he lives on an island and all."

"Just like you told Nip to 'take care' of Charlie," I said.

Peter had been careful not to be alone with me since that incident. His brows knitted together as though he were offended that I would even mention it after so much time— eleven whole days!—had passed.

"It's not my fault Nip misunderstood," Peter said, his eyes pressed to the corners of their sockets, sly and sure. "And anyway, you'll have your chance to kill him in Battle soon enough, and take your revenge for his frightening your little duckling."

"He killed Del," I said.

I was trying not to lose my temper over this, trying not to let him draw me out.

"Del would have died anyway. He had that annoying coughing thing like Ambro. I can't believe you'd fight over a boy who was half dead."

And there was my temper, surging up, making me want to grab the nearest rock and smash it against his head until I could see the white skull underneath.

I'd had enough of Peter dismissing the boys who were dead. They loved him. It was hard for me to remember why at the moment, but they loved him, and he didn't care what happened to them at all.

I don't know what I would have done then—shouted or hit him or picked up that rock—but he spoke again, and it stopped me.

"I know you'll beat him. You always do."

He'd caught me wrong-footed, and the confusion punctured some of my anger. "What?"

"Nip," Peter said, all earnest sincerity now as he sat up and looked at me. "I know you'll beat him because he hurt one of the boys, and you always look out for the boys, don't you, Jamie? Even me. Even when I don't deserve it."

He looked terribly contrite. I couldn't believe my ears. Was *Peter* actually admitting he'd done something wrong? This had never happened before in the history of the island.

"Peter, I—" I began, wanting suddenly to mend what was torn between us, to feel the way I'd felt about him always.

Peter's eyes widened then, and I saw something I rarely witnessed on his face—shock. He pointed over my shoulder.

"Jamie! The pirates!"

"What?" I twisted around, half certain this was a joke, expecting Peter to push me face-first in the water or some such thing as soon as my back was turned.

But Peter wasn't lying, for a change. The pirates *were* there.

Their great tall-masted ship rounded the promontory that sheltered the mermaid lagoon.

"They never come to this side of the island," I said.

It was one of the truths that seemed written into the bones of the island—the pirates stayed on their side, by their camp. They might sail away from the island, but they always returned to the same place. They didn't sail all the way around. They didn't trek through the mountains or the forest. They just *didn't*.

And yet there they were—sailing directly toward us.

"They won't be able to get close to the beach," Peter said. "It's too shallow. They'd ground the ship."

"It's not that shallow here by the rock," I said. "And those cannons will reach the shore for certain from here. We've got to get the boys back into the forest."

Nod and Fog and Crow hadn't noticed yet. They were all getting along, for a wonder, and had just hauled a net full of fish onto the rock. Kit and Ed had stopped swimming halfway out to us and were wrestling in the water, splashing and pushing each other under the waves.

"None of us have weapons," I said to Peter, for he had that look in his eye, the one that said he'd like to swim out and board the ship, the one that said there was nothing better than killing pirates.

"You take the others back," Peter said, almost dreamily.

"What will you do?" I asked.

Peter grinned at me and dove into the water. He had nothing but his skin and his brains with him, but I'd no doubt that if he managed to make it aboard that ship, he'd cause havoc.

The other three crouched over the net, arguing how best to bring the fish back to shore. Nod and Fog wanted to pull the net of live fish behind them. The thinking was that if the net broke or some other catastrophe occurred, the fish could swim free and this was fairer for the fish.

Crow didn't care in the least about what was fair for the fish. He wanted to smash their heads with rocks and then drag them to shore.

"You can't do that!" Nod said, smacking Crow in the head. "If you smash them they'll get all bloody and then sharks come cruising."

"The sharks don't come just because there's a little blood in the water," Crow scoffed.

"Yes, they do. It happened to us once," Nod said. "Fog scraped his leg out here on the rock and when we swam back to the shore this big old shark followed him the whole way. Jamie and Peter had to beat it away from Fog or else I'd have no brother to this day."

They could have gone on like this, and I didn't have time to break it up the usual way. I ran across the rock to where they were crouched and kicked the fish over the side and into the water, net and all.

"Jamie!" Fog shouted. "We worked for those! Peter wanted fish! And you've lost the net."

"Pirates," I said, and pointed to the ship that was getting closer unbelievably fast.

It seemed to cast a shadow on us, a shadow that stretched from the ship back to the shore of the island. They weren't supposed to be there. They just *weren't*.

Nod and Fog stared at the ship, as astounded as I'd been.

"Pirates . . ." Fog said.

". . . don't come to this side of the island," Nod said.

"I know," I said. "Look, everyone has to get back to the forest before the cannons start. You three grab Kit and Ed on the way in and go straight back through the dunes. Don't wait for us, all right? I'll collect the others."

They nodded and dove into the water. Crow followed,

always happy to do what the other two did, even if he didn't understand why it was so astonishing to see the pirates there.

I glanced back at the ship again. There was no sign of Peter—not even the bobbing of his head above the water. I hesitated, wondering if I should go after him. I would have, if Charlie wasn't on the beach. But Charlie was on the beach, and then the first cannon boomed.

The cannonball left the ship and arced up. For a moment I was mesmerized by the shape of it, by the way it looked small and then got bigger and bigger, and then I realized that it had been launched at me.

I leapt for the water, scraping the side of my ankle on the sharp side of the rock. The ball crashed into the rock behind me. I heard it bounce once and then it hit the water, just a finger's length away.

I stopped when I felt it whoosh by me, peered into the clear blue water and watched it fall down, down, down. My ankle bled freely, making a little cloud of red in the water, and the salt stung the wound. I would have worried about sharks except that I thought any shark would be smart enough to stay away from that pirate ship and its noisy, smoking cannon.

Several brightly colored fish darted out of my way as I resumed swimming. The triplets were all enthusiastic swimmers, though not very good ones, and I caught up to and passed them easily.

When I stumbled onto the shore I saw that the rest of the boys had gathered down the beach, where the sand ended and became that wonderful jumble of rocks to climb on. That was exactly what they were doing, playing some kind of follow-the-leader game with one in front—I thought it might be Billy; his hair was yellow like Charlie's—and the rest strung out behind him like a long snake. Charlie and Sal were still wading in the water, their backs to the sea. I was amazed that none of them had heard the cannon shot, but then, the crash of the surf was very loud by those rocks.

I yanked on my trousers and coat and buckled my knife belt around me. Nod and Fog and Crow and Ed and Kit made it to shore while I did this and they all scrambled into their own clothing.

"Back to the tree," I told them.

"Wait—where's Peter?" Ed said. "Wasn't he on the rock?"

"He's gone to cause trouble for the pirates," I said.

Ed grinned. "Taking all the fun for himself."

The pirates hadn't fired again, and I'd expected them to do so right away. It was possible that Peter was causing enough trouble that the pirates were distracted.

I waved the others in the direction of the forest and ran barefoot down the beach, leaving my moccasins behind. The scrape on my ankle didn't hurt but the blood splashed down my foot and onto the sand, making a trail behind me.

Sal and Charlie looked up when I was about twenty

lengths away from them, the two of them smiling and slightly pink from the sun.

"Jamie, look—" Charlie called, holding up a large peach-and-white shell. "You can hear the ocean in it!"

"Get away from there!" I yelled. "There are pirates!"

Sal appeared bewildered, but one glance over his shoulder had him hustling Charlie out of the water at a run.

"Take him back to the dunes and then to the tree," I said. "I have to get the rest."

The others were at the very top of the rocks, strung in their long snake tail. Just then Billy stopped, and it seemed he had just noticed the pirate ship. He pointed at it, and the others peeked around him. There were six of them in that row—Slightly, Billy, Terry, Sam, Jack and Jonathan.

The cannon boomed again, and a second later they were all gone.

CHAPTER 10

I'd never seen what a cannonball could do before. I'd seen a lot of blood in my time, though, and a lot of death. But I never saw death like that.

The ball tore through Billy first. The rest of them might have been all right except that they were directly behind him, and so that cannonball just ripped through all the boys like a finger flicking over a line of dominoes.

It hardly seemed to slow at all, just smashed in their ribs and pulled their hearts and guts out and then all that was left of them were heads on their bloodied bodies. The ball bounced off the rocks and tumbled in the direction of the marsh.

I cried out, and ran for them, unable to believe what my eyes told me. They couldn't all be gone. But when I reached the top of the rocks, all six of them were nothing but mangled meat.

The pirate ship had anchored near Skull Rock, and I saw a rowboat with five or six of them lowering in the water. I didn't see Peter, and the rest of the boys had disappeared into the forest.

I took off my red coat and covered the dead boys, then climbed back down and into the water. I didn't know whether the pirates had seen me up there on the rocks and I didn't care. I wasn't thinking of anything except killing all of the pirates, every last one.

The pirates were not going to follow the boys into the dunes. I would not lose any more of my friends. I would not.

I don't remember swimming out to their rowboat. I don't know how I got there so quickly, or how they missed seeing my shadow in the water. They must have been looking into the dunes for the boys who had run that way.

I surged out of the water and grabbed one of the pirates closest to me, and he was in the water with his throat slit before the others knew he was gone. I swam under the boat while they were all yelling and shouting and looking for their sinking fellow, and I took another from the other side and did for him the same as the first.

There were four of them left now, but they'd been spooked and none of the remaining pirates had managed to see me yet. I swam around under the boat while they peered like idiots over the sides and then gave it a great push. Two of them must have been standing for they fell in the water and made my task easier.

Blood churned everywhere in the water now, spewing from the bodies of the pirates. They couldn't see me in that red fog. I was nothing but a shadow, a sharp-toothed hungry thing, and when I climbed over the side of the boat one of them was so terrified by my appearance that he jumped in the water and tried to swim back to the pirate ship.

I say "tried to," because by then the sharks were coming in. He screamed, high and thin, and then the water churned and the scream was gone.

The last pirate was stringy and toothless and looked like he might have survived a lot of battles. Any other day he could have beaten me, maybe. Any other day but that one.

My dagger was in my hand and his throat tore into that long open smile and then I kicked him over the boat so the sharks could have him.

I stood there, breathing hard, and wished for someone else to kill.

After a moment I was glad of the boat, for the rage burst and my legs shook and I had to sit down on the bench. All around me the sharks—there were three or four of them— tore into my gifts. Chunks of flesh and bone that the sharks had missed bobbed to the surface for a moment before sinking again. Their huge silver bodies bumped the boat as they swam by, close enough for me to touch.

Any other day I might have had the sense to be afraid, but not that day.

The pirate ship pulled anchor and sailed away again, into the horizon this time. I wondered how many of them were left on that ship. Had they seen me kill all the ones on the rowboat?

Had Peter killed more on the ship? I wondered if the pirates were going away forever, deciding that it was no longer worth staying on this island, promise of eternal youth or not.

I wondered, in a vague and unworried way, what had happened to Peter.

I put my hands to the oars and pulled back to shore. The sharks stayed all around me until I was past the drop-off and the rowboat scraped against the sand. I stumbled out of the boat and through the water to the dry beach, where I fell facedown.

I breathed in the smell of the sea salt and the clean sand and the green of the forest and the coppery blood all over my hands and choked back the cries that wanted to erupt from my throat.

"Jamie?" A little voice, a sweet voice.

"Charlie?" I said, picking myself up to my knees.

Charlie and Sal stood a few feet away. Charlie clung to the striped shell he'd tried to show me before the cannonball shot.

"He wouldn't go without you," Sal said. His face was white and drawn.

I scowled at Charlie. "I thought you were going to mind."

He shook his head yes, and then no, and then yes again. "I am. I will. I'll mind you, I promise, 'cept I didn't want to leave you all alone. We watched from that coconut tree. Sal showed me how to go up and we were safe there if the pirates got to the beach. But the pirates didn't get to the beach."

There was a fierce kind of pride in his voice. I realized

then they'd seen everything, seen me slaughter all the pirates and throw them in the water as shark food. Sal's eyes darted from my face to my blood-covered hands, and something in them made me feel vaguely ashamed of myself.

"The pirates," I said, and then the lump rose in my throat and I could feel the unshed grief there and I swallowed it because I didn't cry in front of the boys. "The pirates—the cannonball . . ."

"We saw," Sal said. "We saw."

I stood up then, and dusted all the sand from me. "I wouldn't lose any more of you," I said.

Sal nodded, but I could tell that some of the shine was off the island for him, just like it was for Charlie. He'd heard us talk about the upcoming Battle, and how it was a fight to the death, but somehow I thought he didn't really believe there would be a death. Until that day Sal thought it was all just in fun, for Peter said it was fun.

Sal didn't understand that Peter's idea of fun was considerably more savage than his.

"We'll help you bury them," Charlie said.

It made me sad then, terribly sad, that this tiny boy was already so inured to death that he knew what came after.

I shook my head. "I don't want you to see them. They're all in pieces."

"But—"

"No," I said, and this time it was gentle. "No, I want you

to mind me now. Go back to the tree with Sal. The others should already be there."

Charlie's mouth set in a stubborn little line, but I found I couldn't lose my temper with him as I'd done before.

"It's my lot, Charlie, not yours," I said. "I look after the boys, and I bury them when they're dead."

"Peter should look after us," he said, and I'd never heard him so fierce. "He's the one who brings us here. He's the one who says we'll have adventures and be happy forever."

He was only saying what I'd thought many times, and things I'd felt in my own heart. Still it seemed a betrayal, somehow, to agree with him.

"Peter only has a mind to play," I said. "So I'm here to look after you all."

"We'll help you bury them," Sal said suddenly.

"I don't want Charlie to—"

"To see. You said," Sal said. "But you can't keep him small forever. He's got to learn to survive here, and so do I. And you can't always be alone, Jamie."

You won't be alone, Jamie. I'll stay with you always.

Peter had said that to me, a long time before, and he'd smiled at me and I'd followed him.

Sal and Charlie, they didn't smile. They didn't promise me they'd stay with me always. But they helped me dig six graves that day, and we didn't weep when we covered the boys, though no one would have blamed us if we had.

* * *

Peter didn't return until the next day, and he was surprised to find only nine of us left. Nip was inside the tree but the rest of us were gathered around the fire, watching Nod and Fog and Crow perform a kind of story they'd thought up, something that had to do with a bear falling in love with a mermaid. I'd no idea where this particular inspiration had struck them.

Like everything involving the triplets, it had quickly devolved into meaningless shouting and punching. I felt that me and Kit and Ed and Sal and Charlie were trying to find this funnier than it was.

Peter strolled into the clearing whistling like he hadn't been gone for almost a day.

"Peter!" Ed shouted, standing up.

The triplets heard Ed's cry and immediately stopped pummeling one another. They ran to surround Peter.

"Peter, where have you been?"

"Peter, did you kill all the pirates?"

"Peter, were you on the pirate ship? How did you get back again?"

He didn't answer any of their questions, only frowned around at the small circle of adoration around him.

"Where is everybody?"

"Oh, all the others were killed," Nod said. "Except for

Nip, of course. He's in the tree being boring, as usual."

"A cannonball hit them," Fog said.

"Jamie said it made a big mess," Crow added.

"All of them?" Peter said. "One cannonball killed all of them?"

Even Peter was taken aback by this. We'd always fought the pirates hand-to-hand, though we'd understood that the cannons were supposed to be a threat. Still, we'd never seen them fired until the day before. And Peter clearly hadn't known what happened onshore while he was off adventuring on the pirate ship.

"Did you kill any pirates, Peter?"

"Mmm," Peter said, by way of answer. He was looking around at the sparse audience for his adventures and not liking it.

"How many pirates, Peter? Jamie killed six. Well, he says one of them jumped off the boat and got eaten by a shark, but he was running from Jamie at the time so that counts, doesn't it?" Nod said.

"Six pirates? That's nothing," Peter said. "Jamie's killed more than that before."

"Not all at once like that," Nod said. "He's always fought them one or two at a time only."

I felt that this was probably true, but I couldn't be certain. The thing I would never tell Charlie or Sal or even Nod or Fog was that I'd killed so many pirates over the years that I couldn't remember how many of them I'd taken on at one time or another.

Nod was impressed not only that I'd slaughtered the pirates but that I'd swum out to the rowboat and taken them by surprise. That was the best part for him. He'd made me tell it all through three times already, and every time I'd left out more details, aware of Sal and Charlie's eyes on me.

Each time I did this Charlie would add back in all the bits I'd left out, and generally make me sound more heroic than I was.

I wasn't a hero. I'd just been angry.

Only I didn't realize at the time who, exactly, I was angry with. I'd thought it was the pirates, for firing a cannonball that took away six of my mates in one fierce swipe.

But it wasn't the pirates. It was Peter.

It was Peter's fault all the boys were dead. Peter had burned the pirate camp. Peter had fed their Captain to the Many-Eyed. All of this was because of Peter.

Because Peter promised them adventures and happiness and then took them away to the island where they died. They weren't forever young, unless dying when you were young kept you that way for always.

In all that time, and all those years, only four boys had not died or grown up—which was the same thing, really, for growing up meant death was closer every day.

Four boys—Nod, Fog, Peter. And me.

And then Peter glanced around and saw that his band

wasn't big enough for him, and he said, "I'll be back soon."

He turned and left the camp as suddenly as he came, and the other boys slumped in disappointment.

"But, Peter, where are you going? Can't we come too?"

He waved his arm back at them, and the few who'd started to follow stopped.

I knew what he was about, and I wasn't having any of it.

"Stay together," I told Sal and Charlie.

I was more worried about Nip since we'd lost so many boys. There were fewer eyes about to watch him. But Sal and Charlie were getting better at looking out for themselves every day, and I had to trust them to do so.

Peter was distracted, and thinking about his plans, and so I caught up with him after several minutes' hard running. I was lucky he hadn't decided to fly, else I wouldn't have been in time.

I grabbed his shoulder and jerked him around. He raised his eyebrows at me.

"No, Peter," I said.

"No, what?"

"No more boys from the Other Place," I said. "You can't look after the ones we have now. I won't let you bring them here just to have them die."

"I don't bring them here to die," he said, clearly insulted. "I bring them here so they'll live forever."

"But they don't," I said. "Can't you see? The island takes them and chews them up."

Peter shrugged. "And then I get new ones. It's always been like this, Jamie. I don't see why it should bother you now."

"You didn't see them," I said. I could see them, just as sure as if they were laid out before me at that moment. I didn't want to see them. I didn't want to see anyone like that ever again. "You didn't see all the boys with a hole in their middle, their insides torn out. There was nothing left of them, Peter."

"It's a good thing the pirates went away, then, so that won't happen anymore."

"It won't happen anymore because you're not *getting* any more," I said, my teeth gritted. "I won't let you."

He laughed then, and my dagger was in my hand. I hadn't thought about it. I just wanted to make that laugh go away forever. It wasn't his happy-Peter-come-play-with-me laugh. It was Peter laughing at me.

Laughing at *me*.

He didn't think I could stop him. He thought it was *funny*. That was the first time I hated him.

His laugh faded when he saw my dagger, and he squinted at me. "What are you going to do, Jamie? Stab me?"

"If I have to," I said. *Oh, how I want to.* I wanted to make that laugh go away forever.

Peter looked at me for a long time. I let him look.

I couldn't guess what he might be thinking. All I knew was that I would stop him if he tried to go to the Other Place. I was tired of burying boys. A permanent sense of grief had settled over me, and every time I saw Charlie or Sal smile, all I could think was that I would lose them too.

Was this, I wondered, what it felt like to be a grown-up? Did you always feel the weight of things on you, your cares pressing you down like a burden you could never shake? No wonder Peter could fly. He had no worries to weight him to the earth.

It was the middle of the afternoon, and the biting flies buzzed all around our heads. I didn't wave them away, because I wanted to be ready if Peter decided to fight. Peter could be very, very tricky in a fight.

A fly landed behind my ear and bit, and blood rolled down the back of my neck to mix with sweat, and still I waited.

Finally Peter sighed, a long, long sigh. "Very well."

"Very well what?" I asked suspiciously.

"I won't go and get any more boys."

My grip loosened on the dagger. I'd held it so hard that it left a bruise on my palm, I found later. "You won't?"

"No, I won't," he said. "But you have to do something for me."

"What?" Just the fact that Peter was asking for something immediately made me suspicious.

"I want you to play with me more. Just me. Not with the others all the time," Peter said, and he sounded very young then. "You hardly play anymore, always worrying about chores and keeping the other boys safe. I brought you here to play and lately you've been acting like a grown-up."

He spit out the last word. I could almost see his disdain dripping from his tongue.

I didn't know how to explain to him that for all that I still looked young, I had been feeling old. The years had passed, so many of them, and they were starting to wear on me. After a while it wasn't fun to always feel like you had to have fun.

And as I thought this, I felt a little twinge in my legs, like the muscles and bones were stretching.

"Well? Do we have a bargain?" Peter asked.

"I won't leave Charlie alone all the time just to play with you," I said. "If this is some kind of trick so you can set Nip on him again . . ."

"No harm will come to your little duckling," Peter said. I checked both hands to make sure they weren't crossed behind his back.

"All right," I said. "I'll play more, and you don't get any new boys from the Other Place."

Peter held out his hand and we shook on it.

"Now," he said, and his eyes gleamed. "How about we bother the crocodiles?"

The day before the Battle, Nip went off in the woods early in the morning and didn't come back until well after dusk. He returned sweaty and scratched from his exertions, but overall he looked much healthier than he had been. His broken cheekbone appeared to be mending, though an ugly ridge had formed where the two pieces joined together.

He was gone so long that day that I wondered if he had gotten lost, or perhaps just decided to keep going straight across the island and join the pirates. It would be better for him if he didn't fight me, though he didn't seem to realize that.

The pirates, surprisingly, had returned to the island a few days before. Peter and I had been out scouting in the mountains (just the two of us, as Peter wanted) and had seen their ship anchored in their usual cove.

We'd crept down for a closer look and found that the previous first mate was now wearing the Captain's coat, and that he'd managed to replace the men he'd lost to Peter and me and the Many-Eyed. They set up a new camp while Peter and I watched from a cliff just above the beach.

"The new pirates look a good deal younger and healthier than the others," I said.

"That means they'll fight better," Peter said. "We should have a raid, and welcome them to the island."

I chose my next words carefully, not wanting to irritate Peter. He'd been in a better mood since our bargain, mostly because he seemed to think he had me on a string that he could tug anytime he liked.

"Maybe we should wait on a raid until after Battle," I said. "After all, I could get hurt in a raid, and then the fight wouldn't be fair."

"You wouldn't get hurt, Jamie," Peter scoffed. "When have you ever gotten hurt in a raid?"

I had, plenty of times. There was a long scar on my right thigh where one of the first mates had managed to slice open the skin and muscle there. That was probably the worst I'd ever gotten.

A boy had lived with us at that time called Rob, and he said he'd once been a servant to a doctor. He told me the doctor sewed flaps of skin together so they would heal, so I tried that with some deer gut I stretched into thin strings. It seemed to work all right, except that the place where the skin and muscle joined was swollen and tender for a long time after, and cutting the deer gut out after the wound healed was more miserable than sewing it together in the first place.

Under my left ribs there was a hard knot of skin where another mate had almost got me, except that I danced away at the last moment before he managed to plunge the knife all the way in. There were assorted other small marks and scars, many of them faded white, but they existed. Peter had just forgotten, the way that Peter did forget about anything that wasn't right in front of him at the moment.

"Still," I said, not liking to remind Peter that he was wrong. "I *could* get injured. And if I was, you'd have to put off Battle until I was better."

"Why?" Peter asked.

"Because you put it off until Nip was better, so you'd have

to do the same for me. It's only fair."

"Oh," Peter said, his mouth twisting to one side the way it did when he was thinking hard. He wanted the raid, was excited about the return of the pirates.

At the same time, I sensed that the ongoing tension of Nip's presence in the camp was beginning to wear even on Peter. Nip never spoke to anyone except to insult them, and he certainly did not come along for games or adventures. He was secretive and angry, and that did not make for Peter's idea of fun. Delaying Battle, even for a few more days, was not appealing to him. Peter wanted the trouble with Nip to be resolved.

"I suppose we could wait until after Battle," Peter said slowly. "But not too long after. I don't want these new pirates getting ideas. The island belongs to me."

Not to us, I noticed. Not to all the boys, or even to Peter and me. Just to him. It was *Peter's* island.

But I didn't let this irritate me. Peter was doing what I wanted. There would be no raid until after Battle.

On the morning of Battle we all woke early. It was a half-day walk to the Battle place and Peter wanted to reach it before midday. It wasn't so far as the crow flies, but it was nestled right in the mountains to the southeast and there was a good deal of climbing to do to get there.

This meant that Peter was cock-crowing us awake before

the moon had set. All the boys except for Nip and Sal and Charlie (who were the only new boys left after the terrible day with the cannonball) had been to the Battle place before, and so were familiar with Peter's routine. We rolled out of sleep and collected our things while Peter scampered around shouting for us to hurry.

I'd carefully prepared all my weapons the night before and packed them—except my dagger, which always went on my waist—in a kind of sling-bag I'd made from deerskin.

Ever since the day Battle had been announced I'd quietly picked up useful rocks that I saw here and there—smooth round ones that would fit inside my slingshot. Those stones were in my bag, along with my freshly strung shot.

I had also found a couple of larger rocks, ones that would just fit inside my hand, with spiky bits on them. They were worth carrying the extra weight. If I got Nip's skull with one of them he'd go down in an instant and then I'd just have to finish him off.

After Del died I'd taken his pirate sword, though I didn't prefer swords, generally. I was good with them, and would take a sword from whatever pirate I fought and use the sword against him, but I mostly found swords unwieldy. The dagger suited me better—I liked to be quick, to dart in and out again, to kill before my enemy knew I was even there.

Swords weren't permitted in Battle, nor daggers either, because Peter liked Battle to be about the boys who were the best fighters—not who was able to steal the best weapons from the pirates. Still, I put Del's sword inside my sling-bag, because I had a hunch that Nip might cheat.

I'd been teaching Sal and Charlie swordplay with it, anyhow. The necessity of keeping Peter company meant that I hadn't taught them as much as I'd have liked, but I'd feel better if they had the sword with them while I battled Nip.

There was a voice whispering to me that Peter was being too nice, too good, that he hadn't forgotten the way Charlie and Sal took me away from him. Going after them while I was distracted by Battle was a distinct possibility.

Nip was cross, as usual, when Peter woke him. This might have had something to do with Peter treading on Nip's hand instead of shaking his shoulder. The other boy woke with an angry shout, and spent several minutes swearing words I'd never heard before while he packed. I've listened to pirates too, and still I hadn't heard some of those words.

Soon enough the ten of us were trekking through the last hours of night toward the mountains. The Battle place was a crater that seemed carved for our exact purpose. It was a bowl-like depression in the rock—the southeastern mountains were rockier and spikier, generally, than the northeastern ones—and about twenty-five boy lengths across. All around the rim of the bowl was a protruding lip that seemed just like a bench for watching what happened inside. When Peter and I found it, so long ago, it seemed as if the island had made an arena especially for us.

Peter took the lead, of course, and I let the other boys get between us so I could walk with Charlie and Sal. Nip, surprisingly, wanted to walk near Peter. I guessed that perhaps he was thinking of what might happen if he beat me. He would have to find his way into Peter's favor again, and from my view it appeared he was laying it on thick.

I didn't mind. I knew that Nip was unlikely to win without cheating, and I was glad of the chance to spend a few hours free from Peter's expectation that I amuse him.

"Jamie," Sal asked quietly, for the night was still and voices carried. "How many of these Battles have you fought?"

I frowned. "I'm not sure. The first one, the first *real* one, wasn't until maybe twenty or thirty seasons after I came to the island. Until then Peter and I used it as a place to practice fighting, but just for fun."

"Nod said Battle is for fun," Sal said, and I heard the question in his voice. *How could it be for fun when one of you dies?*

"Sometimes it is for fun," I said. "Usually Peter sets a Battle day once or twice a year. He picks two teams of boys and then we fight hand-to-hand, no weapons, first in groups and then one-to-one. Whoever wins is the Battle champion until the next Battle."

"How many times have you been Battle champion?" Charlie asked.

I was thankful for the moonlight, which hid the blood

that rushed to my face at Charlie's question. Sal looked at me curiously when I didn't answer right away.

"I, um . . . I'm always Battle champion."

"Always?" Charlie's eyes glowed in the moonlight.

"Always," I said. Why should I be embarrassed about this? I was the best fighter. But something about the way Sal cocked his head to one side made me feel silly about it.

"So Battle is a way to practice fighting," Sal said. "For when you raid the pirates and things like that."

I nodded. "Yes, and it also helps the boys work things out. When you've got a big group of boys like this, sometimes they go too far with one another, and it's good for them to have a place to fight and clear the air. Else they spend all their time spitting at each other and it causes too many problems."

"The triplets spend all their time spitting at each other," Charlie said.

"Yes," I said, rumpling his hair. I liked the way the yellow strands stood up and caught the light of the moon. "But the triplets like to argue and punch each other. For them it's not clearing the air. It's just as natural as breathing."

"But sometimes, like today, Battle isn't a practice," Sal said. "Today it's real fighting."

"Yes," I said. "Though there are still rules. You can't carry a bladed weapon, only rocks or sticks or things you made yourself, like a slingshot."

"Yes, because it's obviously better if you beat each other

to death with rocks instead of stabbing each other like civilized human beings," Sal muttered, looking away.

"You're not worried, are you?" I asked, trying to peer around to see his face. "Because I've never lost Battle before, and I'm not going to start today."

"Those were play Battles," Sal said, and he was definitely angry. I could hear it.

"Not all of them," I said.

He gave me a sharp look then. "This isn't your first Battle to the death?"

"I've been here a long, long time, Sal," I said, and I felt all the years roll over me when I said it.

I felt that twinge again, the one in my legs, the one I hadn't felt since that day Peter promised he would not bring back any more boys.

"How long?" Sal asked.

I shrugged. "A hundred and fifty seasons, maybe more. I can't really remember."

"You don't remember the Other Place?"

"It doesn't look the same as it was when I was there. Every time I go back with Peter it's different. And we didn't get Nod and Fog here until after I'd been here for many seasons already."

Sal gave me another one of his piercing looks, the ones that made me feel all twisted up inside. It was almost as if he felt sorry for me.

"You're very old, Jamie," Charlie said, and he was so

solemn about it that it made me laugh.

He made Sal laugh too. That laugh rang out in the night and seemed to bring on the dawn faster, as if the sun wanted to hear Sal laughing.

When we reached the steep parts of the mountain, Charlie began to struggle. There were places where there was no path at all, and we had to climb using handholds we found in the rock. Charlie's arms and legs were far too short for this exercise, and he was terrified of falling in any event.

Sal and I took it in turns to carry him on our backs through these parts. It was much, much harder for Sal, who was almost as tall as me but a great deal more slender and not as hardened to life on the island. He refused to let me carry Charlie on my own, though.

"You've got to save your strength for Battle," he said.

I didn't tell him that I could probably carry Charlie on my back throughout Battle and still beat Nip. Sal wasn't impressed, I thought, by my accomplishments at Battle.

Charlie, on the other hand, took my news of permanent Battle champion as proof positive that I was the best boy in the world, something he'd already been mostly convinced of anyhow.

I think that this was, deep down, why Peter disliked him so much. It wasn't just that Charlie took me away from Peter. It was that Charlie *preferred* me to Peter. Peter was used to all the boys thinking he was the best, most wonderful boy there ever was.

Despite the necessity of carrying Charlie, we kept up with the others and we all reached the Battle place by midmorning. Peter wanted to be annoyed that we'd piggybacked the smaller boy, but since we hadn't fallen behind, there wasn't much he could do about it except scowl at Charlie.

The Battle arena was just past a little mountain meadow filled with small white flowers that bobbed in the wind. Though this part of the range was rockier than the northern end, there were still a few green places. A skinny stream full of cold water ran along the edge of the meadow before tumbling over the rocks on the other side, heading down to the crocodile pond and then the sea.

We reached the meadow after a hard climb on a bit of trail that switched back and forth along the side of the mountain. To reach the Battle place we crossed the meadow, heading due east. The carved-out bowl was directly on the other side, a hole that was dropped in between the meadow and the jagged rock wall that rose up on the other side. A dirt track ran from the meadow down to the bowl, and on the fourth side the view opened to the rest of the mountains and a sheer drop down for the unwary.

The rock of the Battle arena was smooth and white, veined with grey, and this rock was different from the rest of the mountains. It was one of the reasons why Peter had declared it special and important.

No matter how many times we fought there, or how much

blood was spilled, the rock remained white and smooth.

It was like the island swallowed up that blood and pushed it out again as magic, magic that kept us boys forever. It was a fanciful thought, but no more fanciful than that of the pirates thinking we drank from some magic spring for eternal youth.

Nod and Fog and Crow and Ed and Kit ran across the meadow and into the bowl, whooping and dancing in circles. Nod and Fog promptly bumped into each other and a heartbeat later their fists were where they always were—in each other's faces. Crow couldn't bear to be left out. He jumped on top of Fog and soon the three of them were doing what they did best. Kit and Ed ran around the three of them, shouting encouragement.

"It seems like it would be exhausting," Sal whispered to me. "To fight like that all the time."

"Strangely enough, they seem to get more energy out of it," I said.

Peter settled himself right at the center of the rim on one side, so he could have a good view of the proceedings. Peter always judged Battle; he never participated.

I put Charlie and Sal a little away from Peter, on the side of the arena that had the security of the mountain wall rising behind it. It would be far too easy to knock the two of them off the open side if anyone (like Nip or Peter, I thought) had such things in their mind.

I drew Del's sword out of my sling-bag and handed it to

Sal. He took it with obvious reluctance. Charlie watched with some jealousy in his eyes. He enjoyed learning how to use a sword far better than Sal did.

"What will I need this for?" he asked.

"You keep yourself safe," I said. "You and Charlie."

"I won't have to," he said. "Because you're going to win, aren't you?"

"Jamie always wins," Charlie said.

"But in case I don't," I said. "You keep yourself safe."

I bent down then, and whispered in Sal's ear the thing that I hadn't let myself think. "If Nip kills me, then you and Charlie won't have a chance here. Peter will find some way to get rid of the two of you. You go as fast as you can to the door to the Other Place and you go back, you understand?"

Sal looked at me, stricken. "I . . . don't know if I can find the way back. We came here in the night. I don't remember the way."

"Then go to the pirates," I said.

"The pirates?" Sal was horrified. "After what they did to the others?"

"You'll be safer with the pirates than you will be here with Nip alive."

I wasn't certain of this at all. It was only a hope. If they stayed with Peter and Nip, then Sal and Charlie would die. If they went to the pirates, then they might live. That was all I could give them, if I didn't make it.

CHAPTER 11

Peter stood and clapped his hands then, and the wild boys running and rolling in the center came to a halt.

"It's time for Battle to begin. Fighters, bring your weapons here to be inspected."

Nip had been lurking on the dirt track behind Peter, just at the edge where the meadow dipped down to the arena. I wondered if he was having second thoughts about Battle. He kept glancing back over his shoulder like he was calculating how quickly he could run away.

When Peter called us he trudged—with some reluctance, I thought—down to the arena to join me.

The other five collected on the seats between Peter and Sal and Charlie. Charlie's legs swung back and forth in excitement. Sal gripped the scabbard of the sword and couldn't disguise his worry.

I took my slingshot and the rocks out of my bag and placed them on the bench for Peter to look over. He carefully checked each one like he was searching for treasure hidden inside, and then took my bag and turned it inside out to make sure I wasn't hiding anything.

"Leave your dagger here," Peter said.

I took it out of my belt and placed it on the seat. Then I collected all my rocks and slingshot in the bag again.

"Here, why's he leaving his dagger?" Nip asked.

"Because we don't use bladed weapons in Battle," Peter said.

"Nobody told me!" Nip shouted. "All I've got is bloody bladed weapons."

He turned out his own bag, and a clatter of knives and axes spilled out.

"You're telling me I'm not to use any of this against him? I thought this was a Battle to the death!"

"It is, but we have rules about how you're allowed to kill each other. This is about skill," Peter said; then he gave Nip a sly sideways glance. "You had thirty sleeps to ask any of us about the rules. Why didn't you?"

Nip's face turned a kind of blotchy red, like there was a thunderstorm in him about to burst.

I peered more closely at the pile of metal that Nip had dumped out. "Where did you get these?"

Some of the objects were quite new and shiny, but most of them were rusted. The axe handle looked like it might rot away from the blade at any moment. There was something about that axe . . . something familiar . . . It looked like an axe a boy called Davey used to carry when he was alive.

"Found them," Nip said defiantly. "There was this field with all these pointed sticks in it and I saw this knife in the dirt so I took it. Then I thought there might be pirate treasure buried there so I dug around some more and found these other things. Found a lot of bones too."

"That's because it's where I buried the boys," I said, anger blossoming in my chest, turning into a red haze before my eyes. He stole from the boys, my boys, my boys that I carried in pieces and covered in dirt. "You took all of these from dead boys, you damned grave thief."

"You *stole* these from graves?" Peter said, looking appropriately horrified.

I knew Peter didn't give a toss where Nip got the weapons. He just wanted to wind Nip up even more.

The other boy seemed torn between fury and embarrassment, especially when Nod and Fog and Crow chimed in.

"That's not right, Nip."

"Yeah, there should be respect for the dead."

"Respect for the dead. That's what Jamie always says."

"And that means you don't go taking things from dead bodies."

"That's against the rules."

"Sod you and sod your bloody rules!" Nip shouted. He pointed at Peter. "I only came here because he said there wouldn't be any rules! And all he's done is lie and make me look a fool."

"Peter didn't make you a fool, Nip," I said. "You did that yourself."

"I'll show you who's a fool," he said, and grabbed the axe.

I wasn't ready for this, though I should have been. Somehow I'd thought he'd take his anger out on Peter, whom he blamed for his troubles. I didn't know that he blamed me just as much, or maybe more.

He swung out at me with the axe and I only just got away, though my movement took me toward the center of the arena and away from my dagger, which waited on the bench because I'd been ready to follow Peter's rules.

If I had my dagger, it would be over in a thrice, for I was certain I could hit him even while he was swinging that axe in a wild rage. But I didn't, and I didn't have time to load up my slingshot while I was dodging the axe.

But I had the big rocks, the ones that fit just inside my fist. I reached into the bag, feeling around for the spiky surface, and my hand closed around one. Nip charged at me again, the axe held high like he wanted to bury it in my head.

I was vaguely aware of the other boys shouting, of Peter saying, "That's not fair play! That's not fair play!" over and over.

Nip didn't care in the least about fair play. He wanted me dead.

As Nip ran at me I ducked away from the whistling blade

and slammed my rock-filled fist into his stomach. This startled him into dropping the axe as the breath left him, and then I was on him in an instant. I heard the boys cheer and call my name, clapping and screeching with glee every time I landed a blow.

I pummeled him fast with both hands, and the one with the rock did more damage but the other one did plenty. In a few moments Nip was on the bottom of the arena, flat on his back, his face an unrecognizable mess. My knees were in his shoulders and I raised the rock once more for a final blow.

The boys all chanted, "Finish him, finish him, finish him."

Nip's little mean eyes looked from the rock to me, and then he laughed. It was a bloody, wheezy laugh, but it made me pause.

"What's so funny?" I asked.

"Doesn't matter . . ." he said, and it took him a long time to say it. ". . . what happens to me. Because they are coming."

"Who's coming?" I asked as Nip closed his eyes. I slapped him and he opened them again. "Who's coming?"

"Pirates," he said.

In an instant I remembered Nip's long trek the day before, and the way he kept looking over his shoulder while he stood at the top of the track.

Like he was waiting for someone to arrive.

Nip had told the pirates where we would be. And in the arena, we'd be trapped. There was no way out except the track back up to the meadow.

I brought the rock down on his head so hard that I

caved in the front of his skull.

The boys erupted in cheers—all except Charlie, who looked pleased but shaky, and Sal, who turned away and retched.

"We have to leave now!" I shouted, but they didn't hear me.

They hadn't heard Nip's words either, because they were too busy cheering me on. They didn't know the pirates were coming.

I had to get them out.

I ran toward Peter, who had stood on the seat and was leading a "hip-hip-hurrah" for me. Nod and Fog and Crow and Kit and Ed were gathered around him with their backs to me.

The shot rang out, and it didn't seem real, the way it echoed all around the rock walls. We didn't use pistols— didn't have them, or the means to fill them with gunpowder, so what was the point? And the pirates had never used them on us before that day.

Everything changed after Peter burned their camp down. They didn't want us for our secrets anymore. They wanted only revenge.

The shot rang out. Then blood bloomed on Fog's back, an opening flower that revealed the hole that passed through his body.

Not Fog, I thought. Nod and Fog had been on the island almost as long as me. How could there be an island without the two of them together, always together? It couldn't be.

Fog fell backward, and the pirates swarmed in.

There were only six of them; else it might have been worse. As it was I think they were tired from the climb—Nip couldn't have described the path very well, having never been there before.

They were tired, and had counted on surprise. And they still thought of us as children.

We were not ordinary children.

Nod saw his brother fall and howled a noise that no human should ever hear, a howl of pain that came from his heart instead of his throat.

I flung my rock, still coated in Nip's blood, at the first pirate down the track. He was the one holding the pistol with smoke curling out of its tip. The rock hit him square in the nose and he staggered to one side, swiping at the blood that erupted there. I grabbed my dagger and leapt over the rim of the arena, landing on top of him. He twisted and fell face-first to the ground. I jammed the blade into the base of his neck and he stilled.

I rolled to my feet, searching for Charlie and Sal. Sal stood over a dead pirate that had Del's sword sticking out of his chest. Charlie was behind Sal, and he didn't seem to be harmed at all.

The other boys had stampeded past me while I dispatched the first pirate, and they'd chased the others up into the meadow. I heard the sounds of their weapons clashing, the hollering of the boys and the curses of the pirates.

It was only Sal and Charlie and me, and four bodies, left in the arena.

Sal was pale and sweaty and had his hands crossed over his stomach like he was going to be sick again.

Then I saw the red seeping between his fingers.

"Sal!" I said, and ran to him just as he fell.

I reached for the button of his waistcoat, a funny affectation of his like the woolen trousers and cap. He batted my hands away weakly.

"Leave it," he said thickly.

"Don't be a fool. I have to see how bad it is," I said.

Sal was too shaky to stop me. I ripped open the waistcoat buttons and then the white shirt beneath, both now sticky with blood.

And stopped.

The wound was in the upper left part of the belly, just below the ribs. It wasn't that deep, though it bled profusely. It looked like the pirate had just got the tip of his sword into Sal.

That wasn't what stopped me, though.

Just above his ribs Sal had wound several pieces of cloth tightly around his chest. It was enough to disguise the truth when his shirt and waistcoat were buttoned, but there was no hiding it once those were off.

Sal wasn't a boy at all. She was girl.

Her face was now terrified and defiant all at once, and she said, very coolly though her voice was weak, "How bad is it?"

I think I fell in love with her then, when she pretended that everything was just the same as it had always been.

"What are those?" Charlie asked, pointing at Sal's chest.

Sal laughed, then coughed. "Getting stabbed *hurts*. Why didn't you tell me?"

"Did you think it would be an adventure?" I said, with a levity I did not feel.

"That's how you and Peter always made it out to be," she said, and coughed again.

I didn't like that coughing. It made me worry that the wound was worse than it looked. I fumbled with shaking hands in the pockets of my coat, where I always had something handy hidden, and yanked out a pirate's head cloth that I'd stolen some time ago. It was covered in dust but it was the best I could do.

I folded the cloth and pressed it over the wound, hoping to staunch the bleeding. Sal cried out when I put pressure on it.

"That hurts too!" she shouted, and hit my arm.

"Do you want to bleed to death?" I said.

"Don't bleed to death, Sal," Charlie said.

"Is that your real name?" I asked.

Her dancing blue eyes looked away. "It's Sally."

Charlie looked from Sally to me and back again to the strips of cloth around her chest. He'd just made the connection. "You're a girl!"

"Who's a girl?" Peter's voice, behind me.

I twisted around. Nod and Crow and Peter had returned to the arena. The three of them were painted in spattered blood. Peter's face said he'd had the time of his life. Nod stared at his dead brother's body.

"Sal's a girl!" Charlie said, standing up and pointing at her.

"You couldn't hide it for long," I said. "Not on the island, surrounded by boys."

"I've hid it for three years, surrounded by boys on the streets, ever since I was ten years old," she said, her eyes sparking. "I'm no fool, Jamie."

"Then you shouldn't have gotten yourself stabbed," I said.

"I was trying not to let Charlie get stabbed," she muttered.

Peter and Crow came over to us. Crow seemed only mildly curious, but Peter's face was thunder. "You're a *girl*."

He said it like he was saying Sally was a slimy thing he'd found under a rock.

"We've already figured that out," I said, getting irritated on her behalf. After all, so what if she was a girl? She'd been here a month and gotten on fine.

"There are no girls on my island!" Peter shouted. His face was red. I don't think I'd ever seen him so angry. His mouth contorted in rage. "No girls! None! None! None! Girls are trouble and they aren't allowed here. You *tricked* me."

"I was keeping myself safe," Sally retorted. "It's more dangerous for girls than for boys when you sleep out in the street at night. I cut my hair after I ran away and I lived like a boy. You liked me fine when you thought I was a boy."

"No, no, no, no, no! You can't stay! There are no girls allowed here and so you have to leave."

"Where will she go?" I asked. I was astonished at his behavior. He was like a small baby having a tantrum. I'd never seen him like this. Never.

"Back to the Other Place!" Peter shouted.

"But, Peter," Crow said. "Nobody's allowed to go back to the Other Place. You said so yourself. It's one of your rules."

"There are no girls allowed on this island!" Peter screamed. "That's a rule too!"

I was less worried about Sally's future home than I was about her living to see a future at all. The blood from the wound had soaked through the cloth and I couldn't really see why. It was just a little stab wound, but it wouldn't stop bleeding.

"Charlie, give me your shirt," I said.

The smaller boy took off the shirt he'd been wearing since the day he'd arrived on the island. I made all the boys wash their clothes as well as themselves every several days or so; otherwise the smell in the tree became unbearable. Luckily we'd had a wash day not long before, so Charlie's shirt wasn't as filthy as it might have been.

"I'll make you a new one," I said, as I tore the shirt into strips.

"Out of deer hide?" Charlie asked. His upper body was thin and pale, though his arms and neck and face were brown from the sun. "Like your pants?"

"Of course," I said, knotting the strips together into a long rope.

"Who the devil cares about your stupid shirt!" Peter shouted. "She's a girl and I want her out. Out, out, out, out, out!"

There's nothing worse than having a fit and no one giving you the proper attention for it. Crow seemed to find Peter's behavior unseemly—he'd backed away and come to kneel next to Charlie and me. Peter ran around the arena, kicking Nip's dead body several times and throwing whatever he could find.

Nod was sitting next to Fog's body, holding his brother's hand and crying, and not caring who saw him.

That was when Fog's death was real to me, real in a way it hadn't been before. I'd never seen Nod cry. I wanted to look after him, but I had to look after Sal first.

I wrapped the strips around Sally's middle, pulling them tight so there would be pressure on the wound.

"I can't breathe when you do that," Sally said. Her face was dead white now and covered in sweat.

"Sorry," I said. "I think you must choose between breathing or bleeding to death."

"Oh, well, when you put it that way," Sally said.

Her natural cheerfulness kept reasserting itself even though she was in a dire situation. I knew many boys who screamed and cried when they took wounds like Sally's, and she'd done none of that.

I closed her shirt and waistcoat around her again and felt the tips of my ears heating. I don't know why it was more embarrassing to cover her up when we'd all been staring at her exposed body for several minutes, but somehow it was.

"Crow, help me get her up," I said.

We each put an arm around Sally until she was standing between us, breathing hard.

"Do you think you can walk?" I said.

"I'll have to, unless I want to sleep alone on this mountain," Sally said. Her hair was soaked with sweat and her cap had fallen off.

Charlie picked up the cap and presented it to her. She shook her head. "Can you wear it for me, Charlie?"

The little boy seem thrilled, turning the cap around so the brim was on the back of his neck, the way he'd seen Sal do it.

"Where are the others?" I said to Crow.

We were all pretending that Peter wasn't screaming and throwing things. It seemed the best course of action at the moment. Charlie couldn't stop himself staring, though, and then looking quickly away before Peter caught him at it.

"Are no others," Crow said. "Just me and Nod and Peter made it."

"Then it's only us," I said.

I wanted to run around in a circle and kick and throw things too. We'd come up the mountain with ten, and now four more were gone—Kit, Ed, Fog and Nip. From sixteen our band was down to six in less than a month.

Nip was no loss, and would have never gone back to the tree in any case, but losing Fog hurt. And the other two had been on the island long enough for me to give a damn for their own sakes, not just because it was a stupid loss of life.

"What I don't see is how the pirates knew to come up here anyway," Crow said as we slowly moved toward the track.

"Nip told them where we would be," I said. "He was always going out on those long walks on his own. I should have known he was up to something."

"You can't always know everything, Jamie," Crow said philosophically.

Peter dragged the corpse of the pirate who'd stabbed Sal over to the edge of the arena and threw it into the drop below, screaming his frustration the whole time. Del's sword was still sticking out of the dead pirate's chest when Peter did this, and I was annoyed that he'd wasted a perfectly good weapon.

We stopped next to Nod, who had not moved or acknowledged anything except Fog's body since reentering the arena.

"Nod," I said. "We've got to go now."

He looked up at me slowly, very slowly, like he wasn't sure what the words I said meant.

"We're going back to the tree," I said.

"What about Fog?" he asked, and his voice was a tiny broken thing.

"I can't stay to bury him," I said. "Sal's been cut and she needs to get back to the tree."

"She?" Nod asked, but it was only a vague curiosity about something out of place.

"She," I said. "Sal's a girl."

"Oh," Nod said. It didn't seem to bother him very much.

"If you want to bury Fog you can do it in the meadow, and catch up to us later," I said. "He'd like that. He'd be near the Battle place."

"Battle was his favorite thing to do," Nod said, rubbing at his dripping nose and eyes with his wrist.

He stood and lifted his brother over his shoulder. We let them go ahead of us on the track. Charlie followed Nod, though whether it was to help or to witness I didn't know. Probably he thought Nod shouldn't be alone.

As I passed the pile of weapons that Nip had brought to Battle, I hesitated, and Sal felt me pause and stopped moving. Crow looked curiously at both of us.

"He took them from the boys' graves," I said.

"But you don't want to waste them," Sal said, nodding.

"The pirates won't stop," I said. "We've killed a bunch of their lot again."

Crow let Sally go, and she leaned all her weight on me. There wasn't much to her, really—none of the boys were anything but skinny and strong from all their adventuring— but it felt different, somehow, when she was pressed up against me. Was it because I knew she was a girl, or because I could feel the tiny curves at her chest that I wasn't aware of before?

For her part, I think Sal only wanted to rest. The short hike across the arena seemed to have drained her.

Crow gathered up the weapons and put them in the bag

Nip had carried, then slung it over his shoulder. He took up his place on Sal's other side and we continued our slow, deliberate way.

Behind us, Peter was still screaming.

Nod had found a place for Fog in the meadow. I think Charlie wanted to stay there with him, see it through until the end, but I told him to come along with us. Nod needed to be alone with his twin, this one last time.

It took us a long while to get back to the tree. I carried Sal on my back down all the parts where climbing was necessary, and Crow took Charlie. Nod caught up with us fairly soon (he had Fog's knife slung at his waist, the one they'd fought over) so he and Crow took it in turns to carry the smaller boy.

Peter did not return with us.

It was night when we staggered into the clearing, numb and exhausted. Nod and Crow and Charlie collapsed in a heap together just inside the tree, all three clinging to one another. Sal muttered incoherently, and I was afraid she might be building a fever.

I got her settled in a pile of skins and then lifted her shirt to check the wound. The blood had soaked through the bandage, and it was still fresh and red.

This might have been because the wound was so much worse than it looked, or it might have been because Sally hadn't been able to rest since she'd been injured. I took off her shirt and waistcoat entirely, carefully ignoring the wraps around her chest, and cut off the strips of Charlie's shirt that I'd tied around the wound. Some scabbing came away when I lifted the cloth and Sal cried out.

"I'm sorry, I'm sorry," I said.

I ran outside to get some water from the skins that collected rainwater. These were hung all about the tree on the branches. The water was warm but it would do.

I poured some water in Sally's mouth, holding her head up so she wouldn't choke. She coughed and spluttered anyway and half of the water ended up on my face. I released her head back and she closed her eyes, drifting into sleep.

My own eyes were gritty from sleepiness and worry, but I washed out the wound as best I could and then put some spicy-smelling green leaves on it that I knew would make it stop bleeding. That boy Rob had also showed me this when he'd lived on the island.

How long ago was that? Fifteen seasons? More? It didn't matter. I wrapped the wound again and hoped it would stop bleeding in the night. It was one thing to experiment with sewing up myself. I didn't think I could do it to Sal.

Sally. Her name was Sally, not Sal.

I covered her up with one of the best skins, a nice soft fox-fur one. Then I lay beside her on my side, and watched her breath rise and fall until I fell into a deep and dreamless sleep for the first time since I'd lived on the island.

PART III

SALLY

CHAPTER 12

Peter didn't return the next day, or the next, or the next after that. In fact, he was gone for more than a week. He'd never done this before, and I might have worried about it, except that Sal did catch a fever.

The next morning when I woke up her skin was like fire. The wound had ceased bleeding, but she moaned and tossed and turned and it was hard to get her to swallow any water or broth. She soaked through any skins we put on her but if we took them off, she would cry out piteously that she was cold.

Nod and Crow were, surprisingly, a good help to me. They took it in turns to watch her and to bully her into swallowing soup, and even washed all the dirty clothes and skins so she'd have something clean to sleep in. Charlie ran back and forth collecting water and bathing Sal's head with a cloth.

If the pirates knew where the tree was, they could have crept up on us and killed us all, for none of us was aware of anything except Sally.

On the fourth day, her fever broke.

We all cheered, and I think I never loved those boys more than at that moment. We had saved her. We'd all done it together.

Together wasn't something that Peter understood, not really. He liked all the boys to be in one group, but he didn't like sharing and he certainly didn't like it when the boys banded together to do anything without him. He liked to sow discontent, to cause fights, and this, I realized, was why he never played at Battle. It was much more fun for him to watch us run to and fro and hurt each other. If we hurt one another, even in fun, then we could never like one another best—only him.

On the sixth day, Sally sat up and scowled at me when I changed the poultice.

"Must you put that foul-smelling stuff on there?" she said.

"If you enjoy living, then yes," I said. "That foul stuff probably saved your life."

"I thought Crow said it was your magic broth that saved me," Sally said, her eyes twinkling. It was nice to see that twinkle again, to know that Sal was almost back to normal.

Nod, who was good at sewing, had made her a fresh pair of deerskin pants that stopped at the knee, and a matching shirt with silver wolf fur trimmed all around the edges. It was one of the finest things he had ever made, and he'd presented it to her with a blushing face that morning.

Sal had thanked him very prettily, her own cheeks pink,

and then asked for some privacy so she could change into Nod's gift.

She'd washed and changed while the four of us stood outside the tree, looking up at the sky and trying not to be curious about what was going on inside.

When she called out that it was all right to come back in, she was wearing her new clothes and sitting up against the cave wall. There was something different about her, something I noticed after a few minutes. She'd stopped binding her chest, and now it was desperately obvious that she was, in fact, a girl.

Crow and Charlie didn't seem to notice, but Nod looked everywhere except directly at Sal, and I tried to keep my eyes right on her face.

"Something saved you, the broth or the leaves or just plain luck," I said, feeling the blood rise in my face as I glanced at her chest.

I had to stop being so foolish. It was only Sal, my friend Sal, and truthfully the curves were so small that she barely looked different from a boy.

But they were there. She was most definitely not a boy.

Nod and Crow and Charlie were outside, and I heard them laughing as they played some game. It was good to hear Nod laugh, though it never quite reached his eyes—the ghost of Fog lingered there.

"Jamie, do you remember your mother?" Sal asked.

I gave her a startled glance. "My mother? No."

"Sometimes you sing a little song to yourself when you're at some task, like you were doing just now," Sal said. "I thought you might have learned it from your mother."

I hadn't even known I was singing, and wondered if this happened often and the other boys just never thought to mention it to me.

"I told you I came here a long time ago, Sal," I said, feeling unaccountably angry. "I don't remember my life before the island."

"Certain of that?" she asked.

"Yes, I told you so. Do you think I'm a liar?"

She didn't flinch. She didn't seem even a little bit intimidated by my temper. "I just wondered if you remembered really, but didn't want to say because it would make Peter angry."

I started to say that I didn't care what Peter thought about it, that I did as I pleased.

But that wasn't really true, was it? I didn't do as I pleased. I did what I thought was best and tried to keep Peter happy so he wouldn't destroy everything.

I'd made myself a hostage to him for three weeks just so he wouldn't drag any more boys here to his island, and to keep Charlie and Sal safe from his jealousy.

And I did remember some things from the Other Place.

The song.

Wide blue eyes staring, and a red mouth carved in a smile where there should be none.

"I don't like to talk about it," I said.

I finished up changing the bandage and collected the dirty things to take outside to wash.

"You're a good father to these boys," Sal said. "I thought maybe you learned from someone who cared about you."

"I'm not their father," I said, my voice harsh. "I don't think of myself that way. We're not playing families here on the island. We just work together."

"You look out for them. You take care of them. That's what a father does—or at least, what he's supposed to do. Mine only beat me and my mother until I ran away. After that he only had my mother to hit," Sal said.

She didn't sound sad about this, or like she wanted me to feel sorry for her. It was just a statement of fact, but it arrested my anger.

"Did you love your mother?" I asked curiously.

"When I was small I did," she said. "When I was older I hated her for letting him hurt me."

"Maybe she was scared to try to make him stop." I had a strange impulse to defend Sal's mother.

"I wasn't scared," she said. "I shouted at him. I stood up to him. I hit him with a broken bottle once, made him bleed all over. If a little child can do that, then why couldn't my mother stand between us?"

I didn't know what to say to this. I could see it, little Sal with her dark curls and blue eyes, fierce and small with a bruise on her face and a jagged bottle in her hand.

"That's what you do for the boys," Sal continued. "You stand between them and Peter. You keep them safe. Because it isn't safe, this island. It isn't at all what Peter promised it would be, what I thought it would be."

"What did you think it would be?"

She shrugged, and her hands moved restlessly in her lap. "Like a paradise, I suppose. A happy place that was clean and bright and where everyone was lovely to each other and there was lots and lots of food to eat. I've spent three years eating rats, or moldy bread that I stole off the end of a cart. If ever I had anything—a penny earned from shining shoes, or an apple that wasn't half rotten—some bigger boy would come along and try to take it from me. I always had to fight, every day, just to stay alive. I was fighting when Peter found me, beating an older boy who wanted my cap."

"That's why he wanted you," I said. "If he saw you fighting and thought you were good at it, he would want you here."

"I thought," she said, and she took a deep breath. "I thought that Peter respected me because I wouldn't let the other boy bully me. He said I looked like a boy that deserved an adventure. I didn't believe him at first, about the island, though."

"I didn't either," I said. "I don't know that anyone does. It sounds like a fantastic lie."

"It *is* a fantastic lie," Sal said, and her face was very earnest. "This isn't a wonderful place for boys to play and have adventures and stay young for always. It's a killing place, and we're all just soldiers in Peter's war."

I shuffled my feet, not sure what to say to this. It wasn't that I hadn't thought all of these things before, or even said some of them to Peter. I had. But I was his first choice, his best, his right hand.

And I couldn't, not yet anyway, say out loud to the other boys that Peter was a monster.

"It wasn't always like this," I said. "With the pirates, I mean. We used to just raid them but they never came looking for us after."

"And what changed?" Sal said, her eyes narrow and sharp. She knew the answer as well I did.

"Isn't this place better than eating rats and getting beaten every day?" I shouted, suddenly angry again. "Do you want to go back to that? Because Peter will send you there. I was going to look out for you, and say that he should let you stay, but if you don't like it here, then I should let you go back to that life."

I stomped out of the tree, not waiting to hear what she answered. What did she know about the island or Peter, anyway? She hadn't been here that long, and she wasn't even a boy, even if she pretended to be one. Peter said there weren't to be any girls on the island. He made the rules and I ought to take her back to the Other Place myself.

And while I was at it, I should take Charlie too. He was learning to like it on the island—too much. He'd never seemed so happy as when it was just the five of us, no Peter to growl at him, no Nip to scowl at him. His mother would be missing him. She would be crying every night. I ought to bring him home.

Except that he was part of my heart now, and I didn't want to let him go. And I didn't want to let Sal go either.

Did that make me selfish? Did that make me like Peter?

Maybe it did, just a little.

But I had to believe that I was better than Peter. I wouldn't sacrifice the others for my own amusement. I wouldn't forget about them the moment they were gone.

That made me better, didn't it? I only wanted them near me because I loved them.

Though, of course, it was because I loved them that Peter had to take them from me.

Nine days after the pirate assault on the mountain, Peter reappeared in camp. Nobody jumped up and surrounded him when he strode in like a returning hero. We were playing a game with sticks that Sal had thought up and we didn't notice him at first.

Sal made some boxes on the ground with the sticks, and set them apart at different lengths, some closer and some farther apart. Each boy would take it in turns to try to jump through all the boxes without missing one or breaking the sticks apart. I was the tallest and had the longest legs, so I was winning easily, though Crow seemed to take it personally that he was shorter and was trying to make up for it by jumping higher.

Charlie struggled the most, being the smallest, and we all cheered when he managed to jump through two boxes in a row.

There were three rabbits on the fire for lunch and the smell of meat cooking mingled with everyone's happy laughter and it felt like home.

And then Peter came, and it was like a cloud settled over the clearing, and that home feeling went away. Smiles faded, even from Nod, who used to worship Peter.

But that was when Fog was still alive, and Peter hadn't helped Nod bury his brother. He hadn't seemed to care at all that Nod's twin was dead, though they'd been on the island the second longest. That took a lot of the shine off Peter for Nod, and Crow did what Nod did, more or less.

The shine had come off Peter for Sal and Charlie long before then.

So when he looked all around and said, "What's the matter with all of you? Don't you want to know where I've been?" everyone just stared back at him in silence.

"I've been scouting out a new home," Peter said. "I've found a much better tree closer to the plains."

"There's nothing wrong with this tree," I said. I didn't like to contradict him so sharply, but moving closer to the plains and the Many-Eyed did not seem like an excellent notion to me. "We've lived in this tree ever since we came here."

"But there are so few of us now," Peter said. "And I'm not allowed to get any more boys because you're so boring, Jamie."

The other four gave me curious looks at this. I hadn't mentioned to anyone, of course, that I'd argued with Peter about bringing in new boys. I kept my disagreements with Peter to myself if I could.

The truth was that Peter could have gone off and collected new boys while he was missing for so many days. There was nothing I could have done about it if I didn't like it. But he hadn't, and then he'd come straight in and complained that I was stopping him from gathering new playmates, and I wondered why.

I didn't like the way my thoughts tended. It seemed to me that maybe Peter wanted a clean slate, and that he'd rid himself of all the boys (and that troublesome girl too) by feeding them to the Many-Eyed. Then he would tell me he had to go off and find new boys because all the others were eaten.

"We're not moving closer to the plains," I said. "It's too close to the Many-Eyed and too close to the pirates."

"Well, the pirates have shown they're willing to go anywhere on the island to get at us, so I don't see that counting. I've been surprised at their spirit, you know, Jamie? I didn't think they had it in them, but I guess that old fat Captain was holding them back. When they attacked on the mountain I was really shocked. Though once the shock was over it was sort of nice to have a fight that wasn't planned by us. Those raids were getting so predictable."

Nod moved before I had a chance to do a single thing. One second he was next to me, and the next he wasn't, and Peter had no chance to defend himself, none at all.

I always thought of Peter as a smart and capable fighter, but watching Nod pound him I wondered why I thought this. He always beat the pirates, but then, he almost always fought pirates who were older and slower than he. It was me that fought the young ones, the dangerous ones.

Peter never scrapped with the other boys at all. He watched at Battle, and none of them would dare pick a fight with him because they all adored him.

Or rather, they used to. Now most of them were gone and those who were left didn't adore him anymore.

Nod had knocked Peter down and was pummeling his face over and over. This was Nod's way—to get on top of the other boy and hit him until he didn't know which way was up. Peter was too astonished to fight back, I think.

I dragged Nod off Peter, his fists flailing, his legs kicking out.

"Don't, Jamie! Don't! I'm going to kill him! I'm going to kill him!"

Peter's nose was bloody. He touched it gingerly, like he couldn't believe he was hurt.

I don't think I'd ever seen Peter hurt before. Somehow he never got a scrape, even when we fought the pirates. I might have a list of scars to remember all our battles by, but he didn't.

It was strange that I never noticed this, in all those years. In my defense I was usually patching up another boy, or myself, and had no time to consider Peter's injuries nor the lack of them.

"Nod," Peter said, and he sounded so hurt that Nod stopped shouting and kicking. "Why did you do that?"

Nod seemed to wither under Peter's sad look, as if he was remembering all the fun they'd once had together. I didn't dare put him down yet, though. If Peter said something thoughtless, he might set Nod off again.

"You didn't . . . You said . . . the pirates," Nod said.

"What about the pirates?" Peter asked. I didn't know if he cared so little that he was genuinely puzzled or if he did the best innocent act in the world.

"The pirates killed Fog, and you were talking about it like it was fun," Nod said. His body drooped more after he said this. It seemed to take a lot out of him to admit out loud that Peter wasn't wonderful and perfect.

I knew how he felt. It was why I always found myself making excuses for him, defending Peter even when he was awful.

That was the power he had over us.

"Well, it is fun, isn't it? Killing the pirates is some of the best fun in the world," Peter said.

"Not when my brother dies!" Nod screamed.

It was a good thing that I had a tight grip on Nod, else he would have launched at Peter again. My arm was around his waist and his limbs flailed in front of him, trying to reach Peter.

Peter lifted his shoulders. "Lots of boys die, Nod. It never troubled you before."

"It wasn't my brother!" Nod said, and he let out a long and terrible howl.

The storm burst then, all at once. He stopped kicking and punching and suddenly slumped over my arm. I felt his chest heaving and his tears splashing on my skin.

Sal was up in an instant, prying me away from Nod and putting her arms around him. Nod collapsed on her, weeping into her shoulder.

Peter sniffed at this behavior. He never cried himself, so he didn't see why anyone else should.

"I'm going to the mermaid lagoon, since none of you want to see the marvelous tree I've chosen for us," he said.

"Nobody's moving to that tree, Peter," I said.

"Oh, I see," Peter said, his eyes narrowing at me. "I've been gone too long, is it? Now they're *Jamie's* boys on *Jamie's* island."

"No," I said. "It's not that way. There's no reason to leave this tree, and it's safer here."

"Well," Peter said, his voice silky and dangerous. "It seems that way. It seems that they're all following you now. What's to stop me from collecting a new band of boys from the

Other Place so I'll have some boys to follow me?"

"You promised, Peter," I said. "We made a bargain."

"The bargain was that *you* would play with me," Peter said.

"And I have. For many days I have been only with you, just the two of us as you wanted, roaming the island," I said. "I kept my word. So you must keep yours."

"If you don't go with me to the mermaid lagoon, then you're not keeping your word," Peter said. "I want to play and I want somebody to play with. If you won't do it, then I'll have to find another boy."

My eyes met Sal's over Nod's shoulder. She gave a tiny nod, to show that she understood.

"Watch out for Charlie," I told Crow.

Crow nodded. He'd been taking in all of this with wide eyes. I wondered what he thought of Peter at that moment. I wondered if Peter realized that he was losing them all because of what he did, not because of what I did.

Peter clapped his hands when I joined him. The blood around his nose had dried already. He was lucky, as his nose hadn't swelled at all. He didn't seem to notice that I had no enthusiasm for his game. He was simply happy that I was going with him, and that he'd gotten his way.

I trudged beside him through the clearing, hearing him chatter happily about this and that and all the things he'd been doing while he was away—how he'd found this new tree, and also how he'd played some tricks on the pirates who were back at camp so they would think the island was haunted, the way they used to long ago.

"I don't think you should bother the pirates anymore, Peter," I said. "Haven't you made them angry enough?"

"I only made them angry in the first place because of you, Jamie. Don't you remember? You killed the Many-Eyed when you weren't supposed to, and then you wanted to make it seem as though the pirates did it. You asked me to draw the pirates out of their camp and I did, and now you're blaming me because the pirates are mad about it. That's not very fair of you."

"I told you to draw them out, not to burn everything down."

I was ready to take the blame for the Many-Eyed, but not anything else. It was Peter who'd made that choice.

But it was the boys who paid for it. Like they always did.

"None of it would have happened except for you. So if all those boys are dead, it's because of you, Jamie."

All those boys. Billy and Slightly and Kit and Jonathan and Ed and Terry and Sam and Harry and Del and Fog and Jack and Nip, and all the ones before them that I'd buried in the field, so many that their faces swam together and their names were one name. They all watched me, and accused me, but it wasn't because it was my fault that they were dead.

It was because I didn't stop Peter, because I let Peter live, because I let Peter lie to them and promise them things that could never be. All children grow up, or they die, or both.

All children, except one.

CHAPTER 13

Peter spent more time away from us after that, coming and going as he pleased, and nobody really minded. Things were more comfortable when Peter wasn't around, especially as he was inclined to stare resentfully at Sally when he was in camp.

He didn't say anything more about making her go back to the Other Place. I didn't fool myself that this meant she was allowed to stay. It simply meant that he was trying to come up with a good accident for her, so that he could pretend to boo-hoo when she was gone.

When he wanted a companion he always made me go with him, and every hour I spent with him was a misery. There was nothing on the island that we hadn't done a thousand-thousand-thousand times before, and Peter was unaware or didn't care that I didn't want to do it anymore.

What I wanted was to play quiet games with the others, or tell stories, or just laze about the tree and eat fruit if that was all we wanted. I wanted, finally, for there to be some measure of peace, to not face another day where one of the boys would die just because Peter couldn't stand to be still.

One day when Peter had gone off on some mission of his own, I asked Crow and Nod to keep an eye on Charlie, and then I asked Sally to take a walk with me.

She was drawing pictures in the dirt with a stick, and after I asked her to walk, her face reddened.

"I just want to show you something important," I said. Her blush made me respond in kind. It was like this with Sally. Everything would be fine, with all of us treating her like one of the boys, and then she would say or do something that had me feeling like a fool.

Nod watched us curiously as we left. He hadn't been the same since Fog died, not as quick to anger nor as quick to laugh. I'd noticed something else too.

Nod had gotten taller. I noticed it because he and Crow had been more or less the same size, and then one day they just weren't anymore. He had grown.

And so had I.

In fact, it had gotten so that I woke up in the morning and didn't recognize my body most days. All my limbs were longer, and my hands and feet seemed like foreign things.

When I walked, my ankles got tangled up, and I felt big and slow, though in truth I wasn't *that* much bigger than I'd been before Battle. It was perhaps a thumb length, maybe more, but that length felt like miles when Peter was around, who seemed smaller than ever to me. Had I never really seen how young he was until then?

Sal didn't speak as I led her away from the tree. After several minutes where we both determinedly tried not to look right at each other she said, "Where are we going?"

"To the tunnel that leads to the Other Place," I said.

She tilted her head to one side, like she was disappointed in me. "Sending me back, then? No girls allowed on Peter's island?"

"No, no," I said hastily. "Not a bit of it. I just remembered what you said on Battle day—about not knowing the way back. And I want you to know it."

Sal was silent for a minute. "So I can escape, if I need to."

I nodded. "Yes."

She stopped then, and hit me hard in the shoulder. "And what about you, you fool? Do you think I'll run off and save myself and leave you here with *him*?"

I stared at her, rubbing my shoulder. "You hit hard," I said.

"For a girl, you mean?" she said angrily. "I told you, Jamie, I lived on the streets with boys for three years. I can look after myself. I'm not helpless just because I'm a girl. I won't have you treating me like I am. And I don't think you should ask me to run away while you stand and fight. I'm here now, and I'll stand beside you. I won't run."

Nobody had said this to me before. Nobody.

If I told the others to run, they ran. If I said I would be a shield between them and the world, then I was. None of

them volunteered to stand with me, to take the knocks that
I thought were my duty to take.

"Well?" she said.

"All right," I said slowly. "All right. You won't run, and I
won't ask you to. But I still want you to know how to get
back to the Other Place. It's not just about you."

She wilted a little then. "Of course. Charlie."

"I know he doesn't mean as much to you as he does to
me . . ." I started.

"Don't think you can decide for me what's in my heart,"
she snapped. "I love Charlie as much as you do."

"All right," I said again, not knowing what else to say.

I felt as though I were navigating some strange and
undiscovered country, one where perils lurked around every bend.

Girls might not be trouble the way Peter thought, but
they certainly were confusing.

I took Sally off the main path and into a patch of forest
tucked in the border between the swamp and the mountains.
It wasn't that far from the tree, but the course was confusing
if you didn't know where you were going. I showed her all the
things I used to stay on track—a tree marked with an "X" in
the bark, a knife mark scratched on a boulder, a little stream
that bubbled near the entry to the tunnel to the Other Place.

It looked just like a rabbit hole, as it did on the other side.
It was tucked underneath a tree between two knotted tree
roots. There was nothing to show that it was magic, or that

it would take you away from the island entirely.

For the first time I wondered what would happen if the tunnel was blocked. Would you be able to dig out all the way to the Other Place at the end, or would the magic be broken forever? Strange that we had never thought of this, or worried about it. We could have been trapped in the Other Place if that happened.

There was something about Peter, his complete surety that things would always work the way he wanted them to. When he said we could go to the Other Place and return to the island, we believed him. I'd never troubled myself thinking that the magic might go away.

Now I worried about exactly such a thing. What if I told Sally and Charlie to run for the tunnel, and when they got there the tunnel wouldn't take them back because it was blocked or broken?

Worse, what if the tunnel only took you to the Other Place if Peter was with you? I'd never tried to go through on my own, and I was certain none of the boys ever had either.

What if it was Peter who made the magic?

She shook her head. "I never would have found this again. It was dark and I was so excited, and also the tunnel seemed so long."

"It does, that first time," I said. "After that it goes quicker."

Peter's head popped out like a jack-in-the-box, telling me to come on, come on, there were adventures to be had. He disappeared again, and I was afraid to stand out in the dark on my own, out under this tree. I didn't know how to get back home, and the tree seemed huge and frightening, like a dangerous thing that would reach down with its branches and grab me and hold me too tight.

I ran to the hole and peered in, and didn't see Peter. So I called his name and heard him answer, "Come on, Jamie!" though the answer seemed far away.

He was going away from me, and then I would be all alone.

I put my feet into the opening, and after a second I pushed off and followed Peter down into the hole. There was a long drop that I didn't expect and I tumbled to the bottom, getting dirt in my eyes and mouth and nose.

Peter laughed, but it wasn't a mean laugh, and he picked me up and dusted me off and his eyes seemed to glow in the darkness.

"It's not far now," he said, and he took my hand.

It was farther than I thought it would be, so long in the dark, and I would have been afraid except that Peter never let go of my hand.

"Did you ever wonder, Jamie, how Peter found this island in the first place?"

Sal's words startled me out of the memory. I shrugged. "I never asked. I suppose I always thought that he found the hole by accident, when he was just exploring in the Other Place."

I didn't mention my worry that the path only worked because of Peter. I decided that I would explore on my own another day, when Peter was away somewhere, and make sure that you could cross to the Other Place if he wasn't with you.

"I wonder," Sal said, and she looked thoughtful.

"Wonder what?" I asked.

"I wonder if he's not actually *from* the Other Place," Sal said. "If he's from the island, and he found the path to the Other Place from here."

"How could he be from the island?" I asked. "Did he sprout out of the ground like a mushroom? Where are his parents?"

Sal shook her head. "I don't know. But he's not like other boys. There's something different about him."

I didn't say anything to this. There was something different about Peter—the way he knew things about the island, the way that he sometimes seemed like he was *of* the island.

And he could fly. None of the rest of us could fly.

I thought that this was because he'd been there for so long, but maybe Sal was right. Maybe the reason why Peter was so dismissive of mothers was because he'd never had one. Maybe he just appeared on the island one day, unfolding out of the grass just as he was, an eleven-year-old boy forever.

But no. That was silly. Even Peter couldn't have come from nothing. He had to have been born somewhere.

I asked Sal to point out all the markers to me on the way back to the tree, so I could be sure that she understood where she was to go.

She huffed out a sigh. "I told you I'm not stupid, Jamie. There's no need to test me."

"I just want to make sure you won't get lost," I said. "It's easy to get lost here."

If she and Charlie were on their own and got turned around in the dark, they could very easily end up near the crocodile pond. Sal might think I was being ridiculous, but then, she hadn't been on the island when Peter told the story of the crocodile and the duckling.

She didn't worry about Charlie being dragged underneath the water of the pond by sharp, sharp teeth.

Still, she passed my "test," as she called it, and found the way back to the main path without any prompting from me. When we reached it she crossed her arms and looked up at me.

"Happy now?" Then she frowned. "Are you taller? I thought I was nearly as tall as you."

"You did well," I said, avoiding her question. I glanced back over my shoulder in the direction of the tunnel. "Perhaps we should practice again from this side, just to make sure—"

"I'm not doing it again. You'll simply have to trust me," she said impatiently. "Jamie, you didn't answer me. Are you taller?"

This was the other quality that made Sal different from all the boys. She couldn't be distracted by anything. If she asked you a question and you didn't answer, then she would ask that question again and again until you did.

"Yes," I said, and hoped that would be enough.

Sal would never take a one-word answer.

"Are you—" she began.

Then she swallowed before going on, her voice hushed like she was afraid the island itself would hear, and tell Peter.

"Are you growing up?"

Her words seemed to hang between us on the shimmering air, insects flying between them without any notion of how dangerous that question could be.

"I—"

It crashed over me all at once, the truth I'd been pretending wasn't there. I was growing up.

I was growing up, and I was so afraid.

I turned away from Sally, choking on the answer.

She wouldn't let me turn, wouldn't let me cry alone in shame, wouldn't leave me.

Sally would never leave me alone.

She put her arms around me and I covered my face in my hands and sobbed, because I was afraid.

For so long I'd run free with the knowledge that I would never grow up, that I would only die if I got on the wrong end of a pirate's sword.

Even then that sort of death had seemed another adventure at first, when everything on the island was new. It was heroic and also somehow not real, that I might be slashed by a pirate and fall to the ground but Peter would find me and wake me up later.

There were many years when the death of the other boys that we brought here didn't trouble me, because I knew that at least I would always go on. Peter had promised me, and so

I would live forever. It was a very long time before I stopped believing in Peter's promises.

Now the island was fading for me, losing its magic, and I would grow old, and one day I would die for certain.

And I thought it wasn't just because Peter didn't care about the boys, or that he kept secrets. It was because I didn't love him anymore the way that I used to do, when we were both small and he was my best friend in all the world.

"I'm glad," she said fiercely. "I'm glad, because I'm going to grow up and I want you to grow up with me."

I scrubbed at my eyes then and looked at her. Her face was so close to mine. I could smell her hair, flowery and sweet, because Sal took baths even when the rest of us did not. Her eyes were bluer than they'd ever been, dark and full of some promise that I didn't really understand.

"Only, Jamie, you have to not grow up too fast," she said primly. "Because I'm thirteen and I think right now you're about the size of a fourteen-year-old, and that's happened very fast. So you can't get much bigger now, for if you do, then you'll be too far ahead of me."

I knew then that when I stopped loving Peter my heart looked for other things, and Sal was filling up all the space that Peter used to take there.

She pressed her lips against my cheek, something I'd seen now and then in the Other Place. It was called a kiss, I remembered.

A kiss can be made of magic too. I'd never known that.

She blushed again when I stared as she pulled back, but she didn't look away. Sal didn't hide. She always looked at you directly, and made you meet her.

"I'll grow up with you," I said, and took her hand.

It was different from holding Charlie's hand, or Peter pulling me along to a new adventure. Her fingers twined into mine and I held it over my heart, so I could show her all the things that I didn't know how to say.

Then I kissed her cheek very fast and let go of her hand and ran away, and she ran after me, laughing, and all of the world seemed to rise up laughing with her. She had the most wonderful laugh you've ever heard, like silver music that coursed through your blood.

We were still children, for all that we thought we weren't. We were in that in-between place, the twilight between childish things and grown-up things.

Childhood still held out a friendly hand to us, if we wanted to go back to it, while the unexplored country was ahead, beckoning us to come there and see what new pleasures were to be found.

I didn't really understand what that country meant, not really. It had been so long since I'd been near a grown-up who wasn't a pirate. To me pirates were not unlike children themselves, only in bigger bodies. They did as they pleased (or so it seemed to me) and they spent as much time on the island as we boys did. And their lives had just as much blood and adventuring as ours.

The country that called to me now was one I barely remembered, one in which well-dressed husbands and wives talked quietly over supper tables. I remembered, suddenly, seeing just such a pair when I pressed my face against the window of a public house.

I didn't remember why I was there, or how old I might have been, or where my own parents were. I only remembered being cold and hungry and seeing them there, warm and clean and well-fed.

"Sal," I said. "When we grow up we will have a very large house."

"Of course," she said. "For all the boys."

I nodded, pleased that she understood. For when Sal and I left the island to grow up, of course we would take Charlie and Nod and Crow with us. I could never leave them behind with Peter.

The thought of Peter all alone on the island, with no companions to play with, didn't make me as sad as it ought to. I felt a little thrill of pleasure that he would have no one to push or pull or feed to the maw of the island when he was bored.

"When will we leave?" Sal asked.

I explained to her that I wanted to test the tunnel before we tried to cross it without Peter. She agreed that it was a possibility that the crossing might only be there if he was.

She pursed her lips. "I don't like the idea of you trying on your own."

"It will be safer and quicker with just one," I said. "And once I'm sure we can make it through to the Other Place, then we can leave as soon as Peter's gone off on one of his trips."

"Why not just leave when he's there?" she asked. "You should look him in the eye and tell him that you're going, not sneak away like a coward."

That stung. I wasn't a coward. I'd never been a coward.

"It's not about cowardice," I said. "It's about safety. You don't know Peter. You think that you know him, but I've been his companion for longer than you can understand. Peter might let all of you go, though I can't be certain of that. But he won't let me go. I think Peter would rather kill me himself than see me leave."

More than that, he'd try to kill the others if he thought it would make me stay. In his Peter-boy-logic he would think that if only he got rid of what distracted me, then I would be happy to be with him instead.

But if I said that out loud, Sal would only tell me that I was trying to protect her when she didn't need protecting.

"You're afraid to fight him?" she asked, peering at me closely. "I can't believe that."

"Of course not," I said.

"Then this is about me or Charlie or some other such thing," Sal said.

It cut me, it really did, the way she just seemed to *know* everything.

"Can't you let me look after you?" I said. "If we're together, then that means we take care of each other."

"Yes, that means I look after you, too, and not allow you to act foolish."

"It's not foolish to keep you away from Peter's anger," I said. "You've never seen it."

"I saw him at the Battle arena," she said.

"That's not anger," I said. Why would she not comprehend? Everything about this plan was much more dangerous than she thought it was.

If Peter caught us . . .

"Please," I said. "Please, don't make me put you or Charlie or Nod or Crow at risk just because it offends your sense of honesty. You can be as honest and forthright as you like, Sal, but you should know that Peter won't be. This is his island. He'll do anything to keep it exactly as he wants it."

There must have, finally, been something in my face or voice that convinced her, for she gave a reluctant nod.

"All right," she said. "We'll do it your way."

"And don't mention anything to the others yet," I said. "Not until it's time to go."

"Yes," she said, and then her hand came up suddenly, blocking her eyes.

"What's the matter?" I said.

"Something bright," she said, lowering her hand and pointing behind me. "Like a flash."

I twisted around, looking for what had startled her, but I didn't see anything. I thought I heard a faint tinkling sound on the wind.

"Where did it come from?" I asked, suddenly worried that pirates might be roaming the forest searching for us. The flash might have been the sun off a blade, and the tinkling the sound of buckles jingling as they walked.

She showed me, and we carefully explored all around checking for any sign of pirates—footprints, broken brush, the smell of rum that they left behind them in a cloud.

After I assured myself that there was nothing to find, we agreed to go back.

"It must have been a bird," I said.

"What sort of bird flashes in the sun?" she asked.

"You'd be surprised," I said. "Some of the birds here have feathers so white that they shine. You haven't seen all of the island, Sal. I have."

She would have liked to argue about this, I thought, except there was no denying that on this one subject alone I was more knowledgeable than she. The only person in the world who knew the island better was Peter.

I returned to camp feeling more lighthearted and hopeful than I'd felt in a long time. I even smiled at Peter when I saw him sitting at the fire with the other three. Peter took that grin in stride, but Nod looked sharply from Sally to me and back again, which made my smile fade. I wondered how much he could see there, and how much he understood.

Charlie was sitting beside Peter, which surprised me very much. He was holding a little piece of carved wood in his hand, and I recognized the thing Peter had been whittling the day I killed the Many-Eyed. That day seemed so long ago, a lifetime ago.

So very many boys ago, when they were all still alive.

"What's that?" I asked.

Charlie's eyes shone as he held up the wood. "Peter made me a toy! Look, he said it's a little fairy to keep me safe."

He handed the toy to me and I inspected it. The carving was that of a very tiny girl with wings. Somehow Peter had managed to make the wings appear gossamer and light, carving little lace patterns there. Her hair was long and curled past her shoulders and she wore a dress made out of leaves. Her feet were small and bare. The face was full of mischief and delight, a face that drew you, invited you.

It was very finely done, so fine that it seemed that the girl might suddenly fly away from my hand.

"A fairy, eh?" I asked, looking at Peter.

"Oh, yes," Peter said. "I know all about fairies. I met them in the gardens in the Other Place."

This was the first I'd heard of such a thing. The most I knew of fairies were the stories that other boys told when they came to the island, stories about creatures that granted wishes or stole a child away from its parents and left a changeling in its place.

"When did you ever meet the fairies?" I asked.

"Oh, it was long before I met you, Jamie," Peter said.

I could always tell when he was lying. His eyes went from one side to another, looking everywhere but directly at me.

"Peter told me that if you find a fairy and make a wish, it will give you whatever you want!" Charlie said excitedly. "I wish I might find a fairy."

"And what would you wish for?" Peter asked.

Charlie fingered the fairy toy's delicate wings. "I'd wish I could fly just like them. Wouldn't it be wonderful to soar on the air above everything?"

Peter smiled, and it was the smile of a crocodile.

"Yes," he said. "Wouldn't it be."

CHAPTER 14

Peter stayed in the camp for eight days in a row after that. I would have snuck off to check the tunnel during that time except that he was suddenly showing an unnerving interest in Charlie.

Wherever Peter went and whatever he did, suddenly it just wouldn't do unless Charlie was by his side. Charlie might have been reluctant except that Peter had softened him with the gift of the toy. Now the smaller boy was convinced that Peter liked him best in all the world.

Charlie began to copy Peter's walk, a little rooster swagger, and stopped wearing his shoes from the Other Place because Peter went barefoot. If Peter thought that sunshine was wonderful, then Charlie did too. If Peter thought that hunting was boring, then Charlie did too. He would no longer help around camp because Peter never would. More than once I caught the two of them whispering to each other and laughing at the rest of us.

Peter was making Charlie a smaller version of himself, full of fun and heartless with it.

I knew that Peter was up to something, that he wasn't really interested in Charlie at all. Because of this I was afraid to leave Charlie alone with Peter for even a few minutes.

That meant that when Peter took Charlie off to swim or climb or what-have-you, I always followed along, and the others went because I did.

Peter was happy because he had all his boys (and one girl) around him all the time and everyone was doing exactly as he wished without arguing about it.

Sometimes Sally would look at me, and that look would say that I needed to go and scout out the tunnel so that we could leave. I knew, and she knew, that leaving was the only possible way we could save Charlie.

But I was afraid that the moment I left, Peter would see his chance. If I looked away for even a breath, then Peter would put a knife in Charlie's heart, and that would be as good as putting one in mine.

So I stayed in that in-between place, between the future with Sally and the past with Peter, because I didn't know how to set us all free without losing Charlie.

Finally, one evening Sally pulled me aside while the others were distracted by Peter capering and tumbling about the clearing. Charlie was laughing like he'd never seen anything so funny in all his life. Peter would turn on his hands and then spring to his feet again, pulling faces and making ridiculous noises that had Charlie howling. Crow was laughing too, and even Nod was smiling as though he wanted to scowl but couldn't quite do it.

"You have to go tomorrow," she whispered.

I looked from her to Charlie, who had fallen under Peter's spell.

"We've got to leave before Charlie's in love with him any more than he already is," Sally said. "He won't even look at you anymore."

It was true. Far from being my trailing little duckling, Charlie now disdained me as boring, the way that Peter often did.

"If you don't go in the morning, then I will," Sally said.

I thought this was unfair in the extreme. She was asking me to choose between keeping Charlie safe and letting her do something potentially dangerous.

"I'll watch out for Charlie," she said. "You have to trust me."

Peter picked Charlie up, turning him upside down and making him laugh even harder. Charlie was so happy, but Peter—I could see Peter's eyes, and he was not.

He was plotting.

That night I stayed awake while the others dropped off to sleep. Even Peter closed his eyes and slept, his arm thrown over Charlie like the smaller boy was a possession that he wouldn't share.

I knew I wouldn't have a better chance than that.

Out into the night I went, shivering in the cool air. We never got a proper winter on the island, of course, but it was that time of year when the wind blew a little colder and the sun lowered just a little earlier.

The unchanging moon was hidden by clouds. I thought I smelled the scent of rain. All around me the brush rustled as small animals darted away from my footsteps. I ran fast and quiet, wanting to reach the tunnel quickly. I'd know as soon as I entered it whether the passage to the Other Place was even possible without Peter.

If passage was possible, I would only go as far as the tree at the opposite end. From the tree you could see the lights of the city—the city Peter had taken me from all those years ago, the city that seemed to grow and stretch, reaching its fingers out to the tree that had once been miles from its center.

If I saw the city I would know, and I'd be able to return to our tree just as quickly. I was terrified that Peter would wake up and find me gone, and come looking for me. He seemed to be able to sniff you out like an animal if he wanted to find you. I didn't know what lie I might tell him if he did follow me. He would never believe that I was going to the Other Place to find new boys to play with.

I turned off the path, finding my way despite the lack of moonlight. I'd walked that stretch so many times I was certain I could find it in my sleep.

And yet when I reached the place where the tree was supposed to be, I thought I'd made a mistake. Because the tree wasn't there.

It was dark, but even with the dark I should have been able to see the shape of the tree against the sky. The stream that was supposed to bubble nearby was silent, and the ground underfoot was strangely squashy, like the land near the marsh.

I must have walked the wrong way in the dark, and I imagined how Sal would laugh at this after my insistence that she test her memory of the path. Feeling foolish, I started back to retrace my steps when the clouds parted and the moon revealed what had been hidden a moment before.

The tree had been cut down.

In truth, it looked as though it had somehow been *torn* down. The break in the trunk was less like an axe-chopping and more like it was ripped away by an angry giant.

If I had walked even a few steps farther, I would have bumped into it, for it blocked the way completely. It partially dammed up the flow of the little stream, which had caused the water to seep around it and soak the grass.

My heart pounded as I approached the broken trunk. Just because the tree was gone didn't mean that the tunnel was gone. Why should the tree falling affect it? The roots were still in place . . .

The roots were there, but these had definitely been cut by something that bit sharp and deep. And every place the roots were sliced, there was something filling those cuts, something dark and sticky that looked like blood.

I touched it, and it clung to my fingers, and when I sniffed it the stuff smelled like blood too.

The hole between the roots was gone.

It wasn't just filled in. It was entirely gone, as if it had never been. There was grass growing over the place where it used to be.

"Peter," I breathed, and fell to my knees.

Somehow, Peter had discovered our plan, mine and Sal's. Had he been in the woods that day? Had he seen Sal kiss me, heard us talk about leaving the island?

It would explain the flash that Sal saw, and why there had been no sign of anyone nearby. Peter knew how to cover his tracks.

Peter had snuck away from the tree, probably in the night when we all slept, and destroyed the gate back to the Other Place so that we could never, ever leave.

It was Peter's island, and we were now his prisoners.

"No," I said, and stood up again.

I was not going to stay there. The island was surrounded by water. We could make a boat and sail away. We could *steal* a boat from the pirates. They had those rowboats that they used to come ashore. It would be hard going on the ocean in a boat that small, but we might find a ship of friendly folk who would take us aboard.

And if we didn't, well—anything, even dying at sea, was preferable to staying there one more moment in the company of a mad child who would jail us on his island paradise.

If Peter tried to stop us, tried to hurt any of the others, I would kill him.

I knew then that I could do it. For a long time the memory of our former happiness had stopped me, but no more.

Peter wasn't my brother. He was my enemy.

I knew what to do with an enemy.

My dagger was in my hand, and I ran.

I wasn't away from the tree that long, but it was long enough.

When I reached the clearing I don't know what I intended to do—to wake Peter and make him fight me or to slit his throat in his sleep. I just knew that I wanted to know his blood, to see his green eyes dull, to end his power over me forever.

I could hardly remember why his smile had once meant so much to me. There was only one smile I wanted from him then, a long thin red one where a smile should not be.

(*a flash of silver in the darkness*)

(*what have you done?*)

(*small hands covered in blood*)

The dream-memories were in my way. I shook them off, entered the tree, ready to confront Peter and end it all forever.

He was gone, and so was Charlie.

"No," I said, and kicked the skins they'd been sleeping on. "No, no, no, no, no!"

Sal and Crow and Nod sat up, all three still bedazzled by sleep.

"Where's Peter and Charlie?" I shouted.

Crow and Nod looked like they didn't understand what I was saying, but Sal was on her feet right away.

"They must have gone while we slept," she said, and her face was white and scared.

She reached for my arm, and I shook her off. "I thought I could trust you."

"Jamie, I'm sorry," she said. "I'm so sorry."

"Why are you yelling just because Peter and Charlie are gone?" Crow said.

"Because Peter hates Charlie," Nod said. So he understood, too, what Peter's game was about. Before Fog died, he wouldn't have even noticed. "We could track him."

I shook my head. "No, it's hard to track Peter in the day. It's impossible in the night."

"Where would he take him?" Sal asked.

I immediately thought of the crocodile pond, and then realized Peter would never take Charlie anywhere so obvious. He would know that I would think of the story, and run to save Charlie there.

There was only one place where he'd go, because he would think we'd never guess.

"The Many-Eyed," I said. "He's taking Charlie to the nest."

"Would Charlie follow him there?" Nod asked, and now his face was white too. Nod never went near the plains, or even the border of them, if he could avoid it. "He's scared of the Many-Eyed."

While we were talking I was gathering anything that might be useful—bows and arrows, knives, rocks, slingshot, sharp sticks, the special stones that we used to start fires. I thrust all of these things in my sling-bag.

"Peter's got Charlie now," I said. "He'll believe anything Peter says, do anything Peter does. If Peter said it was a wonderful lark to cross the plains at night, then Charlie would do it."

I started out of the tree and the others followed, though Crow still looked like he didn't really understand what was happening.

Instead of taking the trail that led in the direction of Bear Cave, I went toward the forest on the opposite side. From there we could cut through the trees to the central plains, which was where the Many-Eyed nested.

Before we entered the trees, I stopped. I couldn't take a chance that I was wrong.

I would lose Charlie forever if I was wrong. That story—always that damned story, chasing Charlie and me.

"Go to the crocodile pond and make sure they aren't there," I told Nod and Crow.

Nod's face hardened. "You don't have to keep me from

the Many-Eyed just because I'm afraid."

"I'm not," I said. "I just don't want Charlie to die if I'm wrong about where Peter took him."

He looked into my eyes hard and believed me. Nod grabbed Crow and took off running in the other direction.

Then I started to run too, toward the plains of the Many-Eyed.

Sal ran beside me. She never stumbled; she never slowed; she never hesitated. She just stayed right beside me, driven by the same fear that was riding me.

My little duckling, wrapped in a Many-Eyed's silk, nothing but food for their babies.

The branches lashed me but I didn't feel them. Bears and wolves and cats ran from us, for we didn't slow when we saw them and that meant we were something to be feared.

The moon went down. The sky turned purple-orange, and we broke out of the trees and into the plains.

Charlie and Peter were just before us. Peter was whispering into his cupped hand, and Charlie's hand was wrapped around it.

Then Charlie caught sight of us, wild-eyed and sweaty, and his face lit up.

"Jamie! Jamie! Peter's showing me how to *fly*!"

"No!" I said, but I couldn't run fast enough.

Peter grinned down at me as the two of them floated up into the air, high above, and he pulled Charlie over the long yellow grass. Charlie laughed in delight, and Peter laughed too—laughed because he'd won. I watched, chest heaving in despair, as they flew toward the center of the plains.

I couldn't outrun Peter in the air. He would carry Charlie to the Many-Eyed nest and drop him there, and that would be the end of my trusting duckling.

No. There had to be something I could do. I couldn't just let it happen. I couldn't let Peter win.

I threw down the sling-bag in frustration. All my weapons, all my plans—they were useless against a boy who could fly.

The fire-stones rolled out of the bag. The breeze went through my hair. The wind was blowing from the south, almost directly from the south.

"Burn them," I said, and grabbed the stones. "Burn them all out."

Sally understood immediately. She always knew precisely what I was thinking. She ran to collect wood that would be useful for torches.

If we burned the plains, then the Many-Eyed would have nowhere to go but the sea—if they survived the flames. The wind would help send the fire where I wanted it to go—toward the nest and away from our forest.

Peter might still try to drop Charlie in the middle of the plains and hope the little boy cooked to death. I was going to run ahead of the fire for just that reason.

Nod and Crow shot out of the forest just as I lit the first torch.

"Good, this is better," I said when I saw them. "Nod, you take this torch and go west. Light all the plains grass all the way to the sea on that side."

I touched the tip of the torch to another piece of wood, and when it caught I handed it to Crow.

"You do the same going east, all the way to the mountains."

They didn't even ask why. They just took the torches and ran, lighting the grass as they went.

I pulled some cloth out of my pocket to wrap around my face. Sal took it from my hand and tore it so she could do the same.

"I'm not staying behind," she said. "Don't ask me to. It's down to me that Peter got away with him."

There was no time to disagree, no time to talk about what she ought to do or who was at fault. Maybe it was Sal, for sleeping when she ought to be watching. Maybe it was me, for underestimating Peter.

Or maybe it was Peter, because he was a monster.

We ran, and we set fire to everything.

Soon the smoke billowed and surrounded us, and the flames were curling at our heels, trying to catch us, to drag us down, to eat us alive. Sweat poured off my face and over my body, soaking my clothes. My throat was parched, scorched by the smoke despite the cloth I'd tied to prevent that.

The fire roared all around, a hungry, mad thing that swallowed everything before it, and I realized that we needed to run for our own lives, not just Charlie's.

Then I heard, just above the howl of the flames, the terrified screeching of the Many-Eyed, and I smelled them burning.

We ran straight into the nest. The egg sacs were all aflame, and any adults that were in their silks had caught fire as well. Most of them were running ahead—I heard their mad buzzing as they tried to escape the fire.

There was so much smoke, so much heat.

I didn't know it would be like that.

I didn't understand fire was that kind of monster.

We kept running. The nest was enormous, a series of spun silk caves connected by longer threads, one after another. If Peter dropped Charlie, it would be here.

But if he was here, how would I find him? I hadn't reckoned on the smoke, a black billowing cloud that was drowning everything.

And the noise. The fire was so noisy, a roaring, howling thing. Calling out for Charlie was pointless.

Then Sal grabbed my shoulder. Her eyes were streaming from the smoke and so were mine, but she pointed to the ground ahead of us.

There was my Charlie, half wrapped in Many-Eyed's silk, his arms and head exposed.

"Not dead," I moaned. "No, not dead."

I ran to him, and picked him up, and held his little body to mine.

And felt his heart beat.

Sal tugged me up. The fire was already there, hunting us, relentless.

We ran and ran and ran toward the sea, and I held Charlie close to me and promised that I would keep him safe. Over and over I promised that, if only he would live.

And then somehow we were out of the grass and falling on the dry sand of the beach. Before us were the Many-Eyed that had outrun the fire.

There were so many of them. So many I couldn't count. I'd never really understood.

They filled the space between the plains and the water, and they didn't seem to notice us at all. The ones that were closest to the sea were screeching in terror, as were the ones that were being burned by flame. All the Many-Eyed in between were pushing and buzzing and trying to find a way out when there was none.

I scrambled, exhausted, toward some jumbled rocks on the west end, and Sal followed me. We stayed low, crawling, avoiding the Many-Eyed's teeth and legs and stingers. I clutched at Charlie with one arm and pulled myself along with the other.

We reached the rocks and I made Sal go up first, so I could pass Charlie to her. Then I followed, taking Charlie again, and we climbed until we were well above the sand. Sal collapsed at the top, pulling the cloth off her face and coughing. There was no flat space to rest on—all those rocks were jumbled and sharp—but the sea air was fresh and we were away from the madness of the Many-Eyed.

I took the cloth off my own face and then cut the silk off Charlie's body with my dagger. I pressed my ear against his chest and listened. His heart still beat, but slowly, and his breath wasn't easy.

Sal watched me with frightened eyes. "Is he . . . ?"

"He's still alive," I said.

My voice was strange and croaking and my lungs burned. I felt like I was still inside the smoke, even though it was billowing away from us, up above the island. I wondered what the pirates made of all this.

I wondered where Peter was now.

I propped my back against one of the rocks and pulled Charlie into my lap, his head on my shoulder.

Below us the Many-Eyed were now in a frenzy. At first I was too exhausted to realize why. Then I saw about a dozen of them knocked off their feet and swept into the ocean.

The tide was coming in.

The tide was coming in and the fire in the plains had reached its peak fury, the flames twice as high as the grass that burned. As the Many-Eyed in front ran from the seeking ocean, the Many-Eyed in the rear caught fire. Some in the middle were trampled as others panicked and tried to run.

There was nowhere for them to run.

We stayed on the rocks for a long, long time, watching the destruction of the Many-Eyed. It should have given me more satisfaction than it did. I'd always wanted to rid the island of that vermin. I'd finally succeeded.

Soon the beach was littered with the bloated, stacked corpses of the Many-Eyed as far as my eye could see. Some of the dead ones closest to the fire caught and burned, and the air filled with the acrid smoke from their flesh.

Charlie's eyes did not open. And I didn't know how to tell Sally about the tree.

We'd thwarted Peter. He hadn't been able to kill Charlie, and he wouldn't have another chance. The smaller boy wouldn't believe in him a second time.

But we were still trapped on the island. The tunnel to the Other Place was gone.

Sally didn't speak for a long time. She stared dully out at the slow massacre of the Many-Eyed. Then she said, "Did you know he could fly?"

"I saw him once," I said, and the words seemed thick and heavy in my mouth. I was so tired. "I never could catch him at it again."

"How?" she said.

"If I knew, I would have flown after him," I said.

"Maybe Charlie will tell us," Sally said, and stroked his yellow hair.

It seemed so overwhelming then, so impossible. How could I defeat a boy who could fly, a boy who had destroyed our best means of escape?

I wanted to tell Sally—so she could understand, so she could help me. She would be angry with me if I tried to solve it all on my own, if I didn't let her stand by me as she said she would.

But I was tired. So tired.

I closed my eyes, and I remembered.

CHAPTER 15

Mama? Mama?"

She wasn't in the kitchen. She liked to be there by the fire, in her chair, mending clothes or polishing cook pots or just rocking while she stared into the flames. She liked it because it was far away from Him, the He who stalked through our house like an angry shadow, the He who staggered home from the pubs stinking of ale and searching for a reason to be angry at us.

He would never hit me if she was there, because she would stand in front of me and tell him to leave off her boy, her blue eyes sparking fury.

My eyes were not blue. They were black like His, dark and pupilless, like the eyes of the sharks that swam in the sea. But my hair was like hers, soft and dark, and I would put my head on her knee while she stroked my head and we would both cry and pretend that we hadn't. She would sing a little song, a song that went into my heart and stayed there, a song that I would sing all the long years of my life.

He had gone out as He always did every evening, before I came home from the bookbinders'. Mama hoped I would apprentice there when I was older, but for now I fetched and carried and cleaned up after the older men, and at the end of the day they would give me a coin or two to bring home to her.

She was saving all those coins in a secret place, a place He didn't know about, and no matter how hard He hit her she wouldn't tell. I wouldn't tell, either, because I didn't know where it was. But she was saving them, so that one day we could run away to a place where there were no fists and no fear, just me and Mama, happy for always.

I went into the cottage and called for her, but she didn't come to the door with a smile the way she always did.

He wasn't home, I knew for certain, for when He was in the house He filled up all the empty space. Even when He slept He did this, the sound of His drunken snores echoing through the cottage, the smell of drink and sick overwhelming any fresh air that might come in the open window.

"Mama?" I called, and when I went through to the kitchen she wasn't there, and I started to worry.

Our cottage was only four rooms, and when I went through all of them I didn't know what to do. She might have gone to the market, except that it was late and the market was closed. She would never have gone out with Him, for she said that drink made Him disgusting, and He didn't want her with Him anyhow.

I stood in the kitchen and wondered if I should look for her, or if I should stay exactly where I was so she wouldn't worry if she came back. I hated to make her worry, for she already had so many cares and I didn't like to add to them.

Then I noticed that the back door of the cottage was open, just a little.

Mama would never go out and leave the door open like that. There were rats that lived in the narrow way behind our home, and Mama hated rats, and an open door was an invitation to them—she always said so.

And the candles were lit and so was the fire. Candles were dear, and Mama wouldn't waste them. She wouldn't go out and leave the fire untended.

I went to the door, and pushed it all the way open. I trembled all over as I peered in the dark, the flickering light of the kitchen behind me. I couldn't see anything except the shifting shadows, but I heard the scurrying of the rats and I shuddered. I didn't like rats either, though I wouldn't tell Mama that. I wanted Mama to think I was brave.

I didn't want to let the rats in the cottage, but I didn't want to go out into the dark either, so I stood there and called, "Mama?"

She didn't answer.

I wasn't certain what to do. The door was open, so Mama must have come this way. And the candles were lit, so she must have meant to return soon. But she didn't answer.

She might be hurt, I decided. And if Mama was hurt I would have to be brave, so that she would be proud of me.

I took a candle from the kitchen, and walked out into the night, closing the door behind me. The sound of the door closing made me jump. Candle wax dripped on my hand with a hiss.

It smelled funny, not like the smell of rotting and rats like it usually did. There was something else, something that made my nose itch.

I walked out carefully, the stones ringing under my boot heels. They were so loud in the darkness, though from out on the street in front of the cottage came the noise of people laughing and talking and shouting at one another. Those people seemed very far away from me.

The circle of light cast by the candle was small, so that the dark pressed all around it. I thought I saw, just for a moment, a wink of silver ahead of me, a flash that reflected the faint light and then disappeared.

First my foot trod on something, something soft. Then the glow from the candle found it, and she was there.

Her eyes were blue and empty and her dark hair was all around her head in a tangle. She lay on her side and her arms were thrown out in the direction of the cottage, like she was reaching for something, like she was reaching for me.

Her mouth was open and so was her throat and the blood was all over her blue dress, seeping from the smile where no smile should be.

"Mama?" I said, and my voice was very, very small.

I reached for her then because it couldn't be, it couldn't be that my mama, my mama who kissed me and hugged me and held me so tight, was there on the stones with her throat cut and blood on her dress.

I tried to pick her up, to make her wake up, to make her stop pretending to be gone forever. The candle fell from my hand and went out.

"What have you done?" A voice ringing through the darkness.

"My mama," I sobbed.

A boy appeared from nowhere, a boy I thought at first I'd never seen before and then realized I had. He was a little older than me and had green eyes and ginger hair, and more than once I'd seen him on the street near our cottage. He didn't seem to belong to anyone and sometimes I thought he was watching me when I went home at the end of the day but when I tried to get a good look at him he would be gone.

Now he stood over Mama and me and looked sternly down at me.

"What have you done?" he said again.

"I didn't do anything," I said. "I found her."

"There's blood all over your hands and when the constable comes he'll think you killed her and then they'll hang you," he said.

"But—" I said.

"You have a very bad temper, don't you?" he said. "Don't you sometimes run at your father and hit him with your fists? Don't you sometimes get so angry that you break the crockery in the kitchen?"

I did, but I didn't see how this boy could know that. I

sometimes ran at Him and punched Him as hard as I could, when I couldn't bear letting my mama stand between us any longer, and it would make me angrier because He seemed to like me better then. He would say that I had spirit and that at least I wasn't hiding behind Mama's skirts. I hated to do anything that made Him happy but I hated it when my mama was hurt too, and sometimes all these feelings would push and pull inside me until I wouldn't know what to do and I would smash and break things until they went away. Then when it was all over Mama would put her arms around me and hold me until I was better.

"Everyone around these parts knows you have a bad temper, and when they find her"—here the boy jerked his chin at the thing that used to be my mama—"they'll know it was you because you get so angry all the time and because your hands are covered in blood."

I looked at my hands then, and though it was dark I could see the stains on them, and I was terrified that what this boy said would be true.

"But I didn't hurt her," I said. "I would never hurt her. I love her so much."

Tears rolled out then, and the other boy smacked me hard.

"Stop crying," he said. "Boys don't cry like that. Now listen— you have to come with me. I know a place where you'll be safe and they'll never catch you."

He had me all confused now, tangled up and turned around. I believed that when the constable came they would arrest me and they would throw me in a dark, dark place full of rats until it was time for me to hang.

"If you come with me we'll go to my island. It's a special place, only for boys like you and me. And there you can run and play and no one will hit you and you'll never, never grow up."

"How can you never grow up?"

"The island is magic," he said, and he smiled. "And I live all alone there, and I want you to come there and play with me and be my friend for always."

He tugged me up, tugged me away, and I was confused and scared and already forgetting my mama and her empty blue eyes and her arms thrown out, reaching for me. Peter pulled me away and told me all about the wonderful place that we were to go to, a place that was only for us.

We walked all night and reached the tree and tunnel and then I was so tired, and Mama seemed like she was a story from a far-off time.

We went through the tunnel and I smelled the island for the first time, smelled the trees and the sea and the sweet fruit, and the scent of the city was washed away. And later Peter and I were picking fruit from a meadow and he showed me how to take the skin off with his knife. There were red stains on the knife but I didn't wonder about them at all, for all I could see was Peter smiling at me.

* * *

Jamie, you're squashing me."

"Jamie, let go of him. He can't breathe."

I opened my eyes, and found Charlie awake in my lap. Sal leaned over me, tugging at my arms.

"What is it?" I asked.

"You're squashing me!" Charlie said, and he pushed at my chest.

"You were dreaming," Sal said.

I let Charlie go and he scrambled free. I scrubbed at my face with my hands. My face was wet, though I couldn't tell whether it was from sweat or tears.

"What were you dreaming of?" Sal asked.

"The same thing I always dream. A woman with blue eyes and black hair with her throat cut," I said. "I didn't know until today that it was my mother."

"And?" Sal said, for she knew there was more.

"And it was Peter who killed her."

I don't know how I could have forgotten her, forgotten the mama who loved me so much, forgotten how she stood between my father and me and kept me safe. I felt a wrench of shame, that she would be lost to me so easily, that I would run away with a strange boy and leave her there.

I'd left her alone. Alone with the rats who would gnaw at her until someone found her—maybe my father, maybe a neighbor, maybe a happy drunk stumbling into the alley to take a piss.

But Peter had confused me. He had. He'd told me that it would be my fault, that I would be blamed. I was scared and confused and the only person who ever mattered to me was staring up at me with blank blue eyes and his hand offered an escape from the hanging I was sure would come. Who would believe a little boy, especially a boy covered in his mother's blood?

So when he took my hand it was easy to leave her there, easier to run away from the horror, easier to forget that she loved me, especially with Peter telling me all the time to forget, that nothing from the Other Place mattered, that it was just him and me now.

I'd loved her, and I'd forgotten her. That was partly Peter's fault, but it was also mine. I'd wanted to forget.

My anger at Peter burned brighter than it ever had, but my grief and my shame were almost worse. I'd remembered my mother only to remember what I'd done.

I'd left her there, her arms thrown out, reaching for me. The last thing she thought of was me and I *left* her.

To run away with the monster who'd killed her.

Sal gasped and covered her mouth at my words, though I don't think she was surprised—not really. It seemed precisely the sort of thing that Peter would do, if he wanted someone and there was somebody else in his way.

Peter didn't care about obstacles, even if they were shaped like people. They were only things to be jumped over, to be knocked down. You didn't *care* about them.

He'd done it all so well, really. He'd looked for me—not just any boy would do for Peter—and found a boy who had the potential he wanted. Then watched me, and waited for his chance. And when he had it, he'd killed her, and then twisted me up so I was afraid. Once I was afraid, he could make me do anything he liked, and he made himself my savior, and he made me feel special and loved and then he pushed all the memories of my mother out of me.

Peter had chosen me first. He'd cut me away from the herd and taken me to the island, and I was too much of a boy to remember what I had lost. I could only remember all the days when it was just Peter and me, and we were happy then.

But the song had stayed, the song that my mother sang to me. No wonder he hated it when he heard it. He wanted me to shed all my life in the Other Place like an old skin, but he couldn't stop bits of it clinging to me.

Everything I lost swelled up inside me then, the life that I might have had without Peter. Yes, my father was a drunken ass who beat us. But we were saving, my mama and me. We were going to leave him and find a quiet place away from the city where we would be safe.

And I would have grown up and my mama would have grown old but there would have been grandchildren for her to kiss and hug and hold so tight. There would have been a life, a boring, ordinary life to Peter but a full life, one that followed the natural order of things.

It was not natural for boys to stay boys forever. We were supposed to grow up, and have boys of our own, and teach them how to be men.

I felt a sharp stabbing pain in my side, and then in my hands and legs and feet, and something scratchy and prickly at my chin.

Charlie's eyes widened. "Jamie, you've got a beard!"

I rubbed my face, and it wasn't quite a beard, but there was fuzzy hair that hadn't been there before.

Sal hit my shoulder then. "I told you not to grow up too fast! We're supposed to grow up together!"

"I don't think I have a choice, Sal," I said, and there was a little grief there too. What if I kept growing and I was too old for Sal? What then? "It's not something I can stop."

I stood, and stretched, and realized everything hurt—my lungs and eyes, burned by smoke; my legs from trying to outrun the fire; my arms, from clinging to Charlie so tight.

The smaller boy was avoiding my eyes, staring at the mass of dead Many-Eyed on the beach. Behind them the plains smoked still, though all the grass and flowers were gone now and there was nothing except a blackened field as far as the eye could see.

"Peter," Charlie said, and a sob caught in his throat.

Sal reached for him but I shook my head at her. He didn't need to be comforted yet. He needed to say what was in his heart first.

"Peter didn't like me," Charlie said. "He tricked me, and I believed him."

He did look at me then, and his eyes would never be those innocent little duckling eyes again. That was what happened when you were betrayed.

"I believed him, and then he tried to kill me," Charlie said. "You never hurt me, Jamie. You always watched out for me. I shouldn't have believed him."

"We all believe him, at first," I said. "Even me. That's how he lures us here with his promises."

"And then he rips us all to pieces," Sally said.

"He won't bring any more here," I said, and took a deep breath, for now I had to tell her the thing I didn't want to say. "The path to the Other Place is gone."

"Gone?" she said.

I explained what I'd found, that the tree was cut down and the hole to the tunnel covered in grass.

She wilted as I spoke, and for a moment I was afraid she would faint, for she'd gone very pale.

"How did he know? We'll never escape him," she whispered. "Oh, why, oh, why did I ever come here?"

"Because you thought it would be better than what you had," I said. "You thought that you would be happier here."

"I would be happy here," she said fiercely. "If not for him. If it was just us, you and me and Charlie and Nod and Crow, and we could grow up as we should, then I would be happy here."

"But he is here," I said. "And I don't want to stay on the island any longer. I've been here for too many seasons already."

"What do we do?" Charlie asked.

He came to my side then, and wound his fist in my coat the way he used to do, but he didn't put his thumb in his mouth. He wasn't a baby anymore.

"We'll have to sail away," I said. "It's our only hope."

"Not with the pirates?" Sal asked. "Because I don't think they'll be very welcoming to us, not after all that's happened between us."

"That's all Peter's doing, and Nip's," I said sharply. "If Peter hadn't burned down their camp, and Nip hadn't told them where to find us, then we wouldn't have had to kill any of them. Or at least not so many of them. There might have been a raid, but it wouldn't have been the same."

Everything was Peter's fault. My mother was killed by Peter. The boys he brought here died because of Peter. The pirates came looking for a war because of Peter, and were massacred by us because of Peter. Charlie had nearly been fed to the Many-Eyed because of Peter. It was all down to Peter.

"It doesn't matter now if it's our doing or Peter's," Sally said, and she shook her head at the look on my face. "It *doesn't*. The pirates think all of us are the same now. If we go to them for help, if we ask them to take us away in their ship, then they'll hurt us."

She added then, in a small voice, "They'll hurt me more

than you if they know I'm a girl."

I didn't really understand this then, but I remembered that the pirates sometimes brought girls back to camp with them after they'd been away from the island, and that the girls spent all their time screaming and crying.

So I took Sal's word. After all, she'd found it so unsafe to be a girl that she'd pretended to be a boy, which was how she'd ended up on the island in the first place.

"We'll have to build a boat," I said. "Build it in a secret place, where Peter won't find it."

"He can find everything," Charlie said. "Because he can fly. He told me how he flies all over the island and he sees everything. It was nice to fly, even if it did end when Peter threw me on the ground. It was scary then. This big Many-Eyed made all this noise and then Peter told the fairy what to say and the fairy told the Many-Eyed that Peter brought me as a present for them to eat."

His eyes welled up then. "I thought he was my friend and he tried to feed me to monsters."

Again, Sally wanted to pick him up and comfort him, but I stopped her.

"Charlie," I said. "What fairy are you talking about? The toy that Peter gave you?"

Charlie shook his head. "No, silly, a toy's a toy. This is a *real* fairy, a fairy that lives on the island. She can talk to the Many-Eyed and she showed Peter how to fly."

"There are no fairies here," I said. "I've never seen one."

"There *are*," Charlie said. "But they only like Peter and not the other boys, so they don't come out where we can see them. Only Tink does because she's Peter's special friend."

"Tink?"

"That's what he calls her, because she makes a kind of tinkling noise when she talks."

I gave Sally a significant look. "I heard a tinkling noise that day when we were on the path talking about leaving for the Other Place."

"Do you think she was spying on us for Peter?" Sally said.

"She always spies for Peter," Charlie said. "And it's easy for her, because she seems just like a firefly unless you get a close look."

"And she taught Peter how to fly?" I said.

"Well," Charlie said. "She didn't really teach him. She shakes her dust on him and the dust makes him fly."

"So if we had some of that fairy dust, then we would be able to fly away from the island," I said slowly.

"It doesn't last very long," Charlie said. "That's what Peter said. You have to keep a fairy with you so she can keep dusting you. I don't think Tink would do it anyway. She doesn't like anyone except Peter, and I don't think it would be very nice to catch her."

"What about the other fairies? Where do they live?" I asked.

"In the fields," Charlie said, and pointed at the desolation.

"Oh," I said.

"If any of them survived, then they won't want to help the ones that burned their homes down," Sally said sadly.

"Then we've got to go back to the idea of sailing away," I said.

"But Peter flies everywhere and knows everything," Sally pointed out. "And if he doesn't, then this fairy will spy us out."

"We've got to do something," I said. "We can't stay here. What about taking a rowboat from the pirates? There are only five of us."

"How would we do that?" asked Sally. "We'd have to swim out to the pirate ship, and I can't swim."

"Me either," Charlie said.

"That's all right," I said, warming to my plan. "Nod and me can swim out at night and get the boat, and then take it around to the mermaid lagoon and meet you there."

Sally looked doubtful. "Won't the mermaids tell Peter what we're about?"

"They won't know until it's happening," I said. "I don't share secrets with mermaids. And anyway, the mermaids don't have any special love for Peter. They love themselves best."

"And when will we do all this?" Sally said.

"Tonight," I said. "We'll go back and find Nod and Crow; then we'll collect all the things we'll need."

"Then Crow and Charlie and me will go to the lagoon,"

Sally said. "And you and Nod will go for the rowboat."

"Yes," I said.

"What if Peter tries to stop us?" Charlie asked.

I didn't answer. I think we all knew that it was down to him or us.

If Peter tried to stop us, I would be ready for him.

CHAPTER 16

None of us wanted to climb over the corpses of the Many-Eyed or cross the smoking fields. We clambered over the rocks for several minutes until we came to the lagoon side, then skirted around the edge of the lagoon until we reached the main part of the forest.

Three or four mermaids were sunning on a flat rock in the center of the lagoon, their fish tails lolling in the water. They didn't give any sign that they noticed us but I was sure they did—mermaids noticed everything. It was the only way for them to stay alive in the ocean, with sharks and sea monsters all around.

We stayed on the border where the forest met the plains. Crow had done a good job of it—all the grass had been burned here too, right up to where the plains, the forest and the lagoon met. Smoke curled from the ground, and there was a lingering heat in the air.

By unspoken agreement Sally and I took it in turns to

watch both the air and the forest. Now that we'd made our plans I felt a lingering unease, sure that Peter would somehow discover the plot.

If he did find out, it didn't mean that he would face us and fight us. No, it meant that he would try something crafty— like removing the rowboats from the pirate ship so we couldn't get at them, or even burning the whole ship itself.

Peter had killed my mother so I would stay with him for always. He'd destroyed the tunnel to the Other Place so I couldn't get away. I was sure he'd do anything he thought he must to keep me there with him.

I was first for Peter, and it didn't matter whether I wanted to stay or not. Peter always got what he wanted.

Then I saw him just ahead of us, kneeling on the ground over something. I let out a cry, and he stood and looked back at us, and I saw the bloody knife in his hand.

"This is your fault, Jamie!" he shouted at me. "Your fault! None of this would have happened if not for you!"

My dagger was out and I ran at him, Charlie and Sally forgotten. All I saw was Peter and the red haze that covered my eyes.

He killed my mother.

Peter killed my mother because he wanted me to play with him.

"It's your fault!" I roared. "You took Charlie! You burned the pirate camp!"

You killed my mother, I thought, but I couldn't say the words because the rage was choking me, consuming me.

"I did everything because of you!" Peter shouted. "All for you!"

I should have known he wouldn't fight fair. Before I was within throwing distance of him he rose into the air, high above where I couldn't reach him. Blood dripped from his hand and his knife and onto my face as he flew above me, and away.

"That's not fair play, Peter!" I shouted after him. "Not fair play at all!"

Sally screamed then, and her scream shocked me away from Peter. Then I saw what he'd been kneeling over.

It was Crow. Peter had arranged him so all his limbs were pointed out like an "X." Crow's throat was sliced from ear to ear, and then Peter had done the final thing to hurt me.

He'd cut Crow's right hand off.

That was my mark, the thing that I did to pirates. Peter wanted me to know that this was about me, not about Crow. Crow had died because of me.

Sally covered Charlie's eyes, pulled him to her, but it was too late. The little boy had seen. He didn't cry, though. He only said, "There's so much blood."

"Yes," I said.

Yes, there was so much blood. That was what Peter brought. He didn't bring magic and fun and eternal youth. He brought fear and madness and death, trailing blood behind him, trailing all the corpses of all the boys behind him.

And yet it didn't weigh him to the earth at all. Every drop of spilled blood only made him lighter, gave him the freedom to fly.

"We have to find Nod," I said. "And get away as soon as we can."

"What if he's already killed Nod?" Sally said.

"We still need to know," I said.

"There might not be time for the rowboat," she said. "You have to go all the way across the island for it."

"What about the other one?" Charlie said.

"What other one?"

"The one you left on the beach the day you killed all those pirates," Charlie said.

"That boat is probably gone now," I said. "I didn't anchor it, and the tide would have taken it out to sea."

"Isn't it worth finding out?" Sally asked. "The Skull Rock beach is much closer than the pirate camp. Me and Charlie will go and see while you find Nod. It will be faster if you go on your own anyway."

She was right; the pirate camp was much farther away, though getting there was safer now that the Many-Eyed were gone. But there would be the difficulty of crossing the camp under cover of dark, as well, and then swimming out to the ship. If by some lucky chance the other rowboat was still there . . .

"I can't believe it wouldn't have drifted away," I said. "I

think you'd be safer just going to the mermaid lagoon like we planned."

There was at least a small chance that the mermaids' watchful eyes would stop any mischief Peter might try on Sally or Charlie. The mermaids had their own set of rules, and I hoped that they wouldn't let Peter kill anyone right in front of them.

"Stop talking to me about what's safer," Sally said. "Nobody is safe here. It's not safe as long as Peter is alive. Whether I'm with you or at the mermaid lagoon or at Skull Rock, I'm not safe. Peter took Charlie right from under our noses while we slept. There is no safe."

She made me all knotted up inside, because she was right, but I didn't want her to be. I only wanted to be sure she was still alive when I returned, but there was no way to be sure anymore.

"All right," I said.

I wanted to hug her again, or touch her hair, or just stand close and breathe her in. I didn't do any of those things. I didn't know how. I was only a boy, for all that I was beginning to look like a man.

And there was no time.

Sally and Charlie went south, to cut through the forest and then the dunes and down to the beach. I went toward the tree, which was where I thought Nod would go if he couldn't find us. That was what we always did. We always went back to the tree.

I ran, because I wanted to find Nod before Peter did, because I wanted to get back to Sally and Charlie before Peter did. I ran because everything I loved had been taken from me again and again and I was tired of Peter taking more.

I didn't know what day it was anymore, or how long the sun had been up. It seemed I'd been running since Peter took Charlie away, but I wasn't tired. Fear and anger drove me on, made my legs stretch longer, made my feet barely touch the ground. Somewhere I'd lost my moccasins, though I couldn't remember when that might have been. Perhaps my feet had grown out of them and I hadn't noticed.

My red coat caught and snagged on branches and I tore it off and threw it away in the woods. It didn't matter anymore. Peter had always wanted the coat. He could have it now.

I ran, bare-chested and barefooted, wearing only my deerskin trousers and my knife. I looked, finally, like the wild boy that Peter always wanted me to be, but I would never be so much of a boy again.

Peter wanted me to stay a boy, but it was Peter, finally, who made me a man.

Then I was at the tree, and there was Nod, sitting on the ground with his back against the trunk, holding his left hand over the bleeding wrist of his right.

Nod gave me a weary smile as I ran to him. It was a very grown-up smile, not the smile of the boy he'd once been at all. "I was a little harder to kill than Peter thought I'd be."

"You'd think he'd know that, having watched you at Battle all these years."

I inspected the wound. Peter had done a bad job of it. He'd cut into the inside of Nod's wrist but not come close to taking the whole hand off. There were a few other nicks and cuts on his chest and arms but the wrist was the worst thing.

I went for the bandages and water, and wrapped Nod's wrist up tight so that the bleeding would stop.

"Where are Sally and Charlie?" he asked; then he looked at me closely. "Jamie, you have a beard."

"So do you," I said, scraping my hand down the side of his cheek.

He seemed surprised by this, and touched his face. It was only a few stringy hairs, but they hadn't been there before.

Nod laughed, and I was struck by how different that laugh was, how much older it sounded.

"We're growing up, Jamie," he said. "I wonder why, after all this time."

"It's because we don't love Peter anymore," I said. I'd only just figured this out when I saw Nod's face. "Because we don't want to be boys and do boy things for always. The island will keep you young if you want it, and Peter never wants to be a man. But we don't want it anymore."

"No," Nod said. "I had enough of being a boy when Fog died."

I finished patching Nod up and then ran to collect all

that I thought we would need on the boat—water, food, rope, weapons. I made certain to pack one of the pirate swords as well as an axe and several small daggers.

There was a great deal to carry, but there was no sense in pushing a rowboat into the sea without supplies. All we would be doing was trading Peter's death for the slow death of starvation.

I let Nod rest until I was ready. He wanted to carry some of the supplies, but I wouldn't let him. He'd lost too much blood and I was worried he wouldn't be able to make it to Skull Rock as it was.

Somehow night had fallen again. How did the days pass so quickly then? I felt as though I'd just left to find Charlie, to save him from the Many-Eyed. I felt like I'd been on the island forever, running in circles, trying to escape Peter's trap.

Once, a long time before, I'd found a wolf's paw inside one of our rope traps. Just the paw, not the rest of the wolf. It was mangled and torn and horrible-looking, for the wolf had chewed off its own foot rather than be caught.

I should have chewed off my foot long ago, but I didn't know that I was in a trap. Peter smiled and made me think there was only joy. Even when there was blood he made me think it was only play, until there was so much of it even Peter couldn't pretend anymore.

Fireflies lit the night in the forest. I used to love to watch them light up, sparkling like stars close enough to touch, but

I swatted any that came near me. I wasn't certain anymore that they were fireflies. They might be fairies in disguise, spying for Peter and telling tales back to him.

And if they were fairies, they would have no love for me, for I'd burned all the plains where they'd lived.

Would I have still burned the plains if it meant getting rid of the Many-Eyed and saving Charlie? Yes. I would have. But I would have warned the fairies, if I'd known they were there. This was another fault to lay at Peter's door.

If he hadn't kept the fairies secret, then they might have been saved. Peter had wanted them all to himself, to keep their magic just for him.

Peter wanted to fly, but he wanted the rest of us bound to earth.

I tried to hurry Nod along, but he was tired and bloodless and not driven by the same fear that I was. He cared about Sally and Charlie, but it wasn't the same.

Or so I thought.

We'd hardly spoken since leaving the tree. I could think only of Sally and Charlie and Peter and what might happen while I was gone.

Sally wanted me to trust her, to believe that she could look after herself because she had done so for years before she met me. But Sally didn't know Peter, not really. Peter wasn't like the boys that Sally fought for food on the streets of the city.

We'd crossed into the dunes, and the sky opened up above us. So many stars wheeled overhead it was hard to imagine them all. They were brighter that night than they'd ever been and they seemed to cry out to me, "Hurry, hurry, hurry."

"I know she loves you," Nod said.

He startled me. I wasn't thinking about love. I was thinking about getting Sally and Charlie off the island and away from Peter. "What?"

"Sally," Nod said.

I thought he might be blushing.

"So?" I said. I wasn't certain why we were talking about this now.

"I was hoping it would be me, but it's you. And I just wanted you to know that's all right."

It felt strangely like he was giving us a blessing, and it made me feel awkward in a way that I'd never been with Nod before.

"Okay," I said. I didn't want to talk about it anymore.

"You've always been the best of us, Jamie," Nod said, and his voice cracked. "Me and Fog, we always looked up to you. We always wanted to be just like you, only we never were."

If he was crying I didn't want to see. I only wanted to get to the beach. The night was spinning on and Peter could have found them by now.

"I wasn't as good as you think," I said.

"You kept us alive. You looked after us. We all knew it, even if we didn't say so. We knew it made Peter jealous."

"Peter's not jealous of me," I said. "Only of anyone that takes me away from him."

"He is," Nod insisted. "He knows no one will ever love him the way we all loved you."

My throat felt clogged suddenly. I cleared it noisily, but found I couldn't say anything. What could I possibly say?

"We all loved you, and so we loved Peter too, because you did. But when you stopped, so did the rest of us. You always made us see him through your eyes."

If I'd known I had that kind of power over the boys . . . I might have left sooner. I might have saved more of them.

It took such a long time for me to see Peter as he truly was. He blinded me, and shame wriggled in my stomach.

Was this, too, part of growing up? Was it facing the bad things you'd done as well as the good, and knowing all your mistakes had consequences?

Peter made mistakes all the time—he was thoughtless; he hurt people. But it never troubled him, not for a moment. He forgot all about it in an instant. That was being a boy.

I wasn't a boy anymore.

Then she screamed, and screamed again. It echoed over the dunes, high and shrill.

Peter. Peter had found them.

I dropped everything I was carrying and ran for my life, for Sally's life, for Charlie's life.

One more time, I ran.

CHAPTER 17

Nod ran with me, or tried to, but he soon fell behind. I heard him panting and coughing, trying to keep up. Sally's scream went on and on.

I don't know how long I ran, listening to that scream hovering in the air, and then it stopped.

When it stopped, I ran faster, though I didn't know that I could. My body already felt like it was pushed far past the point of pain or exhaustion. I didn't feel anything except fear, except the pounding of my heart driving me along.

In my mind I saw Sally on the beach, her arms spread out in an "X" like Crow, a big red smile at her throat where there shouldn't be one at all.

Her blue eyes empty and open, a cloud of dark hair around her head. Just like my mother.

Because that was what Peter did. If I loved someone he took them away. I should never have loved her in the first place. Or Charlie. Or Nod.

Or Fog or Crow or Del or anybody.

Not even my mother. I'd loved her, and so Peter had cut her away from me, just as quick as the pirate he was. He took what he wanted and left what he didn't behind.

The moon was full, like it always was on the island, watching with its cold, cold eye. The seasons changed but the moon never did. The moon was Peter's brother, never changing.

It lit up the sand and the ocean like daylight, but at first I didn't see them. I did see the rowboat, though—Charlie had been right about that. But what good was the boat if Charlie and Sally were dead?

Then I did see them. And everything was worse, much worse than I'd imagined. Peter hadn't slit Sally's throat and left her for me to weep over.

He'd brought a crocodile to the beach.

I knew Peter must have done it on purpose, for the crocodiles always stayed near the pond. None of them would have roamed the forest or cruised as far as the place where the marsh met the sea. In all the years I'd been there, I had never seen such a thing.

A huge crocodile, its belly round and dragging in the sand, sprinted after Charlie with surprising speed.

Peter was high above the sand, laughing in the air as Charlie ran, trying to reach the safety of the rocks at the other end. The little boy was so scared he was zigzagging this way and that, always just out of reach of the crocodile's snapping jaws. I heard his thin cry of terror streaming behind him.

I was sure that if Charlie managed to reach the rocks, Peter would grab him and drop him into the crocodile's open mouth. Peter was well past the point of pretending to care anymore. No one remained to pretend for—almost all the boys were gone, and the ones who were left no longer believed in him.

I ran, not knowing how I could do it again, knowing only that if I didn't reach him in time, Charlie would be eaten for certain. And I wished I'd thought to bring some arrows, for nothing would have pleased me more than to shoot Peter out of the sky and watch him fall like a burning star to earth.

There were trails of dark blood in the sand. I caught a glimpse, just from the corner of my eye, something that looked like Sally.

Or something that used to be Sally.

If Sally was dead, I couldn't help her. Charlie was what mattered now.

Peter didn't appear to have noticed me yet, for he was too busy laughing himself silly at Charlie's struggle to reach and climb the rocks.

The last time I was at those rocks I'd had to scrape off what was left of six boys and bury them all. I didn't want to do that again. I didn't think I could bear it, to put Charlie in the ground.

The crocodile snapped and this time it caught Charlie's

leg. He screamed in terror as the croc ripped away his pants and teeth grazed his leg, but he wasn't caught, not yet.

I put on a burst of speed, my dagger out in my left hand, and leapt onto the back of the crocodile. Its scaly back scratched my bare chest and I felt all the muscles of the creature bunching. The animal bucked, trying to roll over and throw me off, but I dug in my knees hard and wrapped my right arm under its jaw to hold it in place and then I slashed as hard as I could across its neck with my other hand.

It wasn't quite enough, though blood poured over my arm, and the crocodile twisted back and forth, trying to get me off so it could bite and claw.

Peter cried, "That's not fair of you, Jamie! That's no fun!"

I didn't know where Charlie was, but I hoped he was hiding from Peter. It was difficult to see anything except the heaving animal underneath me, lashing its tail and tossing its head to and fro in a desperate attempt to make me go away.

I stabbed at the croc again and again, trying to reach the soft underbelly, and finally it slowed. Hot blood gushed from its many wounds, and then it stilled.

I rolled off its back and away from its claws and teeth, not trusting that it was entirely dead yet. Blood coated my hands and arms and sand stuck to it so when I tried to swipe the sweat from my eyes I got a face full of the fine grains.

Spitting and trying to clear my eyes I called, "Charlie!"

"Jamie!" he said from somewhere in front of me, and he

didn't sound happy or relieved that I'd killed the crocodile. He sounded terrified.

I shook the sand off, my eyes still blurry, and then the world swam into focus again.

Peter was holding Charlie tucked in one arm, almost the way I did, like he cared about Charlie, except that in his other hand he held his knifepoint over Charlie's heart.

Peter watched Charlie's face and mine, though Charlie was looking only at me. His eyes were pleading for me to do something, do anything, to save him.

I'd told him I would protect him.

"Caught your little duckling now, haven't I?" Peter said.

His voice was singsong and somehow very young. His eyes darted between Charlie and me, sure that I wouldn't be able to stop him. I saw the cruel glee at this certainty, his enjoyment of our distress.

"Thought you could get away from me but you won't. Nobody ever leaves the island, Jamie. Nobody. Especially not you. And certainly not this little duck, who went wandering from his mama. Should have stayed home like you were supposed to. Should have listened and minded. Now you've been naughty and you have to be punished. All the boys must follow my rules, for this is *my* island."

He stroked the knifepoint down Charlie's chest toward his belly, and the smaller boy tried to shrink away but Peter held him tight.

"It's me you want to punish," I said. I tried hard not to sound scared, not to sound like I would do anything if he would only let Charlie go. "Why hurt him?"

"Because it *will* punish you if I kill him," Peter said. "I know you, Jamie. I know your heart, even if you think I don't. It will hurt you more if you can't save him than it would if I killed you outright."

"Why not just let us go?"

"Because who would I play with if you all were gone?" Peter said. "No, you have to stay here with me, Jamie, the way you said you would always. And for you to stay here with me means the rest of them must die. They keep you from me."

"I'm not going to stay a boy, Peter. I'm going to grow up," I said. "I already am."

He seemed to look at me then for the first time, really look at me. He hadn't, not properly, since before he took Charlie to the Many-Eyed. Now he took in my taller body and my bigger hands and the hair on my face that hadn't been there before.

His face twisted into something awful then, something monstrous and terrifying. He pulled Charlie tighter to his body and the younger boy cried out in pain.

"No," Peter said, stalking closer to me. "No, no, no, no, no! You're not allowed to grow up. You're supposed to stay here with me forever, for always. Who am I to play with if you grow up, Jamie?"

His eyes, I saw, glittered with tears, but I couldn't believe in them. Peter wasn't really hurt. He only wanted to have his way, like always. But he was coming closer to me, closer and closer, and I waited for my chance. The dagger was still in my hand.

"It's over, Peter," I said. "No one wants to play with you anymore. And you destroyed the tunnel to the Other Place, so you can't bring any more boys here. You're going to be alone here forever unless you grow up."

"No, I'm not growing up! I'm never growing up!" Peter screamed.

Then he screamed again, this time in surprise, and he dropped Charlie. I lunged to scoop him up as Peter flailed at the back of his thigh, reaching for something.

Nod had snuck up behind Peter while he talked to me, so quiet and careful I hadn't even noticed Nod there, and had thrown his knife at Peter, right into his leg.

Peter pulled the knife from his thigh and howled in pain and also, I think, in shock that he was actually hurt. He rose straight up from the ground, cursing all the terrible words he'd ever heard from the pirates.

A little golden firefly light bobbed around his head as he shouted his fury at us. Then he abruptly soared away, leaving us on the beach.

Nod's expression was fierce and proud. "I got him back. He got me but I got him back."

"And you saved Charlie," I said.

I sank to the ground then, the world gone all wobbly, and Charlie rolled out of my arms.

Nod ran to me, pushing me over so I didn't collapse on my face but on my back instead. I shook all over, every muscle trembling from exertion and shock.

I'd been running and running and running for days, it seemed, trying to stop the inevitable, trying to stop Peter from slaughtering them all.

My breath came in thready gasps. Nod and Charlie leaned over me, identical expressions of worry on their faces.

"Jamie?" Charlie asked.

I flopped my hand at him. It was all I had the energy to do. "I'm fine."

"No, you're not," Nod said. "You're white as bone under all that blood and sand."

I tried to nod my head yes, to say that I was fine. I must have fainted then, for the next thing I knew the stars were gone and the sky above me the pale blue of just after dawn.

Charlie held my right hand in his smaller one. Tears streamed down his face. My left hand was still closed around my dagger.

"Charlie? Where's Nod?"

"Burying Sally," Charlie said, and pointed behind me.

I sat up straight then. I'd forgotten, forgotten the long trails of blood in the sand, forgotten the thing that I saw out of the corner of my eye as I sprinted down the beach to save Charlie from the crocodile.

I'd forgotten the girl who wanted to grow up with me.

Now she never would.

I managed to stand very slowly, every part of me stiff and sore. The crocodile's blood had dried on my hands and arms and fell off in flakes.

"You don't look good, Jamie," Charlie said. "You look sick. Maybe you ought to sit down again."

I shook my head, unable to speak. I walked slowly, limping because my right ankle was swollen. I had no memory of how or why this might have happened. Charlie trotted along beside me, holding out his hands toward me when he thought I might fall, as though he might be able to stop me.

Nod was at the place under the coconut tree where I had buried the others the day that the cannonball took them. He had a wide flat stick that he was using to dig a hole in the sand.

On the ground beside the hole was what was left of her.

Nod paused for a moment and saw me coming. He scrambled out of the hole and ran toward me, waving his hands and shaking his head no.

Nod had gotten taller since last night. He was almost as tall as me, though he'd always been a lot smaller when we were children. His blond beard was thicker than mine. He seemed almost completely grown-up, not in-between as I was. There was no more of the boy about him at all.

He put his hand on my chest to stop me from going any

farther. That hand was big and thick-knuckled and covered with curling yellow hair.

"No," he said. His voice was all grown-up too, deep-throated and rumbly. "I don't want you to see her."

"I need to see her," I said.

"You don't want to," Nod said. "I wish I hadn't."

"The crocodile ate her," Charlie said in a very little voice, his eyes downcast. "I'm sorry, Jamie. It only ate her because she was watching out for me like she said she would."

I rumpled his hair, his little yellow duckling hair, and watched it stand up in the sunlight. Charlie was still a small boy, because he hadn't been on the island long enough to stop growing the usual way and then start again like me and Nod. He was very tiny now compared to us.

"It wasn't your fault, Charlie," I said. "It was Peter's."

Charlie kicked the sand, his fists clenched. "It's always Peter's fault. Always, always. It's because of him that Sally's gone."

Nod's restraining hand was still on my chest. I looked at him for a long time, and he looked back, and finally he let me pass.

There wasn't much left of her, not really. The crocodile had taken most of one leg entirely, nothing there except some ragged skin and sheared-off bone. The opposite arm was stripped of flesh, and there was a big chunk torn out of her middle. Everywhere there were claw and bite marks, on her hands and face and chest.

She'd fought. I didn't need Charlie to tell me that she'd

stood in the way of the crocodile and told him to run. It was what she would do. It was what I would do, and our hearts were the same where Charlie was concerned.

Her blue eyes were milky grey and empty. Her laughing blue eyes, the eyes that promised me we'd be together for always, the eyes that promised me things I didn't really understand—there was no Sally in them anymore, no fierce happy girl that I loved.

I should have cried, but all my tears had been wrung from me already. My grief couldn't overwhelm me anymore because it was a part of me forever, all the names and all the faces and all the boys that I hadn't protected from Peter.

All the boys, and one girl.

Charlie and me, we helped Nod dig the hole and then I carefully laid her in there, and we covered her face with sand.

After, we sat on the ground near her grave, and all of us kept one hand on the freshly turned sand, as if we could keep her with us as long as we stayed there. And if we stayed there watching long enough, maybe she would push her way out of the sand, fresh and new and young again, for we knew the island could do that if it wanted.

I glanced down the beach where the rowboat was lodged so unexpectedly.

I was so tired. I hadn't slept properly for two days and my ankle hurt from just the short walk to the coconut tree. My head lolled toward my chest.

I shook myself awake again. I couldn't fall asleep. We needed to leave. Peter would be nursing his wound—the first he'd ever gotten, and the shock of it might keep him away longer than usual—and now was our chance. If we waited, then Peter would return, and he wouldn't play with crocodiles this time. He'd stab Charlie and be done with it.

Looking at Nod, I thought Peter would have no luck trying to kill him. Nod was tough as a boy, and now he was almost a man. He'd already managed to score off Peter by injuring him, and Peter hadn't been able to take Nod down when they were the same size.

I stared, startled, at Nod's hands. I'd just remembered that Peter tried to cut Nod's hand off, and the right wrist had been fiercely ruined the night before.

Now all the skin there was whole and pink and fresh and new.

He noticed me staring and turned his wrists this way and that in the sun.

"It happened while I was growing," he said. "It just healed up so fast I didn't even notice it happening. I don't think that would happen again, though."

"It was because you were growing so fast that all your body was making itself new," I said, nodding in understanding. "Once you're completely grown-up you'll only get better the regular way."

Nod narrowed his eyes, like he was thinking something

very hard. "Do you think I'll stop growing up soon? Or will I just keep going until I'm old and grey and hobbled, and then I'll die?"

This hadn't occurred to me at all. I supposed I'd thought we'd only grow to adulthood quickly and then stop. But Nod and I, we were older than even we knew. What if the island's magic, once reversed, would unravel until it reached the end of the skein? What if Nod was right, and we would just get older and older and older every hour until we died?

"No," I said. I had no reason for saying that. It was only a feeling. I thought it would be enough for the island if we grew up, if we felt the creep of old age on our bones the usual way. "You and me aren't even growing up at the same time. You're already older than me, and I've been here longer."

"I think," Nod said, "it's because of what's in our heart. My heart hasn't been young since Fog died."

"It's not such a wonderful thing, to be young," I said. "It's heartless, and selfish."

"But, oh, so free," Nod said sadly. "So free when you have no worries or cares."

I smiled a little then. "I always had worries and cares, mostly so the rest of you wouldn't."

I glanced again at the rowboat. "Do you think you could find the supplies I dropped last night?" I asked Nod.

He followed my gaze. "I'll help you to the boat; then I'll go see if I can find them."

"If you can't, then we should gather some coconuts and push off anyway. We can drink their water when we're at sea."

I didn't like to think how far away the nearest land might be, or what would happen to us if there was a storm on the ocean. But even an ocean storm seemed better than staying one more day on the island, trying not to be killed by a mad child.

He helped me to my feet. My ankle was even more tender than it had been earlier. Nod put his shoulder under mine, acting like a crutch, so I could let the injured foot drag in the sand.

Charlie soon grew impatient with my slow pace but I wouldn't let him run ahead. I wasn't letting him go more than an arm's length from me ever again.

If I did I was sure that Peter would swoop out of the sky and take him away and all I would be able to do was watch, for I couldn't run and I couldn't fly.

We reached the rowboat, and we all stared inside it.

The boat was all torn up, an enormous hole where the bottom of it used to be. It looked like it had been hacked apart with an axe.

Peter had gotten there before us, again, just as he had with the tree.

There was no way for us to leave the island.

PART IV

PETER & JAMIE

CHAPTER 18

The only plan left to us was the original one Sally and I'd thought of—swimming out to the pirate ship and taking one of their rowboats.

"Or," Nod said, when I'd made this suggestion, "to join the pirates and let them take us on their ship away from here."

We were roasting fish over a small campfire on the beach. Charlie was asleep in the sand beside me, curled on his side.

We'd decided to stay there until we knew what to do next. I was sure that the tree would be occupied by Peter, and I didn't want to risk roaming over the island on my sore ankle looking for a better place to hide.

There didn't seem to be any better place to hide, anyway. Peter would always find us. As he told us over and over, it was his island. All its secrets belonged to him. I used to think they belonged to me too, but that wasn't true anymore. There were so many things I didn't know about the island, like fairies and flying and how the magic of it all stayed in your heart. Peter knew those things.

I stared at Nod. "Join the pirates? After what they did to the boys? After what they did to Fog?"

Nod's face reddened. "I know what they did to him. To them. But Jamie—aren't the pirates better than Peter? I'm grown-up now, and you're nearly so. They can't hold what Peter did against us. We're not boys anymore."

"Charlie is," I said.

"We could look after Charlie," Nod said. "You were always the best fighter, Jamie. You don't think you will be now that you're big?"

"I don't know," I said.

The truth of it was that I didn't have much desire left to fight. I was always angry when I was a boy, even if I didn't seem it, even when I seemed unruffled. Part of me was always silently raging, always looking for blood to spill. I never knew why I felt that way, but it made me merciless. It made it easy for me to cut and to hurt, to arrogantly slice pirates' hands from their wrists so I could leave my mark.

It made it easy for me to defeat all the other boys in Battle. It made it easy for me to smash Nip's head open with a rock.

I didn't think I had that anymore. I wasn't angry, not the way I used to be. There was only one person I wanted to kill now, and when he was dead I never wanted to lift a weapon again for the rest of my life.

"Think on it," Nod said. "About going to the pirates, I

mean. We can't run about dodging Peter forever, you know."

"I know," I said.

That night I dreamed, but it was a different dream from one I'd ever had before. I didn't dream of my mother, of finding her in the darkness, of my own hands covered in her blood.

Fog and Crow and Sally were inside the rowboat, the one that had been destroyed by Peter. It was new and whole again, and they were just a few feet off the shore. The three of them sat in the boat and waved at me.

"Don't go," I said, and splashed out into the water.

The boat drifted on the current. I reached for the edge, wanting to climb in, but every time it was just out of reach.

Fog and Crow and Sally watched me with curious eyes.

"Wait!" I cried. "I want to come with you!"

I followed the boat into the deeper water, and soon I was swimming instead of wading, and the boat was drifting away faster and faster.

The sea rose up then, pushing me back, pushing me back to the shore no matter how hard I fought.

The boat disappeared on the horizon.

I woke suddenly, my face wet, the fire burned down to nothing but coals. Nod and Charlie were asleep. I sat up and poked at the fire, feeling my skin prickle.

Peter watched me from the sky.

His eyes were shrouded by the dark, and his skin glowed silvery-white in the moonlight. He just floated there, bobbing up and down on the air, with his little fairy light darting around his head. I could see the tiny flutters of golden dust that drifted down on him.

"Tink is very angry with you," he said. "You burned all of her family when you burned the fields. Now she's the only fairy left."

"I didn't know they were there," I said. "You didn't tell me."

"It's not my fault you never found them," Peter said. "You shouldn't have burned the fields in the first place. What did the Many-Eyed ever do to you?"

"You shouldn't have taken Charlie in the first place," I said. "What did Charlie ever do to you?"

"He took you from me," Peter said. "And so did Sally. Now you won't play with me ever again."

"So you thought it was fine to feed him to the Many-Eyed?" I asked.

Peter shrugged. "It would have saved me a lot of trouble. Anyway, all this happened because you killed that Many-Eyed in the first place when you weren't supposed to, the one at Bear Cave. That was your doing."

I shook my head at him. "This is all your doing. You brought the boys here. You didn't care for them. You used them and then you tossed them in the rubbish pile and you expected me to feel the same."

"You should have!" Peter said. He'd been calm up until then but now I saw the spark of anger. "You were supposed to feel the same as me! All this place, all the fun, all the boys—it was only for you. I did everything for you."

I stood then, and wished like mad that I could grab him out of the sky. "Including kill my mother?"

He gave me a sly look. "I didn't kill your mother. You did. Don't you remember? I found you standing over her and her throat was cut and there was blood all over your hands. You must not have liked your mother very much."

"I don't think it was like that at all," I said. "You killed her so that I would follow you here. You knew I would never leave her."

"That only shows how much I loved you, Jamie," he said, changing tack. "I took your mother away because I never wanted anyone to love you as much as me."

"That's not how you show someone love, Peter," I said. "But you're only a boy, and you'll never understand."

Peter narrowed his eyes at me, and crossed his arms.

"There's only one way to settle this."

"Yes," I said. "The way we always settle quarrels on the island."

"You know where to go, then," he said. "I'll be waiting."

He flew away then, and the night was blacker than it had been before.

"You won't be able to watch this time, Peter," I said. "This time, you'll have to fight me."

Nod sat up and stared at me as I poked the fire.

"Are you going to fight Peter at Battle?" he asked.

"Yes," I said, wondering how much he'd heard.

"Peter killed your mother?"

He'd heard plenty, then.

"Yes," I said.

"I thought you didn't remember her," he said.

"I didn't, until yesterday."

"Oh," he said. "I still don't remember mine. I wish I did. I only remember Fog, and he's starting to fade already. It must be nice to remember your mother. If she was nice."

"Mine was," I said. "But Peter tangled me up and made me forget her."

"He must have made me do that too."

His expression was terribly sad, then, and terribly old.

After a moment he shook his head, as if shaking away the memory, and said, "How will you get to the Battle place with your ankle like that?"

I flexed it, and discovered that it had healed while I slept. I rubbed my hand across my face. My beard was thicker, though not as full-grown as Nod's.

"It's better now," I said.

He looked at my ankle and then my beard and nodded in understanding. "You grew a bit more."

"I want you to take Charlie and go across the island to Bear Cave and wait for me there," I said.

"I don't think you should go to Battle with Peter on your own," he said. "Someone should watch, and judge, like we've always done. He's likely to cheat. You know that. He only cares about fair play when it's not fair to him."

"I don't want Charlie anywhere near Peter," I said. "And we're not going to leave him alone on the beach."

"And what happens if you don't come back?" Nod said, his eyes bright.

"You'll know what that means," I said. "If I'm not back in two days you follow your idea, and take Charlie and go to the pirates."

When the sun rose I took up my dagger and a pirate sword, and I went toward the mountains where the Battle place was, and the other two went toward the forest and Bear Cave.

I felt stronger and better than I had the day before, and my new body was a wonderful thing. I could run faster and climb easier. When I reached the meadow before the Battle place I wasn't even winded.

It wasn't such a terrible thing, then, growing up. Peter was still a boy, and I was big and strong now, stronger than I'd ever been.

I could hurt him with this body. I could kill him.

Peter waited there for me, in the middle of the arena, his hands on his hips.

"You took a very long time," he said crossly, looking me up and down. "I imagine it's because you're old now."

"Not all of us can fly," I said.

I put the pirate sword down on the bench but carried my dagger. Peter already had his knife in his hand.

"This Battle isn't like the other Battles," he said. "There are no rules."

"But it is a fight to the death," I said.

"Oh, Jamie." He sighed, and there was a strange tenderness in the way he said my name. "Do you think I could ever kill you? Look at all I've done for you."

I lunged at him then, not wanting to talk anymore with this child, this mad child who thought that he was showing his love by killing anyone who took my attention away from him.

But though my new body was strong and fast, I couldn't fly, and he darted into the air and around behind me before I could blink.

"Not fair play," I said, in hopes of appealing to his better nature—what little there was of it.

"There are no rules in this Battle," Peter said, laughing. "You agreed to that yourself."

It was his laugh that made me want to kill him, made me want to break open his ribs and carve out his heart, the way he'd done to me so many times before.

He flew in circles above me, laughing and laughing. His laughter echoed off the walls and fed my rage and made me wild, wild as him, wild as he'd always wanted me to be.

That wildness, strangely, also made me calm. I saw some rocks in the arena, left there from previous Battles. I found a small smooth one just near my foot, likely one dropped from my sling-bag the day I fought Nip. It was almost as if it was waiting there for me to pick it up.

Peter didn't notice. He was too busy flying around, feeling so very pleased with his own cleverness.

I watched him carefully for a moment; then I aimed it for his right eye.

I didn't miss. And I can throw very, very hard.

Peter screamed and tumbled down in shock, and then I was on him.

He was so much smaller than me that it was nothing for me to put my knee in his chest and punch him in the face. Two of his teeth—all baby teeth still, like little white pearls—spilled out of his mouth, and blood spilled out of his nose, and his eye was shot through with red.

He wasn't laughing anymore.

I'd dropped my dagger so I could hit him in the face with both hands. I picked it up then, holding his jaw in my right hand and the knife in my left, and I slashed toward his throat.

Just like he'd done to Crow.

Just like he'd done to my mother.

I hadn't noticed that he still had his own knife, and that one of his arms had worked free.

He stabbed the knife into my thigh and ripped it down, tearing open the old wound. Blood ran everywhere, spurted in Peter's face, and he wriggled away from me as I fell sideways, my own knife slash never touching his throat.

It was only then he seemed to realize that it was not a game to me, that I was in earnest.

I meant to kill him.

My blood poured into the rock of the Battle arena and as always, it disappeared, almost as if it had never been.

I struggled to stand again, panting with the effort. Peter watched me struggle, watched the blood that ran from my thigh, and then he smiled.

All his teeth were there again.

His nose stopped flowing. His eye returned to its normal size.

In a moment he was Peter again, whole, unchanged, eleven years old.

"You can't kill me, Jamie," he said. He sounded sorry for me that I would even try.

"The island made me," he continued. "The island made me, and the island keeps me alive. And every drop of blood spilled here keeps me whole and young forever, just like it did for you, when you believed in me. But when you stopped loving me, when you stopped believing—the island let you go, because the island knows your heart and so do I."

"It can't be," I panted. It couldn't be true. It couldn't—that all my rage, all my anger would have nowhere to go and no way to end. How could it be that I'd never be able to kill the one person who, above all, deserved it?

I tried to stand, but my leg wouldn't support me, and the blood was pouring out of me too fast. All that blood that was keeping Peter alive. All my blood had made him whole again.

It was like I'd never touched him in the first place.

I would never be able to kill him. As long as there were boys on the island, as long as blood was spilled here, Peter would live forever.

"That's why you brought me here?" I asked. "So I could keep you alive? That's why we all were brought here? For you?"

"Not you, Jamie!" Peter said. "Never you! I wanted to share all this with you, so you could have fun. You were always sad and angry and that mama of yours didn't do anything to make you happy or make it better. I know, Jamie. I watched you a long time to make sure that you were the right one for me."

"She kissed me and hugged me and held me so tight," I said, echoing the words Charlie had said to me long, long ago.

Peter scoffed. "What's a hug? What's a kiss? Those things aren't like running free or swimming in the ocean or laughing and playing all day with your greatest friend in all the world. You were sad, Jamie, and I wanted you to be happy, and me too. I brought you here so I'd have a friend. I brought the others so I could keep that friend forever."

I laughed then, a horrible angry laugh that sounded nothing like myself.

"Well, I'd say your plan failed, Peter. Because I won't be your friend forever. I haven't been your friend for some time now."

"I know," Peter said. "But that doesn't mean that you're allowed to leave. You know my rules, Jamie. You can't ever leave the island. And I won't let you die either. You won't be able to escape me that way."

I fell over then, unable to stand on my ripped-up leg, and rolled to my back. There should have been a pool of blood all around me but the rock was absorbing it as fast as it came out of me. Everything was going white, then black, then white again before my eyes.

Then Peter stood over me, and he held the pirate sword.

"I curse you, Jamie. I curse you to live forever on this island, but as a grown-up. You'll never be a boy again, but you'll never grow old and die either. If you're hurt you'll always survive. The island won't let you go, and the island will keep you alive because I say so. And so you'll never forget me and my curse, I leave my mark on you."

He raised the sword, and then my right hand was gone.

CHAPTER 19

Peter flew away and left me there, bleeding from my leg and my wrist. I was sure that I would die, despite everything Peter said. I blacked out for a while, and when I woke again the moon was lit and the bleeding had stopped.

I sat up and examined my leg, which was too torn to stand on, even if it wasn't bleeding. White bone protruded from my wrist, and stringy bits of muscle and vein. I didn't want to look at it. I tore a bit of hide from my pants and wrapped the stump up tight.

Then I crawled out of the arena.

As I crawled I remembered every boy I'd fought there. There were some I'd fought in fun—or, at least, Peter's idea of fun, for his idea of fun still meant some blood was spilled, even if it was only from a broken nose.

I remembered every boy that I'd killed when it wasn't for fun. I remembered smashing Nip's skull in with a rock until I saw the gleam of bone beneath.

I remembered how Peter sat there and watched, when it was in fun and when it was not, and how it pleased him to see us there.

How it must have pleased him to see us feeding our blood to the island, keeping him alive.

And every drop of blood had kept me alive too, though I didn't know it. Because I'd believed in Peter. Because he'd smiled at me.

I felt sick and ashamed, and sorry that I'd ever lifted a hand against any boy that came here, thinking they would live forever. I was sorry, but they would never hear me say it.

They were all dead. They were all dead, but I would go on and on, and remember all their faces, and remember how I'd hurt them.

And I would remember the ones who were taken by pirates or crocodiles or sickness or Many-Eyed, and no death would ever bring me relief.

Peter had cursed me, and I would never escape those faces. All the boys and all their bodies were fastened to my heart now, weighing me to the earth.

It took me what seemed like hours just to reach the stream that ran alongside the meadow. I rolled into the cold water and stayed there, letting it wash all over me. The coldness made my leg feel better, and I remained in the water until I started to shiver.

I tried to stand up, and couldn't. If I didn't get help,

didn't get the leg sewn up as I'd done before, then it wouldn't heal properly and I would never walk right on it again.

I found a tall stick to use as a crutch, and managed to prop myself up on it. Then slowly, ever so slowly, I limped across the meadow.

I was halfway there when a figure rose out of the darkness from the trail below. I squinted; then a smaller figure appeared beside the larger one.

Nod and Charlie.

Charlie ran to me, crying, "Jamie! Jamie!"

"You didn't listen," I murmured. "You didn't mind."

"We came to take care of you," Charlie said. "The way that you always take care of us."

"Didn't you believe that I could beat him?" I asked, but there was no rancor in it. "I was always Battle champion, you know."

"Yes," Nod said. "But we knew that Peter would cheat."

The tears came then, the tears that were for everything I loved and everything I lost, the tears that I'd been unable to cry for Sally, the tears that I'd never known to cry for my mama.

All those boys. All those bodies. All that weight on my heart.

Sally.

My mother.

And the one person I wanted dead that could never, ever die.

"He did cheat," I sobbed. "He did."

"He always does," Nod said. "He would never have let you win."

Nod and Charlie looked after me until I was well again. We never saw Peter in those days, nor Tink, nor anyone. Nod showed us the place where he'd buried Fog, and we often found him there just before the sun went down, talking quietly to his brother. I tried not to listen to what he said at those times. It was just between Nod and Fog.

We lived in the meadow until I could walk without the stick. I considered it my punishment to be trapped there near the place where I'd killed so many boys at Peter's behest, killed them because we'd thought it was fun.

Every day I looked at my wrist, at the place where my hand used to be, at the mark that once was mine to give and now belonged to Peter.

On the day I could walk unencumbered again we went away from that place of blood, that place where Peter's life was fed by the boys who died in Battle. I've never returned there since the day me and Nod and Charlie left it.

We went, of course, to the pirates.

They don't call me Jamie anymore. I covered the stump of my hand with a hook, and so that became my name.

It's all right, really, for Jamie was a boy. A foolish boy, one who thought he could do right, who thought he could escape a monster called Peter.

He brings new boys to the island again, for Peter must have playmates. He flies through the night and past the stars and finds them, and when he finds them he gives them the gift he never gave me, and sprinkles them with fairy dust.

When I see their shadows silhouetted against the moon, my heart burns and my teeth gnash and I want to point the ship's cannon at them and shoot them out of the sky.

Mostly I don't, because it's not those boys I want to kill. I've had enough of killing boys. There's only one person I want to die—the person who never will.

And sometimes, sometimes, he even lets them go home again if they don't want to stay. And sometimes he doesn't, and they die up in that mountain so Peter can live.

But that's a freedom I will never have. Peter's curse means that though we sail the ship away from the island we will always return again, no matter what direction we sail.

If we head north, with the island behind us, we will soon find it again, peeking over the horizon. If we sail south or east or west, the same will happen. It's as if we sail upside down and around in a circle, and find ourselves at the top of it over and over and over again.

The other pirates don't know why they're cursed to return to the island, though I think Nod suspects. Nod is the only one who truly understands what happened between Peter and me. Even Charlie doesn't understand it completely.

Peter will never let me go. If I'm not his playmate and friend, then I am to be his playmate and enemy. He brought me to the island and he swore I would never leave and so I haven't.

It will always be Peter and me, like it was in the beginning, like it will be in the end. Peter, who took everything from me and gave everything too.

Peter, who loved me best of everyone except himself.

He tells the new boys I am a villain, and they call me Captain Hook.

If I am a villain, it's because Peter made me one, because Peter needs to be the shining sun that all the world turns around. Peter needed to be a hero, so somebody needed to be a villain.

The anger that I carried with me all the days of my childhood is for only one person now, and if I ever catch him again he'll be sorry.

I know I can find a way. He's given me so much time, all the time in the world, and there must be a way.

Someday. Someday, he'll be sorry he crossed me.

When I hear him laughing, out there in the sky and in the night, and that laugh burns me deep down in my heart, I know I'll find a way to make him sorry.

I will make him so sorry.

I hate Peter Pan.

ABOUT THE AUTHOR

Christina Henry is the author of national bestselling *Black Wings* series featuring Agent of Death Madeline Black and her popcorn-loving gargoyle Beezle. Her dark fantasy novel *Alice* was one of Amazon's Best Books of 2015 in Science Fiction and Fantasy, and came second in the Goodreads Choice awards for Best Horror. Christina enjoys running long distances, reading anything she can get her hands on and watching movies with samurai, zombies and/or subtitles in her spare time. She lives in Chicago with her husband and son.

For more fantastic fiction, author events, competitions,
limited editions and more

VISIT OUR WEBSITE
titanbooks.com

LIKE US ON FACEBOOK
facebook.com/titanbooks

FOLLOW US ON TWITTER
@TitanBooks

EMAIL US
readerfeedback@titanemail.com